D0299147

GALLATIN CANYON

1846 550114 1988 1X

Thomas McGuane

Gallatin Canyon

W.M.
RESERVE STOCK

Harvill Secker
LONDON

Published by Harvill Secker 2006

First published in the United States by Alfred A. Knopf in 2006

2 4 6 8 10 9 7 5 3 1

Copyright © Thomas McGuane 2006

Thomas McGuane has asserted his right under the Copyright,
Designs and Patents Act 1988 to be identified as the author of this work

'Gallatin Canyon,' 'Ice,' and 'Vicious Circle' previously appeared in *The New Yorker*

This book is sold subject to the condition that it shall not by way of trade or
otherwise, be lent, resold, hired out, or otherwise circulated without the
publisher's prior consent in any form or binding or cover other than that
in which it is published and without a similar condition including
this condition being imposed on the subsequent purchaser

First published in Great Britain in 2006 by
HARVILL SECKER

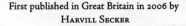

WOLVERHAMPTON LIBRARIES	
184655011419881X	
HJ	481852
	£12.99
GR	2 9 NOV 2006

Isle ⟨ ⟩ ie,

The Random House Group Limited Reg. No. 954009
www.randomhouse.co.uk

A CIP catalogue record for this book
is available from the British Library

ISBN 9781846550114 (from January 2007)
ISBN 1846550114

Papers used by Random House are natural, recyclable products made
from wood grown in sustainable forests. The manufacturing processes conform
to the environmental regulations of the country of origin

Printed and bound in Great Britain by Mackays of Chatham

For Fred and Betty Torphy

To be a human being, one had to drink from the cup.
If one were lucky on one day, or cowardly on another,
it was presented on a third occasion.

—*Graham Greene*

Contents

My deepest gratitude to
Deborah Treisman for her help and advice.

Gallatin Canyon

Vicious Circle

ohn Briggs sat on his porch on a dreary hot August day with a glass of ice water sweating in his hand, listening to opera on the radio. The white borders of the screen doors were incandescent with mountain summer. Through them he could see the high windswept ridge above his house, where the bunchgrass could not get a hold, leaving only a seam of shale to overlook the irrigated valley.

Earlier, at the farmers' market at the fairgrounds, he'd strolled among the pleasant displays of food and craft. A bearded youth offered handmade walking sticks; next to him, with a cage full of rabbits, a woman in Chiapas folk costume sold angora tooth-fairy pillows while tugging strands of angora from a rabbit asleep in her lap. An extraordinary variety of concrete yard animals surrounded a display of bird feeders with expired Montana license plates folded for roofs. A hearty woman with her fists on her hips offered English delphiniums, which, she explained again and again, had never been crossed with Pacific Giants, "not ever." The Hutterites, in suspenders and straw cowboy hats, had a vast array of vegetables; their long table faced lines of people, five deep, eyes fixed upon the produce. A girl in jeans and a bustier played a harp, almost inaudible over the sounds of the crowd, beside a table selling geodes and specimens of quartz.

Briggs had a large shopping bag into which he placed his purchases: carrots, kohlrabi, baby beets bought from a woman in a Humane Society T-shirt, and Flathead Lake cherries from an old man in an "Official Party Shirt" from Carlos and Charlie's in Cozumel. A woman with the forearms of a plumber spotted Briggs and stepped from behind a meager display of home-grown lavender to block his path. She gazed at him fixedly and, as he grew uncomfortable, asked, "Is anything coming to you?"

Briggs shook his head tentatively. The woman let out a vehement laugh with a faint whistle in it. A mirthless grin spread ear to ear.

"Is it possible," she asked, "that you don't remember me at all? Two a.m.? January? Roswell, New Mexico? Ring a bell?"

Trying to conceal his discomfort, Briggs said that he was afraid it was possible he didn't remember.

"You glutton!" she roared.

He could see that the onlookers were not on his side. The woman followed him for several yards, a steady, accusing stare as he made his way through lanes of boxed produce. He heard the word *glutton* again, over the otherwise gentle murmur of the market. He also heard her ask the crowd whether people like him ever got enough. She was right; it was outrageous that such a thing could have slipped his mind, whatever it was. He was dismayed to have shared some potent event with this woman and be now unable to even recall it. He tried again, but nothing came. Perhaps it had been long ago—but no, she'd said *January*. Was he losing his memory?

He stopped to look at the midsummer light bouncing off the hoods of cars lined up alongside the park. Someone touched his elbow, and he turned to a young woman with a blue bandanna tied around her neck. She had on one arm a basket filled with parsnips, heavy August tomatoes, onions shedding golden paper in the hard light. "Don't blame yourself," she said shyly. "She's asked a dozen people the same question, and they couldn't remember either." The woman seemed to redden. He was greatly absorbed by her gray eyes and her fine, clear forehead; it seemed to him the kind of face that only profound innocence could produce.

Her name was Olivia, she said, and she was buying vegetables for herself and her father. Not today, not tomorrow, not until Wednesday could she meet for a drink. In fact, she didn't want to meet for a drink at all, but in the end they could agree on no convenient meeting place other than a bar. He would have to wait.

Olivia was on time. She'd suggested the Stockman Hotel, which had a popular bar and was midway between their homes. Her yellow cotton dress was stylish but out-of-date, maybe a generation out-of-date, and must not have originally belonged to her— an elegant hand-me-down. The bar was busy with ranchers, an insurance man, a woman who drove for UPS, and two palladium miners; everyone was talking, except for three men from a highway crew who didn't know anyone and stared straight ahead, holding their beers with both hands. An empty booth remained, and Briggs led her there, trying not to appear coercive. Olivia sat quickly, clasping her fingers, elbows on the table, and looked around. She seemed happy. Her shoulder-length hair was parted in the middle and pulled behind small, pretty ears that were un-pierced. She had a sensual mouth for a shy girl, though he supposed he ought not to have seen this as a contradiction.

"Do you know something?" she said, almost whispering. "I don't remember your name."

"John Briggs."

"Oh. I see. Just like that."

"What do you mean?"

"I mean . . . it's just two syllables!"

"I know. It's like a dirge or a march, isn't it?" he said.

"John-Briggs-John-Briggs-John-Briggs," she chanted.

"Exactly. In second grade, Roland Ozolinsch sat next to me, and he had such a hard time learning to spell his own name, I became grateful for mine's brevity. I worried about other things instead. I wished for jet black hair that would lie flat like Superman's." His own hair was russet brown and sprang out. He wished he'd said *shortness* instead of *brevity*. There was something silly about the phrase *grateful for mine's brevity*, but it seemed to have gone unnoted.

A barmaid came to their table, in jeans and a T-shirt advertising a whale-watching boat on Prince of Wales Island; the breaching whale in the drawing was bigger than the boat, whose worshipful passengers were lined up like a choir. She knew Olivia, and they exchanged pleasantries. Briggs ordered a St. Pauli Girl and Olivia ordered a double shot of Jim Beam, with a water back.

Briggs was careful not to react. When their order was in, Olivia studied the time on her watch and then on the wall clock, before adjusting the watch. "Four forty-two," she said.

He guessed she was nearly, but not quite, thirty, at least a decade younger than him. She wore no rings or other insignia and, in general, was remarkably undecorated, though a glance revealed possible eyeliner and just enough lipstick, the absence of which might have been odd—not pretentious, but odd. Her eyes traveled around the bar and landed on him, just as their drinks arrived. "Still hot," she said, and smiled brilliantly.

This felt like a journey to Briggs, though he couldn't have said why.

"Still hot," he concurred, thinking, I need to add something. Hot plus what, Dry? Windy?

"Drought-drought-drought," she said, much as she'd said his name, in modest march time. "We lost our well and had to drill another, two hundred feet at I forget how much a foot, but a lot.

Ruined our yard, that man out there with his machine, hammering away."

"I saw on the bank that it's ninety-seven." Jesus Christ, Briggs thought, tell her you saw a zebra!

As she drank, reacting to the bitterness of the whiskey, she looked straight at him. "You know what would be so sweet," she said, "is if you'd get me a paper from the lobby." Smiling in compliance, Briggs got up and went out. At a table in the large bay window, three young Mormons in suits craned to watch the heat-struck pedestrians. One unfurled the sports section of the *Gazette*; another leaned forward, holding his head in his hands. Briggs dropped a quarter into the honor-system jar and took a copy of the paper to Olivia. She had a new drink in front of her.

The bar's manager, Jerry Warren, who was small, ingratiating, and somehow like a frog in a polo shirt, sidled up to the table. Olivia knew him.

"In September," he said, "I'm going to Ireland—"

"Are you Irish?" Briggs interrupted.

"No, to hike the Ring of Kerry, hike all day, booze till two, feel up German girls—"

Briggs glanced at an expressionless Olivia.

"—and visit ring forts or the odd castle. The brochure promises your money back if you don't, like, burst into spontaneous verse by Day Two, though I expect most of the poetry ends up being directed at your raincoat." He rested his hand on the table, then slowly extended a forefinger. "Next round's on me."

"The trouble is, when you just want to get to know someone," Olivia said, with surprising volubility once Warren was gone, "there's no such thing as neutral ground. Like just now, people come up and assume. . . . But, well, here's another round." She raised her face in gratitude to the barmaid. "Jerry always tells me his travel plans, no matter how late it gets. He has some crazy jetlag remedies you ought to hear. By the next morning, I can hardly remember what they were."

"It's five o'clock," the barmaid said. "You're entitled to all of this you want."

When she was gone, Olivia said, "I suppose we did start before five. That woman at the farmers' market, she must've had someone in mind."

"Funny way to figure out who."

"Or she was just, you know, revisiting the experience."

"Anyway, that's how we met!" But this didn't feel right, so Briggs added, "Neighbor."

After thinking about this, she asked, "Have you noticed that out in the country *neighbor* is a verb?"

This struck Briggs as a sudden move away from intimacy. Five o'clock had brought a crowd big enough to elbow up to all surfaces—not just the bar but the walls—and the air of day's-end ebullience was infectious to Briggs, who was a loner, and tired of being one, but seemed unable to do anything about it.

"It's kind of aggressive, isn't it?" he said. "Usually about how someone failed to neighbor."

"Yes." She sighed. "And the speaker always makes you think that *he* neighbors even while he's asleep." She covered Briggs's hands with her own. "How 'bout you?"

"I don't do a lot of neighboring," he said.

Olivia took this in somberly. "I must strike you as desperate," she said. The tone had changed, and her smile was slack.

"You do not."

"Thank you."

She had nearly finished her complimentary double, and Briggs, on his third shell of draft, realized that she'd put away six shots of whiskey, which suddenly seemed to be sinking in; the slow movement of her eyes beneath lowered lids, which he had first taken for flirtatious warmth, now appeared to be the start of some narcosis.

"That Ring of Kerry thing doesn't sound like much fun, does it?" she said into space.

"Oh, I'll bet it's beautiful there."

"But just getting through a wet day to end up in a pub . . . Is that the reward? And where did he get that about German girls?" Only now did she look up at Briggs.

"He was probably trying to entertain us."

Olivia looked surprised. "Oh! Well. Now I'll be grateful. I'm so dense." At that moment, Warren passed their booth. "Hey, Jerry! That was great," she called out.

He stopped.

"What was great, Olivia?"

"About the ring of German girls in raincoats."

Jerry glanced at Briggs before moving on. "If I can just get through this drought," he said, as he plunged into the crowd.

"What does he *mean*?" Olivia asked. "I'm missing connection after connection." She gestured for another round. The barmaid waved back, and Olivia commented, "I really like her, but she's a huge slut. Ready for another?"

"I don't know if I can drink more beer. My teeth are floating."

"Your teeth are—?"

"I'm bursting with beer."

"Maybe you should drink something more concentrated. Beer's mostly water. I wish alcohol came in the same size as an aspirin. You just wear out your digestion trying to cop a buzz. And this stuff"—she pointed—"tastes like *kerosene*. Your teeth are floating! That's a scream."

Briggs didn't feel comfortable doing more to prevent the arrival of another round, but when she'd finished it, he wished he had.

"Olivia."

"What."

"You okay?"

"Where are we going with this?"

"I thought you were about to faint."

"Oh, how wrong you are."

Briggs caught Jerry Warren's eye and made a writing gesture with his right hand on his left hand. Warren winked his understanding, and Briggs turned back to Olivia. "Let's get outside while we have a little of this day left," he said. He could tell that this was heard from a great distance. He stood up to enforce the suggestion and then thought to extend a hand, which Olivia took as she got to her feet and quickly leaned against him.

"Going to have to do it like this, aren't I?"

"Not a problem. Out we go."

— — — — — — — — — —

Briggs escorted her through the front door so deftly that their exit was barely noticed. The one woman who stared was told by Olivia, "No worries," in an Australian accent. Once outside, the heat hit her and she began to topple. Briggs had to take her around the corner to find a quiet spot. "I want to help you here, Olivia. You're having a bit of trouble with your balance."

"How did I let this *hap*-pen? A little birdie says it's time for me to scoot," she said. With her hands at her shoulders, fingers fluttering outward, she did the birdie.

"How about if you let me drive you home?"

"*Bor*-ing."

"I'm afraid I require it. Where is your car?"

"A, we identify make and model."

"Can you do that for me? And parking place?"

She looked left and right. "You know, John Briggs, I'm going to flunk that test."

"No problem. We'll go in mine." He helped her into his twenty-year-old sedan. She told him they'd be lucky if the jalopy made it to her house. The car had old-style seat belts, and fastening hers across her lap produced from Olivia a languorous smile. "There!" he said briskly, to undo the smile, then went around to his side, got in, looked over at her amiably, and turned the key.

"Doesn't look like you're going to try to take advantage of me."

"Nope."

"It wouldn't be hard. All aboard!" She imitated a train whistle.

They headed north and, just as they left town, she said, "Hey, there's my car!" But then she was uncertain. It didn't really matter to Briggs, unless she turned out to be right in wondering whether his car would make it. They were halfway to her house before she spoke again. She said, "Ooh, boy, this is a bad idea."

Grassland spread in either direction all the way to the horizon. From the west, a thunderstorm, zigzagged with wires of lightning, was moving swiftly toward them, until the road ahead began to darken with rain.

Briggs drove without trying to talk until they reached Olivia's town. She pointed out various turns and landmarks, letting her hand fall back onto her lap each time. The trees formed a canopy above the street where she said she lived, a street on which either invidious competition or the boundless love of property had prevailed in the form of one perfect lawn after another, and hedges that seemed to have been purchased in sections. At length, she said, "This is it, with the red shutters. Who else has red shutters? Nobody. Just us. Has red shutters. Have red shutters."

Briggs made sure the coast was clear for assisting her to the house. Olivia had lost some ground since they set out, and it seemed unlikely that she would be able to walk safely. A man in bicycle shorts went by, leading a Newfoundland; there was a Rollerblader, a very old and slow woman pulling a wagon of groceries, a FedEx man delivering to the house next door, and then it was time to rouse Olivia all over again and go for it. "I'm so sorry," she said, as he steadied her beside the car. "I see the jalopy held up better than I thought it would. Shouldn't have said what I said. 'Never ridicule what you don't understand,' my father told me."

Briggs reached for the door but it opened before he touched it, and a severe-looking older man in a starched white shirt appeared. He had a high domed forehead and piercing blue eyes. He inspected Briggs and, speaking to him but looking at Olivia, who stood with her head hanging, said, "We're at it again, I see." Briggs helped her into the front hall and passed her arm to the man he guessed was her father, expecting to retreat to his car, but then the man closed the door behind the three of them and said, "Wait here," with what, in other circumstances, might have seemed an intolerably brusque tone. Briggs stood in the hallway as Olivia went off without a word, climbing the stairs with the aid of her father. He could make out the corner of a dining-room table, a section of transom window, dark wainscoting, old family photographs on either side of the stairway.

"So sorry to leave you standing there," the man said when he returned, guiding Briggs forcefully into the house. "I'm Olin Halliday, Olivia's father. Not too proud to eat in the kitchen, are you?" Briggs obediently followed Halliday through swinging doors. The kitchen met more than the ordinary domestic requirements, with a freestanding chopping block, a commercial-grade stove, and a double-doored freezer. Halliday pointed to a dripping bag suspended over a large mixing bowl. "Making cottage cheese. Not ready yet. I hope you like brisket. I like brisket way too well, and I never seem to get it quite like I want it, though this time I'm close. I try to smoke it long enough to start the neighbors complaining. Then I know I'm on the right track. Like everything else, you have to put in the time."

At last they were seated on stools at the chopping block. Halliday carved the brisket with a broad razor-sharp knife, which he wielded rapidly, each perfect slice just tipping over of its own weight as he started the next. Coleslaw, "my tomatoes," beet greens, corn bread, and iced tea. "Should have beer but I can't keep it in the house," Halliday said. Then he began to eat with the absorption of a hungry man eating alone. Briggs waited a moment before following suit, the food so good it created an appetite.

"As you have seen," Halliday said, mouth still full, punctuating with his fork, "Olivia cannot drink. Cannot but does, and shouldn't. She is the kind of alcoholic usually described as 'hopeless,' but of course she is not hopeless, and I'm not without hope. Are you?"

"I hardly know Olivia."

"There's a difference between taking responsibility, Mr. Briggs, and blaming yourself for everything. There should be a line between the two. Olivia does not see that line."

With every remark, Halliday scrutinized Briggs, and because of his sky blue eyes, his gaze may have seemed more penetrating than intended. Just then Olivia called down in a near screech, *"Tell him what they did to me!"* Halliday and Briggs looked at each other in silence, Briggs alarmed.

He said, "What does she mean by that?"

"It's always something new," Halliday said, looking away. "She has hung on to her job at the hospital. I've helped there; an argument can still be made that she's viable."

"You tell him."

"I'm afraid this could go on. Have you had enough to eat?"

"Yes."

"Don't be worried; this is the best place she could be."

"I hope so."

"I'm her father, Mr. Briggs, and I'm a doctor."

Briggs felt no urgency to respond. After a moment had passed, he asked, "Where is Olivia's mother?"

"Olivia's mother is no longer living. I delivered Olivia, and I adopted her. Olivia's mother was not married."

"Has her mother been dead for a long time?"

Halliday smiled cheerlessly. "She's been dead almost since Olivia was born. She jumped off Carter's Bridge and went all the way to North Dakota before what the fauna of the Great Plains had left of her was found. It was sad, it was unforeseen, and it was certainly not anybody's fault, least of all Olivia's, but Olivia doesn't see it that way."

"What can you do to help someone get over that?"

"Nothing that's worked, as you can see. But now I'm going to try something new and, to tell the truth, I'm optimistic. Olivia is almost pathologically shy, and I'm persuaded that this is connected to the grudge she holds against herself. She is quite dependent upon me, especially financially, which has caused plenty of resentment. That's my only lever but it's a good one. Anyway, long story short, I am going to require Olivia to join Toastmasters International."

Halliday watched complacently as his new idea sank in. Briggs suspected that he wasn't the first stranger on whom it had been floated. He began to wonder what other miracle cures Halliday might have attempted on the poor girl. "I don't get it."

"You don't have to get it. Olivia has to get it. I'm going to help Olivia ground herself. I want to revise her core values. You don't know the boyfriends she's had. I want her to learn to recognize and avoid losers. But she's got to learn how to boldly share her message. She's got to quit going off on tangents. I think if she looked within and learned the skills of public speaking that she would delight audiences with dynamic presentations by simply unleashing her inner self."

"I've never heard of anything this crazy."

"I take that as a compliment. It doesn't bother me to be ahead of the crowd."

Briggs left immediately, making his exit as rude as possible. As soon as he was under way in his car he was aware of the smell of Olivia's perfume, which was somehow more conspicuous in her absence. He hardly had a profound connection to her, but he could not get her out of his mind. For the first time his car actually did seem like a jalopy. Halliday had surely taken him for a loser.

"I don't have a garage," he could have explained. "Why leave a good car sitting out in the weather?" This was the first of his imaginary dialogues with Olivia. One about drinking left him believing that she was possessed, an idea whose tawdry allure was obvious. He imagined a priestly intervention during which evil spirits were exorcised and Halliday, with his pop theories, stayed well to the rear. Briggs understood that these daydreams were meant to allay some heartache.

— — — — — — — — — — —

Briggs spent most of September making repairs on his place, getting ready to go back to work. He repainted the shutters, a maddening job because of all the louvers. He set pack-rat traps and pruned the raspberry patch. He alphabetized his library, a recurrent task since he never put books back where they belonged. He changed the water filter in the basement and removed the ghastly mushrooms that had volunteered there. The lawn seemed to have stopped growing, so he put the mower in the garage. Next to the barn was a stack of old boards that had warped and rotted beyond use; he pulled the truck around in order to haul this trash to a safe place for burning. He was nearly finished when he reached for a heavy sheet of exterior plywood, which he had to raise on its edge to drag it to the truck. As he lifted it, he felt something like the blow of a stick against his leg. He raised the plywood higher and saw the coiled rattlesnake, dropped the plywood, and backed away with a chill. He drew up his pant leg and saw where the fangs had gone in and the slight reddening around the marks. He pulled off his work gloves and decided he'd take the back way to the hospital in his truck. He wondered how bad this was going to be.

It was a half-hour drive, and the serious ache and swelling commenced. He parked close to the emergency entrance, next to two old ambulances, and limped into the waiting room. The nurse, filling out forms, was a long time acknowledging him and when she did so it was by the mere raising of her head. When he explained what was wrong, she told him to have a seat. They must see a lot of snakebites, Briggs thought. The spot where he'd been bitten was now quite enlarged and had acquired a dusky cast that worried him.

Eventually, the nurse instructed him to fill out a form, which he did with growing awareness of the pain. Then she said, "I'll take you to your room. You'll be spending the night." She turned and Briggs followed her down a brown corridor with the usual antiseptic smell and stainless-steel tables on wheels. She left him in the room. He propped one foot on the toe of the other to allevi- ate the rhythmic ache and found himself perspiring. He reached for the remote control, turned the TV on, and then turned it off immediately.

A few minutes later, Olivia entered in a nurse's uniform. "Let's get rid of those pants," she said. As Briggs lay in his shorts, Olivia bent close over the wound and studied it in silence. "Right back," she said, and left the room. When she returned a few minutes later, she had a metal tray with a syringe on it. "I don't like this stuff," she said, "but the poison has spread and we've got to use it. It will help with the pain. We're talking pronto." Briggs had planned a conversation designed to crack this mystery, but Olivia was leaning over him, studying his eyes as she pressed the hypodermic into him, and with the enveloping wave he was overcome. "Feels so good," she said quietly. "Doesn't it?" He nodded slowly, infinitely grateful for the bite of the rattlesnake. She held his face in her hands and gazed at him as he went under. "I just know it feels *so* good."

When he awoke the next morning, he doubted everything he remembered. He checked his leg to see if he'd been bitten by a snake, and thank God he had. He noticed that the pain was gone. He rang the call button next to his bed. A nurse entered, a tall, peevish woman of fifty, carrying a copy of *Field & Stream*. "I'm better, and I'm going home."

"Doctor will decide when you can go."

With Briggs's impatience growing, it was a blessing the doctor came soon. Close to retirement age, he was a well-groomed silver-haired man, exceedingly thin, in polished walking shoes, cuffed serge pants, and a sparkling white smock.

"How do you feel?"

"I feel fine, ready to go home. I suppose the nurse is off today."

"What nurse?"

"The one who treated me last night."

"I treated you last night. You were sound asleep, like you'd passed out. In any case, I couldn't wake you: I went ahead and did what I thought best. I gave you a good slug of antivenin."

"I clearly remember a woman coming in and treating me."

"I hope she was pretty. It was a dream."

"Let me ask you something. Is Dr. Halliday on duty today?"

The doctor looked startled and a little evasive. He said, "Dr. Halliday lost his license to practice a long time ago. Of course, we feel terrible about it. His daughter has stayed with us, and we hope that's some help in a very regrettable situation."

Briggs left the hospital in the same dirty clothes he'd worn to paint and clean his yard. He drove home, parked by the woodpile, and killed the snake with a hoe, then went up to the house to read his mail and check his phone messages. He felt an incongruous sadness about killing the snake, which had tried in vain to get away. The refrigerator was still well stocked, and he started a pot of spicy vegetable soup. He smelled mothballs and remembered the blankets he'd put in storage the day before.

On Wednesday, he took three shirts and a sport jacket to be dry-cleaned. He usually went to Arnold's, where he had an account, but it was closed on Wednesdays so he drove a few extra miles and carried his things into Bright's. The smell of cleaning fluid was a little stronger in Bright's, and he wondered whether that meant they were more thorough or just harsher on the clothes. To the left of the long counter, a broad woman with her back to him operated the electrical revolving rack. She said, "Be just a sec," and compared a slip with that on several garments going past. She found what she was looking for, a tuxedo, and took it down to hang on a rigid rack next to the cash register, before turning to Briggs: it was her, the woman who'd accosted him at the farmers' market. She recognized him first and covered her mouth with her hands. "I wondered if I'd see you again. I so have to apologize to you! I completely and utterly thought you were someone else."

"Don't give it a thought," Briggs said with reserve. He added, "I gather you took a number of other people for someone else."

This puzzled her. "No, just you."

"I was led to think otherwise. Guess it's my turn to apologize."

"Can we call it even-Steven?"

He hoped to have a chance to speak to Olivia about this. So, later in the fall, when he received an invitation to her wedding, his first thought was, Of course I'll go.

In the receiving line, Olivia, jubilant and tipsy, hung around the neck of her new husband, a glass of champagne in her hand. The wedding party was clamorous, gathered under the old trees behind the house with the red shutters. The husband was a specimen of tidy manhood, with black, tightly clipped hair, blue eyes, and ears like little seashells; he wore a perfectly tailored dark summer suit and a colorful tie that spelled out the word *Montana*—not the state but Claude, the French couturier. Briggs wondered if he was wrong in thinking the groom wore eyeliner. Olivia touched the champagne glass to the tip of her nose and giggled when Briggs appeared. He knew right away that he wouldn't be able to ask his questions. He pumped the husband's hand and wished them all the luck in the world. He meant it, even though he felt the same queer longing on seeing Olivia. It was her husband's turn to go for a ride.

During the ceremony, rain clouds had grumbled overhead and now the shower began. The wedding party rushed to the house with hilarity, and Briggs decided this would be a good time for him to leave, but Olivia detained him, resting her outspread fingers on his shirt while the rain fell on them both. She was remarkably heedless in her beautiful wedding gown, and Briggs caught sight of the groom's face in the hall window. "You were so good to me that time and so patient with my father," she said.

"Where is your father?"

"We got him out of here." She was close to him as she spoke. He felt her breath on his face and his heart was racing. "I'm glad I had the chance to"—she smiled—"to give you a lift when you were in the hospital."

The rain redoubled, sweeping down through the canopy of leaves, and they fled to the house, Olivia disappearing into the happy crowd. Briggs didn't know quite what to do with himself. He made his way back to the kitchen where he'd dined with Dr. Halliday. It was empty. He went to the sink and ran the tap until the water was cold, filled a glass, and drank it down. The pandemonium outside elevated for an instant as the kitchen door opened behind him. When he put the glass down and turned around, he was looking into the face of the groom, aggressively close to his own. He stared at Briggs in silence. "I hope you understand that you will never put your nasty hands on her again," he said. "Get over it."

Briggs looked at this handsome well-cared-for man. "It will be hard to give up," Briggs said.

"But you will, won't you?"

"I suppose. It was so intense, the last time, in my car, the air bags deployed. But, yes, you have my word."

The groom reached out his hand and Briggs took it. The hand was so clammy that Briggs had an instant of sympathy. In the groom's face nothing changed. "Have we got a deal?" the groom asked, and Briggs pretended to agonize over the decision. He let the conflicts play themselves out on his face, then heaved a great sigh.

"We've got a deal," he said, his voice resigned.

As they strolled back to the party together, Briggs decided that spicing things up in this way was absolutely the last favor he would do for Olivia. He watched the groom go to her and whisper in her ear. Olivia looked over at Briggs, smiled at him sadly, he thought, and waved. Hello? Goodbye? He wasn't sure.

The rain had stopped, and something caused the wedding party to gravitate to the stately elm shading the lawn, its leaves just starting to change color. Briggs followed until he was part of the half circle of celebrants facing Olivia, who stood on a small dais, placed there, he supposed, for this purpose. "I'd like to propose a toast!" she called out, in a voice that carried remarkably. He barely heard her words but stared, spellbound, at her wide, confident smile, the steady movement of her head as she took in all the guests, and the hand gestures that would have been clear from the nearby mountains. Her voice rang out expressively, each syllable occupying its own time and space. At the end of her toast, she clasped her hands to her chest and bowed modestly to the admiring applause and, without looking, reached out a regal hand to her new husband.

Cowboy

The old feller made me go into the big house in my stocking feet. The old lady's in a big chair next to the window. In fact, the whole room's full of big chairs, but she's only in one of them, though as big as she is she could of filled up several. The old man said, "I found this one in the loose-horse pen at the sale yard."

She says, "What's he supposed to be?"

He says, "Supposed to be a cowboy."

"What's he doin in the loose horses?"

I says, "I was lookin for one that would ride."

"You was in the wrong pen, son," says the old man. "Them's canners. They're goin to France in cardboard boxes."

"Once they get a steel bolt in the head." The big old gal in the chair laughed.

Now I'm sore. "There's five in there broke to death. I rode em with nothin but binder twine."

"It don't make a shit," says the old man. "Ever one of them is goin to France."

The old lady didn't believe me. "How'd you get near them loose horses to ride?"

"I went in there at night."

The old lady says, "You one crazy cowboy go in there in the dark. Them broncs kick your teeth down your throat. I suppose you tried bareback."

"Naw, I drug the saddle I usually ride at the Rose Bowl Parade."

"You got a horse for that?"

"I got Trigger. We unstuffed him."

She turns to the old man. "He's got a mouth on him. This much we know."

"Maybe he can tell us what good he is."

I says, "I'm a cowboy."

"You're a outta work cowboy."

"It's a dyin way of life."

"She's about like me. She's wondering if this ranch supposed to be some welfare agency for cowboys."

I've had enough. "You're the dumb honyocker drove me out here."

I thought that was the end, but the old lady said, "Don't get huffy. You got the job. You against conversation or somethin?"

We get outside and the old sumbitch says, "You drawed lucky there, son. That last deal could of pissed her off."

"It didn't make me no never mind if it did or didn't."

"Anymore, she hasn't been well. Used to she was sweet as pudding."

"I'm sorry for that. We don't have health, we don't have nothin."

━━ ━━ ━━ ━━ ━━ ━━ ━━ ━━ ━━ ━━

She must of been afflicted something terrible, because she was ugly mornin, noon, and night for as long as she lasted, pick a fight over nothin, and the old sumbitch bound to got the worst of it. I felt sorry for him, little slack as he ever cut me.

Had a hundred seventy-five sweet-tempered horned Herefords and fifteen sleepy bulls. Shipped the calves all over for hybrid vigor, mostly to the south. Had some go clear to Florida. A Hereford still had its horns was a walkin miracle and the old sumbitch had him a smart little deal goin. I soon learned to give him credit for such things, and the old lady barking commands off the sofa weren't no slouch neither. Anybody else seen their books might say they could be winterin in Phoenix.

They didn't have no bunkhouse, just a LeisureLife mobile home that had lost its wheels about thirty years ago, and they had it positioned by the door of the barn so it'd be convenient for the hired man to stagger out at all hours and fight breech birth and scours and any other disorder sent down by the cow gods. We had some doozies. One heifer had got pregnant and her calf was near as big as she was. Had to reach in and take it out in pieces. When we threw the head out on the ground she turned to it and lowed like it was her baby. Everything a cow does is to make itself into meat as fast as it can so somebody can eat it. It's a terrible life, and a cowboy is its little helper.

The old sumbitch and I got along good. We got through calvin and got to see them pairs and bulls run out onto the new grass. Nothin like seeing all that meat feel a little temporary joy. Then we bladed out the corrals and watched em dry under the spring sun at long last. Only mishap was the manure spreader threw a rock and knocked me senseless and I drove the rig into an irrigation ditch. The old sumbitch never said a word but chained up and pulled us out with his Ford.

We led his cavvy out of the hills afoot with two buckets of sweet feed. Had a little of everything, including a blue roan I fancied, but he said it was a Hancock and bucked like the National Finals in Las Vegas, kicking out behind and squalling, and was just a man-killer. "Stick to the bays," he said. "The West was won on a bay horse."

He picked out three bays, had a keg of shoes, all ones and aughts, and I shod them best I could, three geldings with nice manners, stood good to shoe. About all you could say about the others was they had four legs each; a couple, all white-marked from saddle galls and years of hard work, looked like maybe no more summers after this. They'd been rode many a long mile. We chased em back into the hills and the three that was shod whinnied and fretted. "Back to work," the old sumbitch tells em.

We shod three cause one was going to pack a ton of fencing supplies—barb wire, smooth wire, steel T-posts and staples, old wore-out Sunflower fence stretchers that could barely grab on to the wire—and we was at it a good little while where the elk had knocked miles of it down or the cedar finally give out and had to be replaced by steel. But that was how I found out the old sumbitch's last good time was in Korea, where the officers would yell, "Come on up here and die!" Said they was comin in waves. Tells me all this while the stretcher pulls that wire squealin though the staples. He was a tough old bastard.

"They killed a pile of us and we killed a pile of them." *Squeak!*

We hauled the mineral horseback too, in panniers, white salt and iodine salt. He didn't have no use for blocks, so we hauled it in sacks and poured it into the troughs he had on all these bald hilltops where the wind would blow away the flies. Most of his so-called troughs was truck tires nailed onto anything flat— plywood, old doors, and suchlike—but they worked alright. A cow can put her tongue anywhere in a tire and get what she needs, and you can drag one of them flat things with your horse if you need to move em. Most places we salted had old buffalo wallers where them buffalo wallered. They done wallered their last, had to get out of the way for the cow and the man on the bay horse.

— — — — — — — — — — —

I'd been rustlin my own grub in the LeisureLife for a good little while when the old lady said it was time for me to eat with the white folks. This wasn't necessarily a good thing. The old lady's knee replacements had begun to fail, and both me and the old sumbitch was half-afraid of her. She cooked good as ever but she was a bomb waitin to go off, standin bowlegged at the stove and talkin ugly about how much she did for us. When she talked, the old sumbitch would move his mouth like he was saying the same words. If the old lady'd caught him at that they'd a been hell to pay.

Both of them was heavy smokers, to where a oxygen bottle was in sight. So they joined a Smoke-Enders deal the Lutherans had, and this required em to put all their butts in a jar and wear the jar around their neck on a string. The old sumbitch liked this okay because he could just tap his ash right under his chin and not get it on the truck seat, but the more that thing filled up and hung around her neck the meaner the old lady got. She had no idea the old sumbitch was cheatin and settin his jar on the wood-pile when we was workin outside. She was just honester than him, and in the end she give up smokin and he smoked away, except he wasn't allowed to in the house no more nor buy ready-mades, cause the new tax made them too expensive and she wouldn't let him take it out of the cows, which come first. She said it was just a vice, and if he was half the man she thought he was he'd give it up for a bad deal. "You could have a long and happy old age," she told him, real sarcastic-like.

One day me and the old sumbitch is in the house hauling soot out of the fireplace on account of they had a chimney fire last winter. Over the mantel is a picture of a beautiful woman in a red dress with her hair piled on top of her head. The old sumbitch tells me that's the old lady before she joined the motorcycle gang.

"Oh?"

"Them motorcycle gangs," he says, "all they do is eat and

work on their motorcycles. They taught her to smoke too, but she's shut of that. Probably outlive us all."

"Oh?"

"And if she ever wants to box you tell her no. She'll knock you on your ass, I guarantee it. Throw you a damn haymaker, son."

I couldn't understand how he could be so casual about the old lady being in a motorcycle gang. When we was smokin in the LeisureLife, I asked him about it. That's when I found out him and the old lady was brother and sister. I guess that explained it. If your sister joins some motorcycle gang, that's her business. He said she even had a tattoo—*Hounds from Hell*—a dog shootin flames out of his nostrils and riding a Harley.

That picture on the mantel kind of stayed in my mind, and I asked the old sumbitch if his sister'd ever had a boyfriend. Well yes, he said, several, quite a few, quite a damn few. "Our folks run em off. They was only after the land."

By now we was in the barn and he was goin all around the baler, hittin the zerks with his grease gun. "I had a lady friend myself. Do anything. Cook. Gangbusters with a snorty horse and not too damn hard on the eyes. Sis run her off. Said she was just after the land. If she was, I never could see it. Anyway, went on down the road a long time ago."

―――――――――――

Fall come around and when we brought the cavvy down, two of them old-timers who'd worked so hard was lame. One was stifled, the other sweenied, and both had cripplin quarter cracks. I thought they needed to be at the loose-horse sale, but the old sumbitch says, "No mounts of mine is gonna feed no Frenchmen," and that was that. So we made a hole, led the old-timers to the edge, and shot them with a elk rifle. First one didn't know what hit him. Second one heard the shot and saw his buddy fall, and the old sumbitch had to chase him all around to kill him. Then he sent me down the hole to get the halters back. Liftin them big heads was some chore.

I enjoyed eatin in the big house that whole summer until the sister started givin me come-hither looks. They was fairly limited except those days when the old sumbitch was in town after supplies. Then she dialed it up and kind of brushed me every time she went past the table. There was always something special on town days, a pie maybe. I tried to think about the picture on the mantel but it was impossible, even though I knew it might get me out of the LeisureLife once and for all. She was gettin more and more wound up while I was pretendin to enjoy the food, or goin crazy over the pie. But she didn't buy it—called me a queer, and sent me back to the trailer to make my own meals. By callin me a queer, she more or less admitted to what she'd been up to, and I think that embarrassed her, because she covered up by roaring at everyone and everything, including the poor old sumbitch, who had no idea what had gone sideways while he was away. It was two years before she made another pie, and then it was once a year on my birthday. She made me five birthday pies in all, sand cherry, every one of them.

I broke the catch colt, which I didn't know was no colt as he was the biggest snide in the cavvy. He was four, and it was time. I just got around him for a couple days, then saddled him gentle as I could. The offside stirrup scared him and he looked over at it, but that was all it was to saddlin. I must of had a burst of courage, cause next minute I was on him. That was okay too. I told the old sumbitch to open the corral gate, and we sailed away. The wind blew his tail up under him, and he thought about buckin but rejected the idea, and that was about all they was to breakin Olly, for that was his name. Once I'd rode him two weeks, he was safe for the old sumbitch, and he plumb loved this new horse and complimented me generously for the job I'd did.

We had three hard winters in a row, then lost so many calves to scours we changed our calving grounds. The old sumbitch just come out one day and looked at where he'd calved out for fifty years and said, "The ground's no good. We're movin." So we spent the summer buildin a new corral way off down the creek. When we's finished, he says, "I meant to do this when I got back from overseas, and now it's finished and I'm practically done for too. Whoever gets the place next will be glad his calves don't shit themselves into the next world like mine done."

Neither one of us had a back that was worth a damn, and if we'd had any money we'd of had the surgery. The least we could do was get rid of the square baler and quit heftin them man-killin five-wire bales. We got a round baler and a DewEze machine that let us pick up a bale from the truck without layin a finger on it. We'd smoke in the cab on those cold winter days and roll out a thousand pounds of hay while them old-time horned Herefords followed the truck sayin nice things about me and the old sumbitch while we told stories. That's when I let him find out I'd done some time.

"I figured you musta been in the crowbar hotel."

"How's that?"

"Well, you're a pretty good hand. What's a pretty good hand doin tryin loose horses in the middle of the night at some Podunk sale yard? Folks hang on to a pretty good hand, and nobody was hangin on to you. You want to tell me what you done?"

I'd been with the old sumbitch for three years and out of jail the same amount of time. I wasn't afraid to tell him what I done, for I was starting to trust him, but I sure didn't want him tellin nothin to his sister. I trusted him enough to tell him I did the time, but that was about all I was up to. I told him I rustled some yearlins, and he chuckled like everybody understood that. Unfortunately, it was a lie. I rustled some yearlings, all right, but that's not what I went up for.

The old man paid me in cash, or rather the old lady did, as she handled anything like that. They never paid into workmen's comp, so there was no reason to go to the records. They didn't even have the name right. You tell people around here your name is Shane, and they'll always believe you. The important thing is I was workin my tail off for that old sumbitch, and he knew it. Nothin else mattered, even the fact we'd come to like each other. After all, this was a goddam ranch.

The old feller had several peculiarities to him, most of which I've forgot. He was one of the few fellers I ever seen who would actually jump up and down on his hat if he got mad enough. You can imagine what his hat looked like. One time he did it cause I let the swather get away from me on a hill and bent it all to hell. Another time a Mormon tried to run down his breeding program to get a better deal on some replacement heifers, and I'll be damned if the old sumbitch didn't throw that hat down and jump on it, until the Mormon got back into his Buick and eased on down the road without another word. One time when we was drivin ring shanks into corral poles I hit my thumb and tried jumpin on my hat, but the old sumbitch gave me such a odd look I never tried it again.

—————————————————

The old lady died sittin down, went in there and there she was, sittin down, and she was dead. After the first wave of grief, the old sumbitch and me fretted about rigor mortis and not being able to move her in that seated position, which would almost require rollin her. So we stretched her onto the couch and called the mortician, and he called the coroner and for some reason the coroner called the ambulance, which caused the old sumbitch to state, "It don't do you no never mind to tell nobody nothin." Course, he was right.

Once the funeral was behind us, I moved out of the Leisure-Life once and for all, partly for comfort and partly cause the old sumbitch falled apart after his sister passed, which I never suspected during the actual event. But once she's gone, he says he's all that's left of his family and he's alone in life, and about then he notices me and tells me to get my stuff out of the LeisureLife and move in with him.

We rode through the cattle pretty near ever day, year-round, and he come to trust me enough to show how his breedin program went, with culls and breedbacks and outcrosses and re-placements, and he took me to bull sales and showed me what to expect in a bull and which ones was correct and which was sorry. One day we's looking at a pen of yearlin bulls on this outfit near Luther, and he can't make up his mind and says he wishes his sister was with him and starts snufflin and says she had an eye on her wouldn't quit. So I stepped up and picked three bulls out of that pen and he quit snufflin and said damn if I didn't have an eye on me too. That was the beginnin of our partnership.

One whole year I was the cook, and one whole year he was the cook, and back and forth like that but never at the same time. Whoever was cook would change when the other feller got sick of his recipes, and ever once in a while a new recipe would come in the *AgriNews*, like that corn chowder with the sliced hot dogs. I even tried a pie one time, but it just made him lonesome for days gone by, so we forgot about desserts, which was probably good for our health as most sweets call for gobbin in the white sugar.

The sister had never let him have a dog cause she had a cat, and she thought a dog would get the cat and, as she said, if the dog got the cat she'd get the dog. It wasn't much of a cat, anyhow, but it lasted a long time, outlived the old lady by several moons. After it passed on, we took it out to the burn barrel, and the first thing the old sumbitch said was, "We're gettin a dog." It took him that long to realize his sister was gone.

Tony was a border collie we got as a pup from a couple in Miles City that raised them, and they was seven generation of cow dogs just wanted to eat and work stock. You could cup your hands and hold Tony when we got him, but he grew up in one summer and went to work and we taught him *down, here, come by, way to me,* and *hold em,* all in one year or less, cause Tony'd just stay on his belly and study you with his eyes until he knew exactly what you wanted. Tony helped us gather, mother up pairs, and separate bulls, and he lived in the house for many a good year and kept us entertained with all his tricks.

Finally, Tony got old and died. We didn't take it so good, especially the old sumbitch, who said he couldn't foresee enough summers for another dog. Plus that was the year he couldn't get on a horse no more and he wasn't about to work no stock dog afoot. There was still plenty to do, and most of it fell to me. After all, this was a goddam ranch.

The time come to tell him what I done to go to jail, which was rob that little store at Absarokee and shoot the proprietor, though he didn't die. I had no idea why I did such a thing, then or now. I led the crew on the prison ranch for a number of years and turned out many a good hand. They wasn't nearabout to let me loose till there was a replacement good as me who'd stay awhile. So I trained up a murderer from Columbia Falls; could rope, break horses, keep vaccine records, fence, and irrigate. Once the warden seen how good he was, they paroled me out and turned it all over to the new man, who they said was never getting out. Said he was heinous. The old sumbitch could give a shit less when I told him my story. I could of told him all the years before, when he first hired me, for all he cared. He was a big believer in what he saw with his own eyes.

I don't think I ever had the touch with customers the old sumbitch did. They'd come from all over lookin for horned Herefords and talkin hybrid vigor, which I may or may not have believed. They'd ask what we had and I'd point to the corrals and say, "Go look for yourself." Some would insist on seein the old sumbitch and I'd tell them he was in bed, which was nearly the only place you could find him, once he'd begun to fail. Then the state got wind of his condition and took him to town. I went to see him there right regular, but it just upset him. He couldn't figure out who I was and got frustrated because he knew I was somebody he was supposed to know. And then he failed even worse. They said it was just better if I didn't come around.

The neighbors claimed I'd let the weeds grow and was personally responsible for the spread of spurge, Dalmatian toadflax, and knapweed. They got the authorities involved, and it was pretty clear I was the weed they had in mind. If they could get the court to appoint one of their relatives ranch custodian they'd have all that grass for free till the old sumbitch was in a pine box. The authorities came in all sizes and shapes, but when they got through they let me take one saddle horse, one saddle, the clothes on my back, my hat, and my slicker. I rode that horse clear to the sale yard, where they tried to put him in the loose horses—cause of his age, not cause he was a bronc. I told em I was too set in my ways to start feedin Frenchmen and rode off toward Idaho. There's always an opening for a cowboy, even a old sumbitch like me, if he can halfway make a hand.

Ice

The drum major lived a short distance from our house and could sometimes be seen sitting pensively on his porch wearing his shako, a tall cylinder of white fake fur, the strap across his chin, folding the *Free Press* for his paper route. I was reluctant to so much as wave to him, since this was a time when my greatest concern—originating I don't know where—was that I was a hopeless coward. Although we saw each other every day at school, any greeting I sent his way fell on deaf ears, and I had long since given up getting any sort of response at all, a situation said to have begun when he scored 156 on the school-administered IQ test. I had the route for the *News,* so it was unremarkable that we didn't speak.

When one Thanksgiving he single-handedly captured an AWOL sailor and escorted him to the brig at the nearby base, I began to study him in the hope he held the key to escaping my cowardice.

I delivered papers in the evening and, as the year grew late, was often overtaken on my bicycle by darkness and by fear. I flung my rolled papers toward porches and stoops and onto lawns, and I was sometimes pursued by dogs, once taken down in an explosion of snow and bicycle wheels by a wolfish Irish setter. I had a recurrent fantasy of a muscular ostrich pursuing me in the dark and pecking down through my skull into my brain, another of several fears stemming from my single childhood trip to the zoo.

I always delivered my papers as promptly as possible; the drum major delivered his whenever he felt inclined to do so. One afternoon in early October, he unexpectedly chose to address me; he accused me of making him look bad by getting my papers onto people's porches and lawns before his. When I tried to respond, he cut me off and directed me to wait until his papers had been delivered before delivering mine. I complied with his instructions, tossing my papers onto lawns at all hours and dodging any customers who tried to complain.

I went to great lengths to observe the drum major practice on the big windblown and sometimes snowblown football field, where he would strut toward the goalposts trailing a stingy cape, the gray wintry lake just beyond, twirling his baton, the white shako tilted back arrogantly, culminating in the blissful high toss and recapture of the spinning chrome-plated baton, preferably without getting beaned by one of its white rubber ends. At actual game time, when he was leading our cacophonous marching band in disordered frenzy, the entire drama depended on his actually catching the baton, so that what was meant to accent a larger spectacle became the focal point of an otherwise lurching rigmarole. There was something about his haughty gaits and their seeming disconnection from the confused uproar of the band behind him, in its modest and unattractive costumes—threadbare maroon with gold piping, led by a hugely overweight youngster doing a Grambling State–style shimmy while flogging his glockenspiel with a felt-covered hammer—that was more attractive to a modest crowd that sometimes threw horse chestnuts at the drum major.

What lay behind this behavior? I think drum majors were about to be replaced by majorettes and what had once been honorably athletic had become effete and clouded with some unspoken sexual ambiguity, however inappropriate with reference to our own drum major, all of whose pert and blossoming girlfriends seemed to wind up losing their reputations. Nevertheless, the crowd hoped for a humiliating disaster. *I*, strangely, hoped for his success: I waited for that high toss to produce, as though by the hand of Praxiteles, the most graceful division of space, a split second of immortality for the drum major and for me a lesson in courage. At the same time, another part of me shared the crowd's unspoken wish to see the drum major on all fours with the baton up his behind or wrapped around his neck. As would become habitual for most of us, we wanted either spectacular achievement or mortifying failure, one or the other. Neither of these things, we were discreetly certain, would ever come to us: we'd be allowed the frictionless lives of the meek.

Our school played Flat Rock on the last Saturday of October, when winter was already in the air, the trees shabby with halfshed leaves. I was shivering in the crowd on the rickety exposed bleachers, watching our band wheel onto the field. When the drum major at last tossed the baton in its high glitter, it fell so far behind him that he had to dash into the band to retrieve it. Too late: he was swept aside, forced to stand, hands on hips, until the musicians had passed, his baton on the ground bent like a pretzel. I admit that I joined the baying crowd, our community. As he bent to pick up his bit of wreckage, we were beside ourselves. In that uproar I was without fear. I thrilled to the courage of the mob. Still, it wasn't quite the courage I was looking for.

The following week, the drum major seemed even more isolated at school, though as always he seemed to expect this. Mrs. Andrews, the beautiful young wife of our thuggish football coach who had given up her own remarkable athletic skills to teach us history, made a special effort to console him; I remember how gently she bent beside his desk to correct his work while, across the aisle, Stanley Peabody, with his flattop, pegged charcoal pants, and Flagg Flyer blue suede shoes, attempted to see down her blouse. Mrs. Andrews, with shining auburn hair piled atop her head, a single strand of imitation pearls curling down from her throat, was accustomed to being ogled and seemed to know Stanley only by a quick glance at the roster taped to her desk.

I was surprised by the attention she paid the drum major. From then on, I was a great student of any and all interactions between him and Mrs. Andrews, viewed as scarlet with erotic undertones, and abetted by the smirking of the other boys. But their behavior was no more than a salute to Mrs. Andrews's lovely figure. One incident does stand out, when, after long abstaining, Mrs. Andrews first called on the drum major in class. By now, I believed I sensed something quiet and subtle between the two of them.

"What," she asked, looking straight over the top of his head of curly brown hair, "was the principal result of the Credit Mobilier Scandal?" She seemed timid.

Legs stretched in the aisle, crossed at the ankles, fingers laced behind his head, the drum major said, "You tell me." He gazed at her with quiet annoyance that seemed to intimate possession.

We felt an electric silence, and I thrilled to what I viewed as amorous badinage disguised as classwork. Mrs. Andrews's face colored to the roots of her auburn hair. Stanley Peabody peered broadly. His sidekick, Boly Cardwell, a prematurely wizened teen with lank blond hair cascading over his forehead, grabbed his crotch surreptitiously and rolled his eyes in feigned ecstasy.

"Perhaps," she said, "you feel I have asked you the wrong question."

"Could be." The drum major had the affectless James Dean look down pat.

"In that case, why don't you pose a question for the class based on this week's reading?"

He leaned forward, dropped his elbows to his knees, drew his feet back under the chair, and held his head for a moment before he looked up. He said, "Who's buried in Grant's tomb?"

By the end of the day, he was the most important boy in school. People lingered to watch him pass in the hallway and gave him plenty of space at his locker.

Mrs. Andrews added girls' physical education to her teaching load, and from then on she seemed always to have a whistle around her neck. She moved with a new formality even when teaching history. While Stanley Peabody and Boly Cardwell headed a small group that gathered in the bleachers to run wind sprints, the drum major sat apart, focusing on Mrs. Andrews. On coed gym days, her husband, Bud Andrews, was also on the field, coaching the boys, a classic phys-ed instructor in sweats and a severe crew cut that bared the top of his scalp. One cold, dark afternoon when the windows of the gym were silver with reflected light and the air was sour with sweat, Coach Andrews suddenly sprang into the bleachers, lifted the drum major into the air, and shook him like a rag doll. The drum major managed to retain his smile, even as his head was flung about.

Coach Andrews was briefly suspended and the drum major was assigned a history tutor, though everyone agreed that Mrs. Andrews could hardly be blamed for her husband's freak-out.

I spent my paper-route earnings on small things, an imitation Civil War–era forage cap, a British commando knife, steel taps for my shoes, muskrat traps; I had gotten caught by some magazine coupon swindle whereby I tried to win a baby monkey whose huge eyes dominated the advertisement, but when I fell behind in my payments and began to doubt if the monkey would ever be shipped, I switched schemes and wound up on an easier payment plan with a flying squirrel that bit me savagely and flew around our basement for two days before escaping through the window. My father said, "Next time you've got ten bucks to spare, don't throw it away on a squirrel." My luck changed when, digging up a jack-in-the-pulpit as a gift for my mother, I discovered an old brass compass, which I attributed to voyageurs, coureurs de bois, Jesuits, Récollets, and their various bands of Pottawatamies, Wyandottes, and Hurons. Few facts came my way that could not be magnified. That compass was always in my pocket, an obvious talisman, the one thing that stood between me and the dreaded unknown.

As a test, I went back to delivering my papers on time, but the drum major had forgotten all about me. In January, I skated out onto Lake Erie, which that year was frozen nearly to Canada. I stared at its ominous expanse. I left the shore one evening on my hockey skates, a wool cap pulled over my ears and a long scarf wound around my neck and crisscrossed over my chest beneath my blue navy-surplus pea jacket. I meant to learn courage out on the ice, to avoid the specter of cowardice by skating all the way either to Canada or, if the icebreaker had been through, to the Livingstone ship channel. I struggled over the corrugations of the near-shore ice, then ventured onto glassier black ice that rewarded me with long glides between strokes of my hollow-ground blades. Bubbles could be seen and, occasionally, upended white bellies of perch and rock bass, as the sheen of glare ice, wide as my limited horizon, spread east toward Ontario; I dreamed of landing on this foreign shore, from whence the redcoats once launched sorties against our colonial heroes. I would tell Mrs. Andrews what I had done. Reading schoolbooks had embittered me against the British and the American South, while my uncles handled the job for Germany and Japan. I meant to visit the old British fort at Amherstburg and skate home with tales of imperial ghosts and whatever other secret existences I might discover in places where no human is expected.

Such dreams in the gathering darkness enlivened my skating, and I raced on, stroke after stroke, toward the hiding place of those who once sought to crush our revolution. I would one day see this as the template for many disasters I had much later created for myself, but at the time, risking my life on the same days I worried about paper cuts or infected pimples produced no sense of contradiction. I felt only the allure of the hard, black, and perfect cold-snap ice unblemished by wind during its formation. Impossible to imagine the drum major out here like some animated Q-Tip, I gloated, no prancing among the crows and ice-killed fish.

Except for those crows I was alone out there, out of sight of land or, as I then called it, Michigan, though I knew land lay to the west by the pale sunset still faintly visible. That's how I thought of it: *I can't see Michigan anymore.* I believed that if I let coming darkness turn me back, I would never be any good and the fog of cowardice would forever envelop me.

The ice seemed to rise before me and disappear into the twilight as though they were one and the same; I had to slow down in case the ice came to an end. Lights that had briefly shone on the Michigan shore were gone now, and I had yet to see my first Canadian light or the outlines of the fort I'd imagined. I touched the old compass in my pocket. Then it was dark.

When I stopped to reconnoiter, I felt the cold penetrate and I adjusted my scarf. It was time to go home, I knew, but I couldn't leave this undone at the first wave of panic. I had to press on into the plain blackness long enough to prove that it was I who elected to return and not those forces determined to make me worthless in my own eyes. Such thoughts produced an oddly inflexible rhythm to my skating, by which I reached my feet through a distance I couldn't judge by sight until I contacted the hard floor of ice.

Now the sound of my blades, which had seemed to fill the air around me, was replaced by another as murmurous as a church congregation heard from afar. I glided toward the sound when suddenly a vast aggravation of noise and turbulence erupted as a storm of ducks took flight in front of me; it was water. I heard the ominous heave of the lake. I turned to skate straight away—or not quite straight, because after some minutes of agitated effort I found myself at water's edge again, water sufficiently fraught that it had broken back the edge of ice, heaving it in layers upon itself. I skated away from that too, and, when once more surrounded by darkness and standing squarely on black ice, I stopped and recognized that I was lost. I was suspended in darkness. A step in any direction and I would drown in freezing water.

The feeling of being completely lost was claustrophobic, like being locked in a windowless room. I had an incongruous sense of airlessness; it came to me that I was going to die.

I lashed out first at my entangling fantasies, the hated redcoats especially, the pursuing ostrich—and then against death itself. My bowels began to churn, and I squatted on the ice with the pea jacket over my head, pants around my knees; I recited the Lord's Prayer in a quavering voice. And I was answered: a deep rhythmic throb that gathered slowly into a rumble. I stood and gazed into the darkness; as I pulled up and fastened my pants, a light emerged, followed by several others, streaming toward me in a line. At the moment the sound was most intense, a black all-consuming shape arose before me. It was not the god I expected: a lake freighter whose wake caused the ice to groan all around me, bound for Lake Superior. The lights streamed away and it was silent again.

I extracted the compass from my pocket and began bargaining with death. If anyone was looking on, it would be clear that whatever benefits I might be entitled to would have to be channeled through the old instrument, in whose tremulous magnetic needle I had placed all my faith. It took some concentration to hold panic at bay and rotate the battered brass case until I had north pinned down; then, staring down at the ornate *W* through the cloudy glass held just under my nose, I began to skate as rapidly as I could, moving fast on the cold mirror beneath me, creating my own wind, knowing that if the compass didn't work after its many years in the ground I would skate straight off the ice into a world from which I would not return. Myopic faith kept me stooped over my cupped hands as I pressed on with all I had.

The light of moon and stars was enough to see by if I'd known where I was going; and in a short time I could make out a half dozen squarish shapes in my path, ice fishermen's shanties. There were several of these little villages in the area, and I tried to figure out which of them this might be. They were all quite similar, small houses placed over a round hole spudded through the ice through which the occupants could angle for perch or hang for hours, iron spear in hand, to await the great pike drawn to their hand-whittled wooden perch decoy. By night, the shacks were all deserted.

But one shanty revealed a flickering light, and to it I attached all my hopes. At its door, I made out voices, and I stopped before knocking. They were voices from my classroom, and I listened as if dreaming to what sounded like a quarrel. First the drum major, cocky and bantering. The other seemed to plead and whimper and was, of course, Mrs. Andrews. And then there were different sounds, less precise than words. I had no business knowing what I knew.

I landed a long way from where I'd put on my skates and was obliged to traverse a considerable distance on my blades, tottering upon pickerel grass, water-rounded glass shards, and pebbles, waving my arms around for balance while thanking everything around me for further days on earth. But in a scrap of tangled beechwoods, these pious thoughts soon crumbled before my lurid new vision. Light from the small houses that lined the narrow road to the shore made of my flailing progress wild shadows in the leafless trees. I heard dogs barking behind closed doors, and one homeowner let his beagle out while watching me from his porch. I tried to manage my movements, but I couldn't walk normally nor could an observer see that I was wearing skates. The beagle approached to within ten feet and sat down, emitting a single reflexive bark as I passed his lawn. The owner remained on his porch and in silence watched me pass.

I didn't go on the ice again that winter. It seemed there were better things to do. As the days grew longer, I often saw the drum major starting his paper route as I got home from mine. We didn't speak, but my customers got the news on time.

Old Friends

John Briggs was made aware of the fact that some sort of problem existed for his friend and former schoolmate Erik Faucher by sheer coincidence. A request for news came from the class secretary, Everett Hoyt, who had in the thirty years since they'd graduated from Yale hardly set foot out of New Haven. With ancestors buried at the old Center Church in spitting distance of both the regicide Dixwell and Benedict Arnold's wife, Hoyt was paralyzed by a sense of generational inertia. It was said that if he hadn't got into Yale, he would not have gone to college at all but would have remained at home, waiting to bury his parents. Now, in place of any real social life, he edited the newsletter, often accompanying his requests with small indiscretions delivered with a certain giddiness—which he called *Entre News*—concerning marital failure or business malfeasance, and they almost never made it into the alumni letter.

Hoyt phoned John Briggs at his summer home, in Montana, on a nondescript piece of prairie inherited from a farmer uncle, and, while pretending to hunt up class news, insinuated that Erik Faucher, having embezzled a fortune from a bank in Boston, had gone into hiding.

"I have heard through private sources that our class scofflaw is now headed your way."

Briggs waited for the giggle to subside. "I certainly hope so," he snapped. "I've missed Erik." But he began to worry that Erik might actually come.

"See what you can do," Hoyt sang.

"I don't understand that remark, Everett."

"Perhaps it will come to you."

"I'll let you know if it does."

Faucher's ex-wife, Carol, called around five in the morning, having declined to account for the time change. "How very nice to hear your voice," said Briggs, producing a cold laugh from Carol. "How are you?"

"I'm calling about Erik. He has not been behaving sensibly at all, some very odd things to say the least."

Briggs absorbed this in silence. He knew if he said anything at all, he'd have to stand up for Faucher, and he wasn't sure he wanted to.

"Carol, you've been divorced a long time," he said finally.

"We have mutual interests. I don't know what sort of plan he has in place. And there's Elizabeth." Elizabeth was their daughter.

"I'm sure he's made a very sensible plan."

"I don't want Elizabeth to wind up sleeping in her car. Or me, for that matter."

"I don't think we should argue." This was in response to her tone.

"Did I say we should? I'm saying, Help. I'm saying, It's about time you did." When Briggs failed to reply, she added, "I know where he's going and who to put on his trail."

Briggs's friendship with Faucher had been long and intermittent. Arbitrarily assigned as roommates at the boarding school they'd attended before Yale, they had become lifelong friends without ever getting over the fact that their discomfort with each other occasionally boiled over into detestation. Sometime earlier they had been sold loyalty much as the far-fetched basics of religion are sold to the credulous. When Briggs was in his twenties and had sunk everything into a perfectly legitimate though very small mining company in Alberta with excellent long-term prospects but ruinously expensive short-term requirements, Erik rescued him from bankruptcy by finding a buyer who bought Briggs out at a price that restored his investment and even gave him a small profit to accompany this dangerous lesson. Erik explained that he'd had to waste a valuable quid pro quo on this and waved his finger in Briggs's face.

When Erik was pulled from the second story of a burning whorehouse on assignment for UNESCO as part of a Boston Congregationalists' outreach to hungry Guatemalans, Briggs made a desperate stand to keep the matter out of the newspapers and saw that nettlesome citations on his dossier were expunged.

Against these decades of loyalty, they seemed to search for an unforgivable trait in each other that would relieve them of this abhorrent, possibly lifelong burden. But now they had years of continuity to contend with, and it was harder and harder to visualize a liberating offense.

"I'm glad you called," he said to Erik, while holding a watering can over the potted annuals in his front window. "Everyone else has said you're headed this way."

"Everyone else? Like who?"

"Like Carol, the vulgar shrew you took to your heart."

"Carol? I don't know how she tracks my movements."

"And things are not so well just now?"

"Oh, bad, John. It's not wrong to claim the end is in sight." His voice struck Briggs like a saw.

"I do wish this came at a better time. I'm on a short holiday myself, the theory being rest is indicated—"

"I won't be any trouble."

"Is that so?"

Erik arrived at night while Briggs was preparing his notes for a company stalemate in Delaware for which he was serving as an independent negotiator. It surprised Briggs that Faucher had found him at all, having ventured forth from the Hertz counter at the Billings airport with nothing but a state map. He arrived with a girl he'd picked up on the way. Briggs met her after being violently awakened by Erik's jubilant goosing and her feral screeches. Her name was Marjorie, and Faucher confided that he called her Marge, "short for margarine, the cheap spread." This was not the sort of remark Briggs appreciated and was therefore exactly in the style Faucher had adopted over the years. Around midnight, Faucher reeled downstairs to inquire, with a hitch of his head, "Do you want some of this?"

"Oh, no," John said. "All for you."

Thereafter Marjorie, who seemed an attractive and reasonable girl once she started sobering up, came downstairs to complain that Erik had asked her to brush his teeth for him. John advised her to be patient; Erik would soon see he must brush his own teeth and would then go to sleep. Briggs offered her the rollout on the sunporch, but she returned wearily to Erik, having gone to the front window to cast a longing eye at the rental car. She wore a negligee that just reached her hips and, when she slowly climbed the stairs again, presented a view that was somewhat veterinary in quality. The aroma of gin trailed her. When Briggs went to bed, he thought, Who drinks gin anymore? A full moon made bands of cool light through the blinds. The Segovia he'd put on at minimum volume to help him sleep cycled on, *Recuerdos de la Alhambra*, again and again.

He hadn't been asleep long when he was awakened by noises. In the kitchen there were intruders. Briggs heard them, thumping around and opening cupboards and speaking in muffled tones. He wondered for a moment if he had forgotten that he was expecting someone. Once out of bed, he slipped into his closet, where his twelve-gauge resided on parallel coathooks for just such a time as this. Briggs quietly chambered two shells and lifted the barrels until the lock closed.

In the living room, he knelt behind the big floral wing chair that faced the fireplace and its still-dying embers. From here he could see the intruders as silhouettes, moving around the kitchen, briefly illuminated by the refrigerator light. He lifted the gun and, resting it on the back of the chair, leveled it at the closer figure. Only then did he recognize the man as his nearest neighbor, with whom he shared a water right from the irrigation ditch and a relationship that strained to be pleasant; the other intruder was the man's wife, a snappish, leanly attractive farm woman who was less diplomatic in concealing her distaste for Briggs. Listening to their conversation, Briggs understood that they expected him to be out of town and were raiding his refrigerator for beer. Briggs decided that confronting them would create waves of difficulty for him in the future and that this episode was best forgotten or set aside for use another time. So he put the gun away and crept back to bed. The neighbors departed a short time later with a farewell fling of beer cans into his roses.

Faucher's voice came from the top of the stairs. "Were those people looking for *me*?"

"No, Erik, go back to sleep. They've gone."

Marjorie was the first up: she had a remedial geometry class to teach. "Always a challenge after a long night," she explained to John. She wore a pleated blue skirt and a pale green sweater that buttoned at the throat. Her hair was drawn back from a prettily modeled forehead. She was at the stove, one hand on her hip, the other managing a spatula. "Potatoes O'Brien and eggs. Then I've got to run."

"But you don't have to cook—"

"Oh, I can't have a day with missing pieces." She cast a brilliant smile at him and held it just long enough to suggest he'd missed the boat. Erik wouldn't be getting up for breakfast because, she explained, he had an upset tummy. She held the spatula in the air while she said this, suggesting by a jotting motion that she was only reciting facts as they had been given her. Then she made a tummy-upset face. Marjorie reminded John of teachers he'd had—punctilious, too ready to use physical gestures to explain the obvious, a hint of the scold. They ate together with the unexpected comfort of strangers at a diner. She paid absolute attention to her food, looking up at him intermittently. She raised a forefinger.

"First thing he said to me was, 'You're amazing.' I have learned that when they tell you you're amazing, it's over before it starts."

"Just as well. Neither of you was feeling any pain."

"I never have any idea what will happen when I get drunk. But why would you get drunk if you knew what was going to happen?" she said. "*You* probably get off just watching people make mistakes. That's not a nice trait, Mr. Briggs!"

She smoothed her skirt and checked it for crumbs. "I'm out of here," she said, as she stood up. "What's it like?" She went to the window and craned to see the sky. "Not too bad. Okay, bye."

———— ———— ———— ———— ———— ———— ———— ———— ———— ————

Their boarding school was modeled on English public schools and built with iron ore and taconite dollars. In four years, the boys were made to see America through some British fantasy and believe that the true work of the nation fell to pencil-wristed Episcopalians who sang their babies to sleep with Blake's "Jerusalem" or uttered mild orotundities like *great good fortune* and *safe as houses*. Their hostility toward each other was such that dormitory reassignment was considered, but they seemed always to find a reason to mend their differences. They kept up a sort of friendship at college, but when Erik moved into a rented place on Whitney Avenue with an Italian girl from Quinnipiac, they lost track again. After college, each had been in the other's wedding, and they had, for a short time, lived in the same New Haven neighborhood while they attempted to launch their careers. Then, as John was less and less in the country and Faucher relocated to Boston, they became part of each other's memories, and certainly not ones either enjoyed revisiting, though they continued to make sentimental phone calls on holidays, euphorically recreating soccer triumphs on the rare occasions they were actually together. John Briggs didn't know quite why Erik Faucher was visiting him now. Surely this would be a dumb place to hide; he must want something.

When Briggs heard the shower start upstairs, he went outside and smelled the new morning wind coming through the fields. There were a few small white clouds gathering in the east, and a quarter mile off he could see a harrier working its way just over the surface of the hills. From time to time it swung up to pivot on a wingtip and then resumed its search.

The window of the upstairs bathroom opened and a wisp of steam came out, followed by the head of Erik Faucher. "John! What a morning!" Briggs was swept by a sudden and unexplained fondness. But when Erik began singing in the shower, Briggs found his voice insufferable.

Erik appeared in the yard wearing light cotton pleated pants, a hemp belt, and a long-sleeved blue cotton shirt. Though his hair was uniformly gunmetal gray, he still had the eyebrows that John associated with his French blood. John did not expect much accurate detail about the previous night's bacchanal, as it was clear he held his liquor less well than he used to. It was Erik who'd said that a Yale education consisted of learning to conceal the fact that you were drunk. He raised his vigorous black eyebrows. The wordless greeting made Briggs impatient, and he relinquished the pleasant sense that he could drink better than Erik.

"This is my first day in the American West. Of course I hope to start a successful new life here." Erik claimed to have flown from Boston, only less convenient than Kazakhstan, now that centralized air routes had made Montana oddly more remote. He didn't seem tired or hungover, and his frame looked well exercised.

"I see Marge made off with the rental car," he said.

Briggs made him some coffee and a piece of toast, which he nibbled cautiously while reading the obituaries from a week-old *Billings Gazette.*

"One of these Indians dies, they list every relative in the world. This one has three columns of kinfolks: Falls Down, Bird in Ground, Spotted Bear, Tall Enemy, Pretty on Top. Where does it end? And all their affiliations! The True Cross Evangelical Church, the Whistling Water Clan, the Bad War Deeds Clan. All I ever belonged to was Skull and Bones, and I ain't too proud of that! So please don't list it when I go. I'm no Indian."

Briggs reflected that he could read the paper perfectly well and spare himself the nonsequiturs. He eyed the bright prairie sun working across the window behind the sink. He treasured his solitary spells, infrequent as they were, and wasted very few minutes of them. This one, it seemed, was doomed.

"Look at us, John, two lone middle-aged guys."

"Filled with blind hope."

"Not me, John. But I'm expecting Montana will change all that. What a thrill that the bad times are behind me and the real delights are but inches away!"

Briggs wasn't falling for this one. He said, "I hope you're right."

"One of my great regrets," said Erik solemnly, "is that when we were young, married, and almost always drunk, we didn't just take a little time out to fuck each other's beautiful wives."

"That time has come and gone," Briggs said.

"A fellow should smell the roses once in a while. Now those two are servicing others. Perhaps, in intimate moments, they tell those faceless new men how unsatisfactory we were, possibly including baseless allusions to physical shortcomings."

"Very plausible."

Their wives had despised each other. Carol was a classic but now extinct type of Mount Holyoke girl from Cold Spring Harbor, New York, a legacy whose mission it was to bear forward to new generations the Mount Holyoke worldview. When their daughter, Elizabeth, was expelled from the college for drug use, Erik's insistence that there were other, possibly more forgiving institutions had placed him permanently outside the wall that sheltered his wife and child. When, even with certified rehabilitation, Elizabeth failed to be reinstated at Mount Holyoke, she lost interest in college altogether and joined the navy, where she was immediately happy as a machinist's mate. Faucher was bankrupt by then, a result of habitual overextension, and his inability to support Carol in the style to which she had been accustomed led to divorce and Carol's current position as a receptionist at a hearing-aid outlet on Route 90 between Boston and Natick. Very few years had brought them to this, and neither quite understood how.

Briggs had always been quite uncomfortable with Carol, and he had been greatly relieved when it was no longer necessary for them to speak. His own wife, Irena, was a beauty, a big-eyed russet-haired trilingual girl from Ljubljana whom he'd met at a trade conference in Milan, where she was translating and he was negotiating for a Yugoslav American businessman whose family's property had been nationalized by the Communists. John and Irena were married for only a few years, long enough for her to know and loathe the Fauchers. Briggs wasn't sure what else went wrong, except that Irena hadn't much liked America and had been continually exasperated by Americans' assumption that Briggs had rescued her. With John flying all over the world, she was stuck with the Fauchers. In the end, aroused by the independence of Slovenia, she grew homesick and left, remarking that Carol was a pig and Erik was a goat.

All of this lent Erik's wife-swapping lament its own particular comedy.

Faucher was surveying the hills to the east. "Don't worry about me overstaying my welcome," he said. "I'm quite considerate that way."

"Farthest thing from my mind," Briggs said.

"Do you have an answering machine?"

"Yes, and I've turned it on."

"A walk would be good," Faucher said. "We'll teach those fools to wait for the beep."

"I want you to see the homestead cemetery. It's been fenced for eighty years and still has all the old prairie flowers that are gone everywhere else. I have some forebears there."

They followed a seasonal creek toward the low hills in the west where the late-morning sun illuminated towering white clouds whose tops tipped off in identical angles. The air was so clear that their shadows appeared like birthmarks on the grass hillsides. Faucher seemed happier.

"I was glad to get out of Boston," he said. "It was unbelievably muggy. There was a four-day teachers' demonstration across from my apartment, you know, where they go *Hey, hey, ho, ho, we don't want to*—whatever. Four days, sweating and listening to those turds chant."

Briggs could see the grove of ash and alders at the cemetery just emerging from the horizon as they hiked. About twice a summer, very old people with California or Washington plates came, mowed the grass, and otherwise tended to the few graves: most homesteaders had starved out before they'd had time to die. These were the witnesses.

As they came over a slight rise, a sheet of standing rainwater was revealed in an old buffalo wallow; a coyote lit out across the water with unbelievable speed, leaving fifteen yards of pluming rooster tails behind him. Erik gazed for a moment, and said, "That was no dog. You could run a hundred of them by me and I'd never say it was a dog. Not me."

At the little graveyard, John said, "All screwed by the government." He was standing in front of his family graves, just like all the others: names, dates, nothing else. No amount of nostalgia would land him in this sad spot. "Cattle haven't been able to get in here since the thirties. The plants are here, the old heritage flowers and grasses. Surely you think that's interesting."

"I'm going to have to take your word for it."

"Erik, look at what's in front of you," Briggs said, more sharply than he intended, but Faucher just stared off, not seeming to hear him.

Needle and thread, buffalo, and orchard grass spread like a billowing counterpane around the small headstones, but shining through in the grass were shooting stars, pasqueflowers, prairie smoke, arrowleaf balsam, wild roses, streaks of violet, white, pink, and egg yolk, small clouds of bees, and darting blue butterflies. A huge cottonwood sheltered it all. Off to one side was a vigorous bull thistle that had passed unnoticed by the people in battered sedans; hard old people who didn't talk, taking turns with the scythe. They looked into cellar holes and said, "We grew up here." No sense conveying this to Erik, who mooned into the middle distance by the old fence.

"I could stand a nap," he said.

"Then that's what you shall have. But in the meanwhile, please try to get something out of these beautiful surroundings. It's tiresome just towing you around."

"I was imagining laying my weary bones among these dead. In the words of Chief Joseph, 'From where the sun now stands I will fight no more forever.' Who was in the house last night? I hope they weren't looking for me."

"That was my neighbor and his wife. They stopped by for a beer."

"Well, you know your own society. This would seem very strange in Boston."

From the alcove off his bedroom, which served as his office and which contained a small safe, a desk, a telephone, and a portable computer, he could look through the old glass windows with their bubbles and imperfections and see Erik sitting on the lawn, arms propped behind him, face angled into the sun like a girl in a Coppertone ad. Briggs was negotiating for a tiny community in Delaware that was being blackmailed by a flag manufacturer for tax abatement against purported operating costs, absent which they threatened to close and strand 251 minimum-wage workers. A North Carolina village that had lost its pulp mill wanted the company, and if Briggs worked as hard as he should, one town would die.

He explained this to Faucher as they drove to town for dinner. Faucher made a bye-bye movement with his hand and said *Hasta la vista* to whichever town it was that had to disappear. But it was otherwise a nice ride down the valley, mountains emerging below fair-weather altocumulus clouds, small ranches on either side at the heads of sparkling creeks. A self-propelled swather followed by ravens moved down a field, pivoting nimbly at the end of each row, while in the next meadow, already gleaned, its stubble shining just above the ground, a wheel line sprinkler emitted a low fog on the regrowth. A boy in a straw hat stood at a concrete head gate and, turning a wheel, let a flood of irrigation water race down a dusty ditch.

Town was three churches, a row of bars, a hotel, and a filling station. Each church had a glassed frame standing in front, the Catholic with Mass schedules, the Lutheran with a passage from the Bible, and the Evangelical a warning. The bars, likewise, had bright signs inviting ranchers, families, sportsmen, and motorcyclists respectively. Different kinds of vehicles were parked in front of each; old sedans in front of the ranchers' bar and pickup trucks in front of the local videogaming youth; and in front of the hotel some foreign models from Bozeman and Livingston. The clouds were moving fast now because of high-altitude winds, and when Briggs parked and got out of the car, the hotel towering over him looked like the prow of a ship crossing a pale blue ocean.

Faucher scanned his menu vigorously. "My God, this all looks good and will look even better after a nice cocktail." He was a vampire coming to life at sundown; with each drink pale flames arose beneath his skin.

They ordered from a ruddy-faced girl who seemed excited by every choice they made, especially the Spanish fish soup with which they both commenced. She had a Fritz the Kat tattoo on her upper arm, which Faucher peered at over the top of his menu. John asked for a bottle of Bandol, and when the candles had been lit he thought the way lay clear for Erik to make himself plain. Erik looked down at the table for a long moment, absentmindedly rearranging his silverware. He heaved a great sigh and raised his eyes in self-abnegation. "I feel right at home here," said Erik. "Talk about your fresh start!" Briggs remained quiet and didn't take the bait.

The mayor came to the table with the vibrant merry hustle with which he drew all attention to himself. Briggs introduced him to Faucher, smiled patiently, and did not rise but stared at the mayor's fringed vest. Following a local convention, the mayor asked John when he had gotten back.

"I've been *back* about five times this summer," said John, "from Tanzania, Berlin, Denver, and Surinam." He was always exasperated at being asked this question.

The mayor held his head in his hands. "Surinam! Never heard of it! Denver, I've heard of! What's in Surinam?"

"Bauxite."

"*Baux—*"

"Pal," said Faucher, "give it a rest. We're trying to eat." He made a shooing motion and the mayor left; Faucher raised his eyebrows as he asked Briggs, "How can we miss him if he won't go away?"

The last time Briggs had seen him, Faucher had been insuring marine cargo out of a nice office on Old Colony Avenue in Boston and doing rather well, especially in the early going, when Everett Hoyt had tipped him off to opportunities with far-ranging classmates. Now, Faucher said, he was an investment adviser at a tiny merchant bank in Boston, a real boutique bank. He liked meeting his people in St. Louis Square on warm spring days (he had a key), to lay out the year's strategy, clients who were charmed by his arrival on a Raleigh ten-speed. For a long time he had made cavalier decisions about his clients' investments, but now, in harder-to-understand times, they trusted him less and obliged him to chase obscure indices across the moonscape of U.S. and foreign equities. He vowed to deepen his mystery. He kept a hunter-jumper at Beverly and dropped into equestrian talk to baffle the credulous, using terms like *volade* and *piaffe* and *volte* to describe the commonplace trades he made (and commissioned), or comparing a sustained investment strategy to such esoterica as Raimondo D'Inzeao's taking the Irish bank at Aachen on the great Merano. His own equestrian activities, he admitted, consisted in jumping obstacles that would scarcely weary a poodle, in company with eight- and nine-year-old girls and under the tutelage of roaring Madame Schacter, a tyrant in jodhpurs married to a Harvard statistician. To his clientele, yachts and horses were reassuring entities, things to which one's attention could turn when times were good.

Faucher said, "John, I've got to tell you, nothing makes me happy anymore. I need new work. I want to be more like you, John. *I need a gimmick.* You get the time-zone watch from Sharper Image, and the rest is a walk in the park. Whereas my job is to reassure people who are afraid to lose what they have because they don't know how they got it in the first place. John, it's not that I mind lying but I like variety, and I'm not getting it." His face was mottled with emotion Briggs found hard to fathom. "I desperately wish to be a cowboy."

"Of course you do, Erik."

"That family"—Faucher pointed conspicuously toward a nearby table with a rancher, his wife, and their three nearly grown children—"has been here an hour, and they have *never spoken to each other once.* Don't people here know how to have fun?" The family was listening to this, the father staring into the space just over his plate, his wife grinning at a mustard jar in fear. "We do that when we *hate* each other," Faucher said.

"I don't think they hate each other, Erik."

"Well, it sure looks like it! I've never seen such depressing people."

Marjorie proceeded from the bar with a colorful tall drink.

She was wearing a red tunic with military buttons over a short skirt and buttoned boots, hair pulled tight and tied straight atop her head with a silver ribbon. Briggs was glad to see her; she looked full of life. She said, "May I?"

Briggs got quickly to his feet and drew a chair for Marjorie, steadying her arm as she sat. Faucher looked very glum indeed. He said in an unconvincing monotone, "Sorry I missed you this morning. I understand you cooked a marvelous breakfast."

"It filled us up, didn't it?" she said to Briggs.

"All we could eat and no leftovers," Briggs agreed.

"What'd you do with the rental car?" Faucher barked.

"In front of the bank, keys under the seat."

Faucher lost interest in the car. "Not like I'll need it," he said with a moan.

The ranch family stood without looking at one another, obliging at least two of them to survey the crown molding. The father glared at Erik and dribbled some coins to the table from a huge paw while his waitress scowled from across the room. Karaoke had started at the bar, and a beaming wheat farmer was singing "That's Amore." "Can I get a menu?" Marjorie asked, craning around the room.

"Has it possibly occurred to you that we're having a private conversation?" Faucher said.

Marjorie stopped all animation for a moment. "Oh, I'm so sorry." She looked crushed as she arose. Briggs tried to smile and opened his hands helplessly. She gave him a little wave, paused uncertainly, picked up her drink, and then turned toward the bar and was gone.

Briggs's face was red. "I'm surprised you have any friends at all!" He was practically shouting.

"I only have one: you."

"Well, don't count on it if you continue in this vein."

"I suppose it made sense for me to make two changes of

planes plus a car rental to have you address me with such lofti-
ness," Faucher wailed. "I came to you in need, but your ascent to
the frowning classes must make that unclear."

After dinner, they had a glass of brandy. And then Marjorie
appeared at the karaoke and managed to raise the volume as she
belted out "Another Somebody Done Somebody Wrong Song,"
followed immediately by a Cher imitation, pursed lips and slum-
berous eyes. "I Got You, Babe"—she directed various frug moves
and Vegas gestures in Faucher's direction.

Feeling under attack, Faucher urged Briggs to call for the bill
and pay it promptly. "I can't believe how quickly things have
gone downhill," he said, as if under mortar fire.

Marjorie followed them out of the bar. She was so angry she
moved in jerks. She walked straight over to Briggs and said, "You
think you're above all this, don't you?" Then she slapped him
across the face, so astonishing him that he neither raised a protec-
tive hand nor averted the now-stinging cheek. "You want another one?" she inquired, lips flattened against her teeth.

"I think I'll hold off," Briggs said.

"Ask yourself what Jesus would do," Faucher suggested.

Marjorie whirled on him and John hurried away toward a
boarded-up drygoods store where he'd parked; Faucher joined
him. When they got to the car, they looked back to see Marjorie's
friends restraining her by the arms theatrically. A cowboy with a
goatee and jet black Stetson stared ominously as their car passed
close to him on the way out of town.

"Don't drive next to them, for Christ's sake!" Faucher said.
"The big one is about to come out of the bag!"

Faucher mused as they drove south into the piney hills and
grassland.

"People have become addicted to hidden causes. That's why
you were the one to get slapped. They've been trained to mistrust

anything that's right in front of their eyes. That woman was a turnoff. Everything reminded her of *family*, like it was a substance. Not *the* family or *my* family but just *family*, like it was liverwurst or toothpaste. You can't imagine the difficulty I had preserving the pathetic taco I was trying to sell as an erection in the face of all that enthusiasm for family. I told her she was amazing, and that seemed to take all the wind out of her sails. Oh, John, my path has been uneven. I've made so many enemies. Some of them intend to track me with dogs."

"Outlast them." Briggs listlessly watched the road for deer.

"I hope I can. Really, I've come here because you never quite give up on me, do you?"

"We're old friends," Briggs droned.

"Perhaps once I'm a cowboy, you'll invest your remarks with greater meaning. Anyway, to continue my saga: I knew the noose was tightening; charges were being prepared. But I had been so nimble over the years at helping my clients improperly state assets for death taxes that they saw the wisdom in dropping all complaints against me."

Erik had moved in with his daughter and harassed her with dietary advice until she drove him to the bus station. Settling for a year in Waltham, he lived on the thinnest stream of remaining Boston comforts that shielded him from freefalling disclosure of his curiosity-filled investment days. He might have stayed, but the only job he could find was teaching speed-reading with a primitive machine that exposed only a single line of text at a time, gradually accelerating down the page; that didn't appeal to him. He went back to Boston to "clean some clocks," but important inhibitions were gone and he crossed the line, running afoul of the law at several points but especially attempted blackmail. Nevertheless, he survived until a client—with whom he had reached a mutually satisfactory settlement exchanging forgiveness for secrecy—died; and that brought snoopy children into Faucher's world, followed by investigators, and "Net-net, I'm on the run."

Just before sunrise, Briggs heard Faucher calling to him. He climbed the stairs, pulling on a sweatshirt and his shorts, and entered the guest room. He found Erik kneeling next to the window, curtains pulled back slightly. He gestured for Briggs to join him.

In the yard below, two men stood smoking next to a vehicle with government plates. The smoke could be smelled in Erik's room as he stared hard at them. "They're here for me, John," he said. "I can't believe you've done this. Now I'm going to jail."

"You know perfectly well that I didn't do this," Briggs said. But nothing could prevent him from feeling unreasonably guilty.

"Judas Iscariot. That's how I shall always know you."

They carried Faucher away. Briggs ran alongside in an L.L. Bean bathrobe pouring out offers of help, but Erik waved him off like a man shooing flies.

The weather began to change, and the high white clouds that had remained at their stations for so long moved across the horizon, leaving ghostly streaks in their place. One quiet afternoon, while John looked at the casework that was to follow the demise of the town in Delaware and the new prosperity of the town in North Carolina—mine mitigation in Manitoba, bike paths, a public swimming pool, a library wing in exchange for ground permanently poisoned by cyanide—the phone rang. It was Carol, bringing news that Erik was going to prison. He had been ruinously disagreeable in court, which inflated the sentences to which his crimes had given rise. She aired this as another grievance, as though little good could be extracted from Faucher now. "You were with him, John, why didn't you help him?"

"I didn't know how to help him. We were just spending time together."

"You were just spending time together?"

"I'm afraid that's it. I feel I wasn't very perceptive."

"You have my agreement on that," said Carol. "He left you literally eager for imprisonment. You had a chance to put him back on his feet, and you let him fall."

"Well, I don't know the facts. I—"

"You don't *need* to know the facts. You need to listen to what I'm telling you."

"Carol, I don't think you understand how tiresome you've become."

"Is that your way of commiserating with me?"

"Yes," Briggs said simply. "Yes, Carol, it is."

At times, John worried there *was* something he should have done. The whole experience had been like missing a catch on the high trapeze: the acrobat is pulling away from you, falling into the distance. Or perhaps the acrobat is pulling you off your own trapeze. Neither thought was pleasant.

It was inevitable that he would get worked once more for the newsletter. Hoyt wanted to know how Briggs had found Faucher.

"Breathing," Briggs said.

"You've got good air out there," said Hoyt. "I'll give you that."

In November, on his way to the town in North Carolina he had saved from oblivion, he stopped in Boston, rented a car, and drove to the prison at Walpole but Faucher refused to see him. Sitting in his topcoat in the pale-green meeting room, Briggs rose slowly to acknowledge the uniformed custodian who bore his rejection. He was furious.

But once he was seated on the plane, drink in hand, looking out on the runway at men pushing carts, a forklift wheeling along a train of red lights, a neighboring jet pushing back, he felt a little better. His second drink was delivered reluctantly by a harried stewardess—only because Briggs told her he was on his way to his mother's funeral. At this point, a glow seemed to form around Briggs's seatmate, and Briggs struck up a conversation, ordering drinks for both of them as soon as the plane was airborne. The seatmate, an unfriendly black man who worked for Prudential Insurance, actually was going to a funeral, the funeral of a friend, and this revelation triggered a slightly euphoric summary of Briggs's friendship with Faucher, delivered in remarkable detail, considering that Briggs's companion was trying to read. Briggs concluded his description of his visit to the prison by raising his arms in the air and crying, "Hallelujah!" a gesture that made him realize, instantly, that he had had enough to drink. The seatmate narrowed his eyes, and when Briggs explained that, at long last, a chapter of his life was over, the man, turning back to his open book, said wearily, "Do you actually believe that?"

North Coast

ustin was the more obviously vigilant as they made their way under the canopy of the ancient climax forest, the overgrowth of low alders and ferns towering over him and Ruth. They both had huge canisters of bear spray they'd bought in New Hazelton, but only Austin had ever had to use it—an experience that gave him no confidence since the bear stopped only feet away as the can emptied, and seemingly thanks to mature reflection rather than violent arrest. As he shook the nearly weightless can, the bear, on its hind legs, elevated its nose and just chose not to maul him. He told Ruth the spray worked great. "Point and shoot," he said. "Nothing to it."

They followed a game trail paralleling an unnamed creek that emptied a long way to the south into the main stem of the Skeena River, nearly a hundred miles from its debouchment into the North Pacific. It was mostly forest of cedars and hemlocks, silent except for the small dark winter wrens and the many generations of ravens, the young who squawked and the bearded old with their ominous *kraah* and an inclination to follow the intruders.

This was a world Austin knew. Bearing his heavy pack, he moved with the rocking gait of a Sherpa while Ruth, equally fit, found the near-rain-forest conditions almost impossible. She studied Austin's measured stride and tried to emulate his concentration on the space in front of him, his alertness to the least resistance, and the continuous reference to an objective he somehow kept clear in his head.

Both were in their late twenties. Austin kept his auburn hair cropped close and, combined with the rapier sideburns he affected, the look strengthened his somewhat arranged individualism. He had made a sort of sub rosa living near wild places since his late teens, guiding hikers and heli-skiers around Revelstoke; and he'd helped mining companies search for metallurgical-grade coal in the high country on the Montana–British Columbia border, where from time to time a dope plane flying right on the deck soared down the alpine valleys into the United States. His mother, a Canadian nurse who married an American merchant mariner, had given him half his nationality. He was either a dual citizen or stateless, depending on whom you talked to or, rather, how he felt. When the subjects of religion, nationality, and race came up, he said, "I don't believe in that stuff," and he didn't. What he believed in was money, but he never had enough for his problems—or for Ruth's either.

Ruth came from Burnaby, British Columbia, a tough town whose greatest product was Joe Sakic, the Avalanche center. Her mother left her and her father, a millwright, when Ruth was just a child and Sakic was still playing for Lethbridge. Her father admitted that he didn't know quite what to do with her, and she moved out at fourteen to skateboard, then waitress at Revelstoke, and finally develop her skiing to instructor competency, which provided a seasonal living yet made each year an uncertainty.

Ruth, like Austin, was a heroin user; both would have been more entrenched if their income had been predictable. Their love of the outdoors and great physical enthusiasm sustained the long dry spells; but these always contained some component that led back to using, and that led back to Vancouver, that phenomenal aperture to the drugs of Asia.

Their most reliable connection was a Sikh gallery owner, Sadhu Dhaliwal, who specialized in North Coast art above the table, drugs and protected antiquities under, the most honest junk dealer in Van with a clean business mind under his made-to-measure five-yard muslin turban. Ruth had put Austin on to him: you got a better shot with East Asians who were utterly paranoid about the immigration service and played it straight, at least in the details. There was nothing straight in the big picture, of course, but the big picture always spoiled everything for everybody.

And they were wise; they never went to Vancouver unless, as a kind of enfranchisement, they were prepared to use. To land in that town with empty pockets hoping to improvise your way onto the golden thoroughfare was to risk terrible consequences, and they were far too smart for that. Hence this trip through a primeval forest known with surprising intimacy by Austin. In certain respects, it was a perfect life: you descended from some of the wildest country left on the planet, sunburned and hard-muscled after a season of gazing upon creation, straight down into the city of man where bliss came in a blue Pacific wave and the most beautiful hookers lined up around the cruise-ship termi-nals and chatted about the future.

They were happy to be together and joked affectionately about how they'd met. "Whose futon is this, anyway?" And "You're not my cat!"

Several curious ravens were following, now so preoccupied that they blundered into trees and then croaked in dismay. They really did suggest mischief. Once, when he stayed for a week with the Gitxsan band near Kispiox, Austin heard a story about ravens meeting in the spring to discuss the tricks they'd play that year. He liked his stay with the natives, Christmas lights on the houses year-round. Perhaps they trusted him too much, but that was life. He saw ravens perform a kind of funeral on his lawn at Kamloops, when his cat was afraid to leave the house, the same lawn where they taught their young to fly after they'd been shoved from the nest. Though the neighbors complained about all these noisy birds, he loved them. He went down to Mexico with Ruth on some transaction, and when he got back the ravens were gone. The neighbors had done away with them. He and Ruth were not in such great shape after Mexico, and the raven thing got them so down they ran from it and didn't light until they found another rented house, a trailer this time, in Penticton, where, right after getting his flu shot from the National Health Service, Austin briefly decided he was an American. They had started drinking, which was a feeble alternative though it led to the same place. It was time to go up-country again, this time with a plan that took them to this forest just north of the Skeena with his prized information from the natives.

"*Austin.* I have to take a break."

They stopped and shrugged off their packs, which slumped to the ground, but as soon as they stood still the mosquitoes began to find them. Ruth could feel them against her hands as she tried to wave them away. They rose in clouds from beneath the ferns and forced the two to resume hiking. "We're close," said Austin, his voice betraying a slight impatience with Ruth. He had a GPS, which he took from his pocket while he walked, glancing at its small screen before putting it away. "I can't tell; it's in kilometers, but close."

"I don't know how you ever found it in the first place."

"The old-fashioned way, work. Not a lot of people like to crash around in brush the grizzlies think they own. I had general stuff from the First Nations guys, but I still had to work my ass off."

"I hope we don't see bears today."

"Squirt 'em."

"That's pretty cold. I'm frightened."

He wasn't cold, really; he'd already heard the distinctive *woof* of a bear but declined to worry Ruth about it. He kept his eyes on the lighted swatch of huckleberries near their path and saw the moving furrow in the bushes, but an encounter never came.

He was thinking that if he'd had this GPS with him on the first trip he wouldn't have brought Ruth here at all. They'd be back in Van on the yellow brick road like the time they were so loaded looking at war canoes in the Museum of Anthropology. The security guards kicked them out and they ended up crashing in broad daylight in Stanley Park after being expelled from the Ted and Mary Grieg Memorial Garden for falling on the rhododendrons. Ruth was troubled that they'd found themselves among so many homeless and saw it as a sign. Austin was amused by her love of portents, her belief in symbols, and almost wished he could share it. He considered himself too literal-minded, though he also felt that if he'd been no more practical than Ruth they'd both be doing shitwork around ski resorts the rest of their lives, never really having the merest glimpse of the great beyond.

A couple of times it had gotten away from them. The most humiliating, of course, was when they'd had to move back in with Ruth's dad, the millwright, holed up sick in his basement, but at least they weren't in a program. That had been a close call; yet it seemed after each of their grand voyages they'd moved a little closer to a program. The old guy was off making plywood like the good automaton he was and thought Austin and Ruth just *kept getting the flu.* That's why, when Austin thought about his dual citizenship, he concluded that Canada still had a little innocence left. If you could look at a forest and see plywood you were still innocent.

Austin found the clearing and waited at its edge, in the manner of a host, for Ruth to catch up.

"Here it is."

The totem pole lay stretched out in ferns and moss, strikingly distinct from the forest around it. Shafts of light entered the canopy and illuminated the clearing in pools of brightness. Austin and Ruth moved along its length, staring at the details of the carving, strangely mixed parts of animals, birds, humans, salmon.

Ruth gave a huge sigh, and Austin said, "What'd I tell you?"

Then he walked to the head of the pole, where a fearsome animal head raised fangs toward the canopy. He took out a cell phone and dialed. After a moment he said, "You want me to start at the top? Okay, it looks like a wolf. Is there a wolf clan? Well, it looks like a wolf. Ruth, what's the next one? Ruth says mosquito turning into a human. If I recall my Gitxsan, that's Fireweed Clan. And she says, yes, Wolf's a clan too. Then frog with hawk's beak, followed by another mosquito with a frog on its head, then it looks like a beaver dancing with a raven, and last is two bear cubs, one of which is turning into a boy. They're pretty well separated; I know you could cut them up. I mean, the fucking thing is forty feet long. You'll be happy, Sadhu, and if we're good to go on the you-know-what, I'll just give you the coordinates, and Ruth and I will see you in Van." He stopped talking and took the GPS out of his pocket again. "Hold on, Sadhu, it's finding satellites now. All I gotta do is push MAN OVERBOARD, then I can give you the numbers. . . . " Austin recited the position, longitude and latitude down to minutes of degrees, and then hung up. He turned to Ruth with a huge grin.

She asked, "Is there a lot?"

"Is there a lot!" He thought, We're going to have to pace ourselves or we'll be dead inside a year. "Yeah, Ruth, there's a lot."

The Zombie

Orval Jones, a widower, had a big green willow tree he was very proud of. This thing sat out on their lawn like a skyscraper, and Jones bragged about all the free air-conditioning he got out of it. The neighbors, almost to Harnell Creek, were a Cheyenne family, always working on their cars, whom Jones referred to as "dump bears." After the Indians, the road kept going but in reduced condition until it was just a pair of ruts that turned to impassable gumbo at the first rain shower but finally led to an old ranch graveyard in a grove of straggling hackberry and box elder.

Dulcie Jones came home to introduce her boyfriend to her father, who had trained her in the values of law and order and so understood her difficult and sometimes perilous work. She was twenty-four, a pretty dishwater blonde with a glum heart-shaped face and a distinctive V separating her upper incisors. She held a cigarette between the ends of the first two fingers of her right hand, the arm extended stiffly as though to keep the cigarette at bay. She wore gold earrings with a baseball hat. Beside her stood Neville Smithwick, sly as a ferret in his pale goatee and sloping hairdo. Dulcie was an escort girl and sometime police informant, though her father was aware of only the latter portion of her résumé as well as her day job at an optometrist's office. All-knowing Neville was her dupe. As a fool, he had made her work easier. Under ordinary circumstances, Dulcie served her customers as they expected. If she should suspect they were impecunious, however, she turned them over to the police, who saw to it their names appeared in the paper with varying results: laughter at the office, families ruined, and so on. In such referrals, she got paid by the fuzz. No tips.

Smithwick's father, Neville Senior, had hired Dulcie to do away with his son's virginity on the pretext of Neville Junior's interviewing her for a job, during which exchange Junior was meant to succumb to her erotic overtures. This scheme Neville Junior absorbed but dimly. Rather than be frustrated by his obtuseness, Dulcie quite sensibly went about her day, with Neville in tow so that, should the project collapse, she'd at least get a few errands out of the way.

When she introduced Neville to her father, her father said in a not particularly friendly, half-joshing way, "I may have to give Neville a haircut."

"You and what army?" said Neville.

Orval seemed to sober up. He was pushing sixty but still wore pointed underslung cowboy boots that aggravated his arthritic gait. The snap buttons on his polyester Western shirt were undone around the melon of his small, protruding stomach, the underside of which was cut into by the large old buckle he'd won snowmobiling. He gave off an intense tobacco smell, and his gaze seemed to bounce off Neville to a row of trees in the distance.

"Well. Come in and set, then. If you get hungry, I'll bet you Dulcie'd cook something up."

"I don't eat anything with a central nervous system."

"You what?"

Mr. Jones twisted the front doorknob and kneed the door over its high spot as they went indoors. Dulcie was pleased to have caught her father early. It was only a matter of time before he would begin asking, "Will this day never end?"

Orval brought Neville a Grain Belt and Neville thanked

him politely. "You seem like a well-brought-up feller," said Orval Jones.

"I'm a virgin," said Neville. This remarkable statement was true. But Neville had developed expectations, based on some exceedingly provocative suggestions by Dulcie, which were not so completely lost on him as Dulcie had imagined. From his vast store of secondhand information, he had concluded that he was about to hit pay dirt—3D adult programming. In fact, she told him he'd need a condom and, in the resulting confusion, stopped at Roundup to help him pick one. But, once inside the drugstore, he embarrassed her by asking if they were one-size-fits-all, like a baseball hat, and then balked when the clerk explained he had to buy them as a three pack. Neville told him that the thought made him light-headed.

Orval was on the sofa and seemed defeated by Neville's very existence. Nevertheless, he made a wan attempt at conversation. His jeans had ridden up over the top of his boots to reveal spindly white legs that seemed to take up little room in the boots, just sticks is all they were. The terrible bags under his eyes gave the impression that he could see beyond the present situation.

"Neville, you say you come from a banking background."

"Foreground."

"Ha-ha. You've got a point. And do you—uh, actually work at the bank too?"

"Hell, no."

"Hell, no. I see. And what *do* you do?"

"TV."

"TV sales?"

"I watch TV. Ever heard of it?"

"I suppose that should've been my first guess."

"Uh, *yeah.*"

Neville had learned from television that remorseless repartee was the basis of genial relations with the public. He really meant no harm, but not having any friends might have alerted him to the dangers of this approach. The appearance of harmlessness disguised the violence he had inside him and would save him from ever being held accountable for its consequences, when he quite soon gave it such full expression. "He wouldn't hurt a fly."

Neville Senior managed the Southeast and Central Montana Bank; he was a genuinely upright and conventional individual who worked hard and played golf. His wife had died some years ago, so he had had charge of Neville Junior from early on. In the winter, he went once a month to St. George, Utah, fighting Mormons for tee times, and returned refreshed for work. He was a happy, well-balanced, thoughtful man who had accepted the work ethic he'd been raised with and which caused him to spend too little time with his only child. Their prosperous life was such that there were no duties that his son could be assigned that would instill the father's decent values. And he didn't want him on the golf course with his various hairdos. Walking down North 27th in Billings with his tax attorney, he once passed a youth with pink, blue, and green hair not so different from Neville Junior's. "When I was in the navy," the attorney said, "I had sex with a parrot. Could that be my child?"

Neville Junior worried him. The boy had been raised by a television set, as his father readily admitted. It was bad enough that his language and attitudes came directly from shows he'd seen; he seemed to have found sufficient like-minded companions to keep him from questioning his way of life. What was unsettling was that long after his age would have made it appropriate, Neville Junior had failed to show any interest in girls. As the nice-looking son of a bank president, he should have been cutting a wide swath. Girls liked him and came around to watch TV with him; girls that sent his father's mind meandering in ways inappropriate to his age and state. His frequent attempts to catch his son in flagrante delicto resulted only in an invitation to join the couple innocently watching the late movie. It was not so many years ago that he himself had boogied under the strobes of big cow-town discos where today's dowagers once wriggled in precopulatory abandon.

For a banker, Neville Senior was remarkably free of malice, and his great wish was to overcome the gap of loneliness that lay between him and his heir. It's possible that he imagined that bringing Neville Junior into the randy orbit that seemed to include everyone *but* Neville Junior would have the effect of giving the two some ordinary common ground upon which they could begin to talk like a couple of guys. Boning up on *TV Guide*, as he had once done, proved futile. Real watchers like Neville Junior had a subtle language not easily penetrated by poseurs. He just stared when his father asked if there was anything good on tonight.

"Neville," said the father, "two things: I wish I'd been a better parent."

"You've been all right. Don't sweat it. What's the second?"

"Sex," barked Senior. "Why aren't you interested in sex?"

"Don't get your panties in a wad, Dad. Virginity is no disgrace. At least it keeps you from weighing sixty pounds and being covered with giant sores."

"It doesn't have to be that way."

"It only has to be that way once, and you can count me out."

"It should be seen as a gift, a gift of love and joy that perpetuates the race."

"Perpetuates the race? Are people still in favor of that?"

"I don't know how you've become so cynical at your age."

"You can't accept that I'm happy, can you?"

"Are you?"

"Considering the cards I've been dealt."

"Have they been such bad cards?"

"You tell me."

"I guess I can't."

"Just because you named me after yourself doesn't mean I have to turn out like you."

"No, I suppose that wouldn't be any good."

"I'm not saying that. Different isn't good or bad. It's different is all it is. Get it?"

"You could change your name. I'd understand."

"I've thought about it. I've never thought of myself as Neville."

"What have you thought of yourself as?"

"Karl."

"With a C?"

"With a K."

Much later, when Neville Senior had decided that life was not worth living, he would give this Karl-with-a-K idea a final thought.

— — — — — — — — — —

From his suite at the Northern Hotel, as a summer sun descended on city streets blue with heat, pressed in upon by angular store-fronts and shade-hunting pedestrians, Neville Senior called an escort service. Given that the city police had been recruiting undercover officers lately to nab concupiscent johns, this was risky business, but Neville Senior believed the scrutiny was directed at streetwalkers and so he felt relatively safe, if a bit frightened. Anyway, when it came to your own flesh and blood, risk was unavoidable. He had cash, plenty of it, and he intended to buy Neville Junior out of his dubious virginity and joyless view of things. More than that, he wanted to buy him the high road to the human race, which in his view was bound together more by fornication than anything else. In his life, courtship was fornication, life was fornication, and grief revealed but one road back to the light of day and that was fornication. The only answer to life's complexity: *fornication*.

Dulcie arrived straight from her shift at the optometrist, and Neville Senior welcomed her in his most courtly manner. "Came right away," she said. "Two saps in the waiting room with drops in their eyes." She seemed taken aback at first by his nervousness and perhaps foresaw the long hard work sometimes necessary to overcome the anxiety of skittish customers for the sake of the almighty dollar. Bummer.

Dulcie kept her purse beside her; the cell phone inside it required only a single key to be pressed and her mission would be accomplished, either by an arrest or the heading off of an assault. It seemed she would have to buy time to size up the transaction. Some adjustment of plan was required because unexpectedly this geezer had a plan of his own. After a long day at the optometrist's shop, Dulcie was glad to learn that the heavy lifting would come later, but at the very least they had old man Neville for procuring. That it was for his own flesh and blood was hardly extenuating, and one way or another she'd get paid. Anything to get away from dreary folks reading the acuity chart: "P . . . E . . . C . . . F . . . D—I can't read that last line. . . ." Of course you can't, you need glasses!

He gazed at Dulcie with admiration: at first lustful but, when she noticed, adding avuncular overtones and calling her *dear* so as to assure her he wasn't getting ready to whip it out. She might have been touched if she'd known this modest transaction would later in the year result in his suicide—though it was not easy to say what might get through to Dulcie Jones, barrel racer.

While Dulcie went off to spruce up in the bunkhouse, Orval gave Neville a tour of the place, apologizing for the disorder of the kitchen as they passed through. "It takes a heap of living to make a home a heap!" he said merrily. Neville said he bet Orval had a million more where that one came from. When they were out of earshot, Orval said, "You're kind of a smart-ass, aren't you?" He got right in Neville's face.

"If you say so," Neville said, as though trying to help Orval in the best way he knew how. Orval was thinking of slugging him and stared at the spot on Neville's face where he imagined landing the blow. Overcoming the temptation he asked how Neville had met his daughter, making it clear by his tone that he was sorry it had ever happened. He'd been counting on a cowboy or someone in law enforcement.

"My dad introduced us. She's going to be our new vice president. He wanted me to get to know her on behalf of our business."

"Vice president? Vice president of what?"

"Of our bank, Southeast and Central Montana Bank. Member FDIC."

"What about the optometrist?"

Neville remembered her looking without glasses at the road map that morning.

"I guess she doesn't need him," he said, suddenly wondering if Dulcie was farsighted. He might not feel as safe with her at the wheel. He'd been so relaxed watching his day go by in the rearview mirror, never going rigid against his seat belt as he did whenever he distrusted the driver. He so looked forward to what he expected from Dulcie, and yet he felt the responsibility of considering her as a candidate for vice president of the bank. He realized he didn't quite understand the situation, but knew he would do anything in the world for his father, to whom he helplessly longed to reach out. But this was different. The bank had always been kept from him, so that his father's asking him to do something connected with his livelihood suggested a change.

"You want to drive the tractor?" Orval asked. Neville understood he was being humored, but he hadn't expected Orval to go rural on him this quickly.

"I doubt it."

"Well, what would interest you, Neville?"

"You got any archaeological sites?"

Orval went outside, started the tractor, and backed it up to the loaded manure spreader. It was clear he had decided to go about his business, but Neville followed him innocently as he drove out into the pasture and then activated the PTO, showering the youth with turds. Neville saw right through his apologies and walked back to the house, looking for Dulcie. He had a mean-spirited impulse to tell her that her father would not be welcome at the bank. But all that was tempered by the attraction he felt for her, aroused by her various provocations and double entendres. His girlfriends had always acted as if being available was enough. It wasn't; he required much more. Neville enjoyed this sense that Dulcie was after him like a bad dog, and knowing she was just trying to get the vice president's job made it all oddly spicy.

"What happened to you?" she asked, when he caught up to her in the yard.

"I'm not too sure."

"I think it's time we got us a room."

"Amen to that," Neville said, with a look of terror. She was flicking at him with the backs of her fingernails, loosening some of the debris.

Driving out of the yard, Neville leaned well out the window to wave goodbye. Orval's return wave seemed to say good riddance and confused Neville, who thought they'd hit it off.

Once out of the driveway, Dulcie made the gravel swirl under the tires. They were heading now for the Absarokee cutoff; she told Neville she had a good spot in mind. She held his gaze until he said, "Watch the road."

They wound along well-kept hay meadows, tractors in the field spitting out bales, swathers moving into the dark green alfalfa and laying it over in a pale green band close behind the standing grass. The road flattened, and in its first broad turn was the small, tired motel. Dulcie pulled up in front of the office. As she got out of the car, Neville asked her to be sure there was TV. A crevice of irritation appeared briefly between her eyebrows and she turned to the entrance. When she came back, she climbed in brusquely and threw the key on the seat. She gave him a long look and said, "Room seven," allowing her tongue to hang out slightly. Neville gave a small bounce to show he understood.

When the door closed behind them, they surveyed the room, its brown pipe bed, plastic curtains, and gloomy prints of the Custer massacre and the Blizzard of '86. Dulcie took it all in, and when she turned to Neville he was holding up one of his new condoms. "Americans are coming together to stamp out HIV," he said, with touching sincerity. "Can you help me with this?"

Not at all self-conscious, Neville stripped and stood naked next to his pile of clothes, instantly erect. Dulcie lit a cigarette and knelt in front of him. There was nothing to do but apply the condom. Cigarette held in the V of her teeth, squinting against the rising smoke, she rolled it on deftly. "Now," she said, standing up, "I'll just go into the bathroom and get ready."

"Take your time," said Neville, moving instinctively for the television. As he watched it, she opened the door to the bathroom for an instant and took his picture.

"Memories." She smiled and closed the door again, wondering what the cops would make of a guy with nothing but a channel changer and a rubber. She created a bit of noise with the shower curtain, the faucets, and a cupboard door. It seemed like enough. She stood stock-still and listened. She thought someone else was in the room; then the realization that it was only the television made her doubt her sexuality.

Downhill Racer. Neville was Robert Redford. He locked his knees together and bent into every slalom, concentrating so thoroughly that the condom fell off. After a while, he began to miss Dulcie and rapped politely on the bathroom door. Neville wasn't stupid. He smiled to himself; he knew she wasn't in there. He got dressed and went outside. The bathroom window was wide open, the curtains hanging against the wall of the motel. The car was gone. He returned to the room and tried to kick the condom across the rug, but it just rolled up under his foot. He carried it dangling to the wastebasket and then stretched out to enjoy something reliable. Even the light of the TV flashing on the ceiling seemed pleasant. During the slow parts of the movie, he luxuriated in his relief. He couldn't fathom Dulcie and he wasn't even going to try. Nevertheless, out of fealty to his father, he would confide his intuition that she'd make a poor vice president. It was not out of a sense of having been betrayed but the unseemly picture of a vice president crawling out the window of a cheap motel. In this, he was well brought up, and he loved his poor, confused papa.

Dulcie was at the station house turning in her expense receipts, principally gas, motel, along with film, when they brought Neville Senior in for booking. He stared at her as they tugged him past. The cop at the desk didn't even look up as he stapled her chits to a large sheet. So Dulcie in effect spoke to no one when she said, "He bonds out, he settles, the beat goes on."

When Neville Senior dragged himself through the front door that night, Neville Junior was there to console him, having heard all about what had happened to his father on the local news. They fell into each other's arms. Senior's heart was overflowing, while

Junior felt he was in a school play in which he had memorized the lines without knowing what he was saying.

Finally, Senior spoke. "I was lonely."

"Mom's dead," said Junior, in his odd blank way.

Neville's father explained his scheme so that his son at least would know that he hadn't been on some unseemly quest for his own carnal pleasure.

He had offered Neville Junior numerous pets in the years since his mother's death, hoping that greater familiarity with animals might help him understand his father's urges—and expenses!—but that had come to nothing, as Neville Junior found animals to be little more than a stream of unpredictable images and therefore unsettling. The dog was given away, the cat was given away, and the hamster bit an extension cord and was electrocuted.

"That Dulcie sure is mean!" he now cried. "It's just not right, Dad. I'm going to pay her back."

When the newspaper published his name as a patron of whores, Neville Senior lost his job at the bank. We've all been there, his friends and former colleagues told him, but they hadn't, nor had they forfeited their homes to their own bank as he had, though he was allowed to keep the rather fussy furniture his late wife had chosen. In time, that too would be sold and the funds applied to a rental house on the south side of town, where the homeless walking on their battered patch of lawn reminded the Smithwicks of just what might be next.

Senior's friends had got him a job as assistant greenskeeper at his old golf club, where the summer heat frequently laid him low as he tried to perform work for which he had little training. He was one of eighteen assistants, and when the chief learned the bunker crew on which he'd placed Neville Senior was ridiculing him with requests for car loans or mortgages, he reassigned him to moisture sampling, which allowed Senior to wander the golf course alone with probe and notebook under a hard prairie sun. The greenskeeper himself took subtle pleasure in lording it over someone who had fallen through the invisible ceiling that had separated them for so many years. A former caddie replaced by electric carts, he understood perhaps better than Neville Senior ever had how perilous is all employment, though as a working-man it was unlikely society would bother to take away his job for consorting with prostitutes, as there wasn't enough class separation to produce a stirring fall. In many places, whores were now "sex workers" moving freely between golf courses and no-tell motels like any other independent contractors.

Neville Junior's habits remained little changed, except that because of the danger of muggings his former acquaintances were reluctant to visit him. Since his father had not shared his plan to commit suicide, there was no reason for Neville Junior to imagine a time when the television would be shut off and he would have to bestir himself should he wish to eat or be sheltered from the weather. His father's decision was based equally on his failed career and his now-accepted inability to communicate with his son at any level.

He made his departure as uneventful as possible. For two straight days he watched shows with his only child, including uplifting sitcoms, sitcom reruns, and sitcom pilots that were seeing the light of day that very night. An agnostic, he retained a faint hope, magnified by overpowering loneliness, of meeting his late wife and that gave him the courage—indeed, a certain merry determination—to gas himself in the garage. Before he went there to seal the windows and start the car, he needed final confirmation and so he returned to the living room, whose shabbiness was emphasized by the prissy furniture. The back of Neville Junior's head was outlined against the square of light of the television. "Tomorrow, I'll be gone," he said, but his son didn't hear him. "Goodbye, Karl." The consequences began: the discovery of the body, the unattended funeral, the eviction of Neville Junior, and the loss of all things familiar to him, including those he cared for most: the smell of lilacs and spring perennials filling the air, the sounds of pickup baseball in the park a few blocks away, and television.

Dulcie Jones's days were numbered.

On the Fourth of July, four months after the passing of Neville Senior, Orval looked up the dirt road in front of his house toward the Cheyenne car garden, the crooked line of telephone poles, the mud puddles mirroring blue sky and thundercloud silhouettes, the watchful hawk in the chokecherry thicket, and saw a willowy man in old clothes coming toward him, a man whose still-dark beard and bounding gait marked him as younger than his apparent circumstances might have suggested. Orval sensed he was coming to see him, and indeed he was. There was no reason for him to know that this was Neville Junior, or to know what brought young Neville to his ranch.

He removed his hat rather formally on arrival at Orval's porch, the hair under it looking wet and plastered down close around his small skull, while Orval eyed him suspiciously from his rocking chair. Neville's well-cared-for teeth gleamed through his beard, whose black bristles falsely suggested a hard life. "Mister," he said, "I'm in a bad way. Throwed a rod here a mile or two back and didn't have the do-re-mi to get it fixed. I need a job." Neville had the Appalachian accent routinely heard in Westerns down pat.

"Not hiring."

"A little sumpin' to eat, place to sleep, and a TV; wouldn't have to pay me."

"Wouldn't have to pay you? What exactly is it you want to do for free gratis?"

"I'd work, but like I say you'd need to train me."

"But not pay you?"

"You heard right, mister. Just those things I mentioned."

The two swept out the old milk house, which had a two-stage concrete floor and a place for the creek to run through, though the creek had been diverted long ago and the room was dry enough. Then they assembled an iron bed and rolled out a thin mattress, which they beat until the room filled with dust. "No telling what's been living in here," said Orval, with an ingratiating smile. Neville threw up his hands in wonder. "But I guess that'll do you. Gon' have to."

"TV."

"What's that?"

"I said TV."

"I hadn't got but one and it's up to my house."

"I told you when we started in on this," hissed Neville, "that I'd require a TV."

The reception was exceptionally poor in the milk house, but by adding aluminum foil to the rabbit ears they were able to get two channels, one all snowy with Greer Garson. The tension seemed to go out of Neville's body as he told Orval to call him for supper and then settled down on the pipe bed for some viewing, ignoring the dust that continued to rise and the perhaps-too-vigorous closing of the door by Orval.

In the morning, Orval was determined to see if he could get his money's worth out of this man, who had introduced himself as Karl "with a K." He could tell right away that Karl meant to stay, as he hurled himself into shoveling out the calving shed, a job requiring no experience whatsoever but a strong tolerance for grueling repetition. At one point, he went at this with such demonic energy that it caused Orval to tell him whoa-up, he had all day. Neville wiped his forehead, leaned on the shovel, and asked Orval if he had any family, smiling as he heard about Dulcie as though for the first time. Today he'd parted his hair in the middle, and with the dark beard he had the appearance of an old-time preacher, someone who could talk about Jesus with plausible familiarity. Orval thought he'd have to find him some other clothes if he worked out, something brighter, because he wasn't a hundred percent comfortable with the preacher look. There was always one going up the road with a Bible in the glove box supposedly to convert the dump bears but probably to check out the little squaws.

This one was here for vengeance. "She ever get out to see you?"

"Just on weekends."

"But that's tomorrow."

"The horse sees more of her than I do."

"Could be, now you got a hired man, there'll be more time for the two of you to visit."

"I'm available!"

It seemed like he spent half of Saturday, the set on mute, listening to her gallop up and down the place, wondering when she'd get the curiosity to come over and say howdy. Poor old Orval was doing the vigil thing in his rocker, Saturday beer in hand, but Neville could tell he wasn't getting much in the way of contact either—on a day made for family, a light breeze in the cottonwoods, the Cheyenne sleeping it off up the road, and the rare lowing of distant cattle. Springtime!

She knocked on the door.

Neville had a loose, gangly act ready for this, head tipped to one side, wire lightly wrapped around his left hand as he turned to let her in. Blue light from the silent television jerked around a room that smelled like concrete and once stored an ocean of purest milk. Dulcie wore jeans and tennis shoes, a snap-button Western shirt with the sleeves cut off. She had on sunglasses. He liked her firm arms, the lariats and roses that decorated the pink shirt. She gazed at him and, crossing her arms behind her back, leaned against the door she'd just closed. She raised her forefinger to slide the sunglasses down enough to look over their top.

"I know who you are," she said.

"That's more than I can say!" Neville called out.

"May I turn that thing off?"

"No!"

"Well, I am. I'm turning it off."

Dulcie went past him and bent over the set, reaching for the controls. Neville had the wire on her in nothing flat, called her a lowdown escort service. Though there was a spell of tumult—more like a rerun than anything new—it was the moment when movement stopped that finally produced surprise, and Neville was swept by desire at last. Everything in his life had led to this ravishing stillness. He knew who to dedicate this one to.

Orval went on sitting in his rocker, stubbing out his cigarettes in a tomato juice can. Sooner or later, Dulcie would have to put the horse up and come have a few words with him. At the same time, his new hired man wandered down the darkening road away from the little ranch, away from the Cheyenne and their old cars, weeping at the innocence now beyond his grasp, never to be a virgin again. It was great to feel something so strongly. He hoped to weep forever. If only his father could have been there to see him with tears streaming down his face. It would have been a beginning, something good. He could just hear his voice.

"Well, son, I'll be damned. You feel pretty strongly about this, don't you?"

Miracle Boy

We always went back to my mother's hometown when someone was about to die. We missed Uncle Kevin because the doctors misdiagnosed his ruptured appendix, owing to referred pain in his shoulder. Septicemia killed him before they sorted it out with a victorious air we never forgave. The liverless baby was well before our time—it would have been older than my mother had it lived—but my grandfather's departure arrived ideally for scheduling purposes in the late stages of diabetes; we drove instead of taking the train and en route were able to stay over for an extra day at the Algonquin Inn in western New York, taking advantage of Wienerschnitzel Night, and still make it in time for the various obsequies while reducing prolonged visits by priests. (My father was an agnostic and fought sponging clergy with vigor, remarking that he had "fronted his last snockered prelate" and adding, "Amazing how often it's Crown Royal.")

Before I relate the death of my grandmother, I have to summarize that of my grandfather, because that was where I acquired my short-lived reputation as a worker of household wonders. Ever since I have had great sympathy for those identified as seers or healers; my heart even goes out to those merely called lucky. Like someone drifting lazily down the Niagara River, the big fall is just a matter of time.

My grandfather, though a diabetic, went on occasional sweet binges, cherry pies at Al Mack's diner, and he injected himself with insulin daily, to our agog fascination. He held in reserve giant sugar-filled jawbreakers in his pocket, and when I was too pressingly talkative a single one of those hunks would keep me silent for almost three hours. He was a quiet man, a volunteer fireman who played checkers in the open-fronted firehouse down whose brass pole I was sometimes allowed to slide. In his youth he had read in a newspaper that "Many people persist in making the cemetery a place of recreation, generally a foreign element prompted by ignorance," and thereafter he was a tireless promoter of public parks.

On the Fourth of July, while most of the family was at the parade on North Main Street and after a midday meal of quahog chowder, swordfish, beet greens, and corn, he lay down on his big brown favorite couch and died. He'd never taken up more room than he needed, and in an essentially matriarchal household his death was mostly seen as foreshadowing my grandmother's, though it was widely celebrated among "the foreign element." This was not long after little boys were given dresses to wear, and my mother and aunts sent me off dressed as a hula girl for the Fourth of July parade, a debacle that ended in my breaking a white plastic ukulele with its Arthur Godfrey "automatic" chord changer during one of many clashes with Azorean native Joao Furtado—later known as Meatball—who called me, with sensible directness, "little girl." When I got home from the parade, my grandfather was dead. I studied the adults for clues. They were studying my grandmother for clues. She took to her bed. Three days later, she was still there.

Her absence brought the household to a standstill. My mother and aunts seemed entirely helpless without her ordering them around. She did not even seem to acknowledge them when they visited her room, and a meeting was called where it was decided to send me in. Her idealization of children was counted upon to bring her around before the house and its contents sank into the earth, an eventuality I could imagine to include the opaque projector in the attic with its pictures of long-dead baseball players, the cabinet full of Belleek china in the priest parlor, all the wildly squeaky beds and creaking stairs, the bookless "library" reeking of cigars, and even the souvenir Hitler Youth knife my uncle Paul had given me. As it happened I was the only child available for idealizing, standing around with my mouth open. And so I headed to my grandmother's bedroom, which was on the second floor, and there I acquired my reputation as a performer of miracles, setting myself up for a fall whose effects would never end. (When my father learned of my success, he began calling me Miracle Boy, later M.B.)

I let myself in without knocking, closing the door behind me. From her bed my grandmother followed me with her eyes. I started to say something in greeting but the impulse died, and instead I looked around for a place to sit. The ornate brass bed was to the right as I entered; to the left was a vanity with its silver brush and mirror carefully arranged. At the far end of the room was a door to a small porch over Brownell Street, access to which we were all denied, as it sagged dangerously with dry rot. I took the chair from in front of the dresser, pulled it up beside my grandmother's bed, and sat down. I was perfectly comfortable. My grandmother had turned her head on the pillow to look directly at me, upon me, and I could tell that my presence was welcome. After a while, several formulaic remarks on the death of my grandfather passed through my mind, since even then I was capable of a modicum of glibness in the little-old-man style encouraged by my aunts. But those thoughts vanished and I gazed at my grandmother's long hair, gathered around her face in silver braids. My mind wandered again, and then I spoke.

"I was wondering," I mused, "if Grandpa left me any jewels."

My grandmother stared at me, sitting on my hands in her vanity chair, knocking the toes of my shoes against each other as the silence lengthened. Suddenly she began to laugh, from some deep place and loud enough that the scurrying of my mother and my aunts could be heard outside the door, where they must have been eavesdropping. Then my grandmother sent me away so she could rise, dress, and make our supper. Thus was born my reputation as a child healer, my personal albatross, Miracle Boy.

— — — — — — — — — —

The house was a typical triple-decker on a very small lot, hardly bigger than the footprint of the house itself, with a tiny yard bound by a severely rectilinear and humorless hedge. Any game in the yard had to involve the roof, usually winging a ball up there and guessing which side it would fall off. My uncle Paul, a veteran of World War II, was always willing to do this with me for hours on end; he never really seemed to have a job. Otherwise, all you could do in the yard was stand there and stay clear of the hedge. This being a corner lot, the windows on two sides gave a point-blank view of the faces of pedestrians, and the second- and third-floor windows were ideal for the launching of tomatoes, stink bombs, and rotten eggs. Once when my constant adversary, Meatball Furtado, had chased me all the way from North Park, Aunt Constance was able to pour boiling water on him from the second floor, melting the cast on his recently broken arm. This unambiguous Irish-Portuguese skirmish pretty much reflects the fortress quality of the small neighborhoods of the town, with a church at the center and a pocket park for escalating ethnic conflict. In time, jicks, Portagees, and harps would be partners in law firms and especially in local politics. Then they'd move away and just be Americans—consumers, parents, drivers of minivans. I suppose it's a good thing.

Here in this small yard, on his reluctant and occasional visits from the Midwest, my father sat, reading *Yachting* and contemplating a global circumnavigation, though, he often told me with a conspirator's wink, he would not necessarily return to the same spot from which he'd gamely set sail—by which I guess he really meant he hoped one day to leave us. The closest he came to circumnavigating was a steel cabin cruiser that never left the dock and came with an oil painting of a busty woman walking through a crowded church. It was entitled *A Big Titter Rolled down the Aisle*. This vessel sat in a rental slip on a stagnant lake, and served as a platform for cocktail parties. At the height of these gatherings, my father would start the engine and then look with authority over the transom to make sure the water pump was sending coolant out the exhaust. The feat was performed in silence and suggested that behind the revelry lay a serious world, the world of the sea.

Now my grandmother was dying, the death of a monarch. My father was going to have to visit my mother's cherished hometown and all his in-laws, a dreadful prospect, as he viewed my grandparents' house as a lunatic asylum; its bubbling humanity trained a cold light on behavior that had its roots in his own days as an Eagle Scout and piano prodigy in a four-block area south of Scollay Square, where he was the only pianist, thanks to his iron-willed mother, half paralyzed by an early stroke brought on by her terrible temper. My father hated to play the piano, hated even to see one, and forbade me to join the Boy Scouts.

Between my grandmother's first and second strokes, my mother and I set out in the Nash for this old lunch-bucket city and its mosaic of neighborhoods, the house-rattling trains and worn-out baseball diamonds; my father told my mother he would follow "in due course" for the funeral. She looked him in the eye and asked, "What if she recovers?"

I was inside my grandparents' house on the occasion of her second cerebral hemorrhage. My reputation as a wonder worker had lingered in the years since my grandfather's death, and at each crisis I worried that I would be asked to perform again. As the house filled with family members, including my physician uncle Walter, all gathered hopelessly around the door to my grandmother's bedroom, which seemed to glow with ominous beams of light. Walter came and went wearing a stethoscope, which he had never before done in this house. He was so handsome it sometimes made his sisters gasp, and with all power now in his hands he seemed like a god.

My mother ordered my father to get on the road immediately, and I worried that if his opinions got loose in this atmosphere every one of us would suffer. I was less focused on the impending demise of my grandmother than on seeing my favorite uncle, Paul, my grandmother's youngest, a man in his fifties who sold the occasional insurance policy from his bare office in the Granite Block. He lived in a rooming house named Mohican House after the old Mohican Hotel, and his habits had changed little in many years, consisting as they did in day drinking and reading odd books from the public library. He collected printed mazes; some, he told me, were quite famous, like Welk's Reflection, Double Snowflake, and Jabberwocky. He was keenly interested in the tea clippers and had an old painting that he claimed to have fished out of some Yankee's garbage pail, a portrait of a Massachusetts sea captain dressed in embroidered robes like the emperor of China.

On our drive across Ontario and western New York, I listened again as my mother recited the saga of my grandmother, both hands on the wheel, cigarette in her mouth: the Saga of the Displaced Gael. Orphaned at twelve, Grandma worked a life-devouring job in the textile mills but managed a happy marriage to a fellow she met on the narrows (Grandpa) between North and South Watuppa ponds, where young people gathered. They were to enjoy fertile parenthood, modest gentility, economic sufficiency, and religious security only a block from their parish church; she did, however, occasionally cross the Quequechan River to attend Mass with French Canadian girlfriends she'd met in the spinning room at the Pocasset mill. My grandfather supplied special groceries to the side-wheelers of the Fall River Line including the *Commonwealth*, the *Pilgrim*, and the fabulous *Princess*. His was a tiny business based on special arrangements with a fruit boat that brought bananas from Central America. My grandfather told me of the deadly spiders that sometimes arrived with this cargo, hinted at Spanish treasure from Honduras (probably the origin of my previously mentioned interest in "jewels"), and described the three great steering wheels in the pilothouse of the *Princess* and the chandeliers in its engine room. Even my grandparents' Yankee neighbors, who ranged from mill owners and bankers to broken-down fellows who delivered firewood by horse and wagon, accorded grudging admiration to this honest couple, especially as immigrants even more peculiar than the Irish began arriving from warmer and warmer seas, smaller and browner by the day. If my mother got too caught up in her story, she allowed me to drive on my learner's permit while she kept smoking or chewed her thumbnail.

The children grew up and took their respective places: teacher, policeman, physician, waitress, and finally occasional insurance salesman Paul, who came home from the war having lost to a German booby trap his best friend, a boy from President Avenue with whom he'd enlisted. Paul emphasized that the device was a Leica camera, which seemed to undercut the disparaging term for the thing that had killed his friend. After that Paul began to decline, and the gossip was that he wouldn't have taken the loss of his friend so badly if the pair of them hadn't been queer. But he was smart and resourceful and he managed to go on, usually by selling a policy to one of his drinking buddies. He was tall and well dressed, his auburn hair combed back straight from a high forehead in an elegant look that spoke of success. By evening, the look would change to something wild and slipping.

My mother had always seemed fearless; if she wasn't, she concealed her fear with spontaneous belligerence. But she strove for obedient perfection under my grandmother's eyes and when she fell short, usually in household matters like cooking or cleaning or religious matters like forgetting First Fridays, she responded to my grandmother's well-concealed wrath like an educated dog, performing as directed but with the faint slink of force training. This behavior was disturbing and made me ambivalent about my grandmother, who treated me like a prince. Behind the geniality of this tiny woman, I saw the iron fist. I wasn't sure I liked it.

Paul moved in and out of the house over the years, even had temperate spells. I remember some very pleasant times when my mother and I visited: he threw a baseball onto the complex of roofs for me to field with my Marty Marion infielder's mitt and tried to instill in me his passionate Irish sentimentality and diasporic mythology. The rest of the family was feverishly American and did not care to celebrate the Irish connection; in fact, Uncle Walter on traveling to Ireland announced that the place was highly disorganized and insufficiently hygienic, and that the garrulity of the people was annoying, especially the sharp cracks that were mechanical and tiresome and always about other people.

But Paul had archaic Gaelic jigs on 78s that he played at tremendous volume from his room next to his mother's, and, when drunk, he could roar along to various all-too-familiar ballads—"Mother Machree," "The Wearing of the Green," "When Irish Eyes Are Smiling," and so on—giving me a whack when I accompanied the great John McCormack with such invented lyrics as "my vile Irish toes" or "God bless you, you pest, you, Mother Machree."

Sometimes he tired of his old records and said it wasn't the potato famine that had driven the Irish from the land; they had left to escape the music. It really depended on what the Bushmill's was up to. He also used me to practice his insurance pitch. "Good morning, Wilbur," he would begin—not my name—and it was always *morning* in these pitches even though he was incapable of rising early enough to make a morning pitch. Wilbur was an imaginary Yankee farmer, dull, credulous, yet wily. "Wilbur, we've known each other a good many years and, God willing, more to come with, let's hope, much prosperity and happiness. I know you to be a man, Wilbur, whose family stands just below the saints in his esteem, a man who thinks of everything to protect them from . . . from—*Christ!*—protect them from, uh—*the unforeseen!* Christ, of course! *The unforeseen!*—But ask yourself, Have you really thought of everything?" Here is where the other shoe was meant to drop, but, more often than not, Paul allowed himself an uncontrolled snort of hilarity before refilling his "martini." This was never a martini; it was invariably a jolt of Bushmill's, but he called it a martini, and the delicacy of the concept compelled him to hold the libation between thumb and forefinger, which uncertain grasp sometimes caused the drink to crash to the floor, a "tragedy."

The fact that Paul and I got on so well would be remembered during my seventeenth year, when I was called upon to perform one more miracle. By my humoring him during his Irish spells, I had earned his faith. He'd taken me to see the Red Sox, Plymouth Rock, Bunker Hill, and Old Ironsides; he bought me lobster rolls at Al Mack's diner, a Penn Senator surf-casting reel, coffee cabinets and vanilla Cokes by the hundred. He made me call a drinking fountain a "bubbler," in the Rhode Island style.

Eventually, Paul moved back to his digs at Mohican House, evicted by Uncle Walter, who had replaced my grandfather for such duties. My grandmother was also a disciplinarian, but when it came to her youngest son she reverted to type and viewed him as troubled, broken by the war, while the rest of her offspring were expected to follow clear but inflexible rules. Irish tenors were replaced by radio broadcasts of ball games. For every holiday and the whole of summer, my mother continued to drag me from what she viewed as our place of exile in the Midwest to Brownell Street, which I might not have liked but for our almost daily trips to Horseneck Beach, where I had the occasional red-faced meeting with a girl in a bathing suit. I also made a new friend on Hood Street next to North Park, Brucie Blaylock, who could defend me against Meatball and his allies. Brucie was a tough athletic boy with scuffed knuckles and a perpetually runny nose whose beautiful eighteen-year-old sister had just married a policeman. The couple was still living in my friend's home awaiting an apartment and, while snooping through their belongings, we discovered a *gross* of condoms which we counted, being unsure how many were in a gross. "This cop," said my friend, gazing at the mountain of tiny packages, "is gonna stick it in my sister a hundred and forty-four times!" My mind spun not altogether unpleasantly at this carnal prospect, and my fear of bathing-suit girls at Horseneck Beach rose starkly. From time to time, we would re-count the condoms; by the time the number dropped below a hundred, my friend was suffering and I wandered around as if etherized by the information.

My aunts continued to adore and pamper me while reminding anyone who would listen of my capacity for working miracles. This would have been long forgotten but for the fact that their incentive came directly from their mother, especially my aunt Dorothy, who waitressed long hours at the Nonpareil diner downtown, and my aunt Constance, a substitute teacher who lived two houses away with her husband, a glazier. My uncle Gerry, who had joined the Boston mounted police solely to acquire a horse, was rarely around. Uncle Walter said the horse was all the family Gerry ever wanted. Dorothy's husband, Bob, made himself scarce, too, finding the constant joking around my grandparents' house exasperating. Theirs was a mixed marriage, the first in our family, as Bob was a jick, an English immigrant. It was customary for those of Irish extraction to mimic the accents of such people by singing out, "It's not the 'eavy 'aulin that 'urts the 'osses' 'ooves. It's the 'ammer, 'ammer, 'ammer on the old 'ighway." My grandmother outlawed this ditty out of deference to Bob, who, after all, might one day convert.

I seemed to have been forgotten during the early moments of the crisis, even by my mother. I seized on my brief obscurity to cook up reasons why I was now exempt from the miracle business: one, I was not the same boy who had stirred my grandmother to rise after the death of her husband; and two, it was not a miracle in the first place, except in the minds of my mother and her crazy sisters. I now sequestered myself in my room with *Road & Track*, Dave Brubeck Fantasy label 45s, and *True West* magazine. I was greatly absorbed by the events leading up to the gunfight at the OK Corral. No longer able to enchant me with accounts of the big baboon by the light of the moon combing his auburn hair, my mother tried upgrading my reading habits by offering me a dollar to read *Penrod and Sam*. I declined. But all this was distraction; I feared my call would come and I worked at facing it. I worried that by keeping to myself and playing the anchorite, I gave credence to my imputed saintlike powers; it behooved me to mingle with my relatives and strive to seem unexceptional, even casual. Being incapable of grasping the possible demise of my grandmother, I had no problem sauntering around the house seeing to everyone's comfort. No one suspected the terror in my heart. At one point, as I suavely offered to make cocktails, my mother jerked me aside and asked me if I thought this was the Stork Club. Thereafter, my attempts to disappear consisted of idly scratching my head or patting my lips wearily as I gazed out upon Brownell Street, where every parking spot was taken by my relatives' cars, all except Paul's, which he called a "foreign" car. Anyone pointing out that it was a dilapidated Ford was told, "It is entirely foreign to me." That car was not here, and if it was not over at the Mohican it could be as far afield as New Bedford or Somerset, whose watering holes provided what he called "acceptable consanguinity." These were terrible stewpots mentioned in the paper from time to time in an unflattering light, the one in New Bedford being, according to Uncle Walter, a bucket of blood haunted by raving scallopers and their molls.

My aunt Constance functioned as a kind of hall monitor. She had no legitimate authority, but she enforced the general rules as laid down by her mother, and at a time like this she saw to comings and goings, the hanging of visitors' hats, and the drawing of blinds and the pulling of draperies; she liked to catch me out in little infractions, since I had, besides the unearned affection of my grandmother, the fewest accrued rights around the place. This had to be undertaken discreetly or there would be my mother to contend with, younger than Constance but spoiling for a fight with her. I'd once heard my father say that Aunt Constance's ankles were thick. One day she came to my room where, out of quiet desperation, I was committing self-abuse in consideration of the rate condoms were being consumed up on Hood Street by the homeless cop and his teenage bride. She told me through the door that she would be taking me to see my grandmother. There was a platitudinous tone she used, even when she addressed me as Elvis or when she reminded me that others needed the bathroom too or wouldn't it be nice if I picked up a few of my things so that others didn't have to do it for me. When I emerged, she gave me a stare that insinuated either that she knew what I'd just been doing or that I was unaware of the gravity of the situation.

Is it Miracle Time? I wondered. I already had enough to fear, because I couldn't grasp what was happening to my grandmother. Well, I told myself, we aren't there yet.

As if I lacked sufficient power in my legs, Aunt Constance gave me a last little push into my grandmother's bedroom then followed me inside. My mother was already there, red-eyed and helpless. She was far the prettiest of the sisters and had been indoctrinated somehow in the idea, perhaps by the whole family, that handling crises would not be her strong suit. Years later, she would tell me that at the moment I'm now describing she wanted to curl up on the floor and break down completely; however, even semiconscious, her mother still had strong authority, and such behavior could fall under the proscribed category of *shenanigans*.

My grandmother spoke my name with groggy satisfaction, her face lit by the candles surrounding a figurine of the Virgin Mary that rested on her bedside table, a cheerful statue, trophy-sized and a lovely Bahamian blue. My mother appeared to have been there awhile, and sorrow transfigured her face in a way that I'd never seen it before, which upset me thoroughly. Aunt Constance fidgeted around, disturbed that my grandmother's mouth remained open. My mother caught Constance's briskness, and when she gently tried to close my grandmother's mouth, my mother hissed under her breath, *"Don't touch her!"* Constance's hand rested in midair, her eyes meeting my mother's with a kind of warning. It was like one of the showdowns I'd been investigating. Our awkward vigil didn't last much longer, as Uncle Walter soon arrived and shooed us out. We waited on the first floor for half an hour until Walter came down. He walked straight through us, speaking only as he went out the door: "I'll get the priest." He had a deep voice, and everyone in the family knew he was the law.

It was summertime. Our parish priest, Father Corrigan, had

gone to the Cape for a few days, so we wound up with some alien in a round collar, Father Cox, whom Walter kept on call in the parlor, reminding us that Extreme Unction did not reside in persons. Meanwhile, a bulletin was sent out for Corrigan, who appeared the next morning with a raging sunburn and loftily dismissed his surrogate. Father Corrigan took me aside, to a quiet spot past the stove. I was alert. He looked at me gravely and asked if I had noticed that Birdie Tebbetts had been promoted to starting catcher for the Cleveland Indians. I admitted ignorance in a way that suggested that at another time I would have been better informed. Father Corrigan reminded me, "Birdie went to Providence College with your uncle Paul—say, where *is* Paul?"

"He couldn't make it," I replied impulsively, based on no particular knowledge. Everyone was relieved that Paul had declined to be here, although Aunt Constance had conveyed my grandmother's condition to him by a note to his landlord.

"What'd you do that for?" my mother demanded.

"Ma asked me to," said Constance contentedly.

Father Corrigan, handsome enough that his departure for the seminary had sown heartache, was a priest of old-fashioned certainties who saw nothing cheerless in the present circumstances. He had gone completely bald, not even any eyebrows, but he wore a wig, a small vanity that was considered to have humanized him. He had a redhead's complexion and the wig was auburn. It didn't fit particularly well: the hairline was too emphatic around the front, and when he bent over, as he was usually careful not to do, it pried up from behind and exposed an eerie sanctum of white scalp.

As my grandmother's confessor, he knew she was bound for the ultimate destination, a place whose glory was beyond the descriptive powers of the most effusive travel agent. We fed off his optimism, sort of. He and Uncle Walter consulted away from the rest of us, who tried to read their lips from across the wide kitchen. Uncle Walter worshiped his mother, and it could not have been easy for him to recognize that she was ending her life in his professional hands.

Aunt Constance now brought her two girls, my cousins Kathleen and Antoinette, who viewed me as a corrupt hoodlum because of the then ubiquitous blue suede shoes I wore. My uncle Gerry finally showed up too, in his glossy black trooper boots and Boston police uniform, which seemed thrillingly archaic, like something Black Jack Pershing might have worn. But Gerry was so shy and sweet, he could barely speak. "He gets it from the horse," said Walter. I retired quietly to my room, where I resumed my study of the Old West, a place where do-gooders and mad dogs alike lived free of ambiguity and insidious family tensions. At the moment, the Earps and the Clantons were beginning the open movements of their mortal ballet.

By evening, our two authorities agreed that my grandmother would not live much longer, though she was conscious enough to make one thing clear: she wished to see her baby, Paul, before she died. My mother got on the phone and confirmed that my father had set out by automobile. "He'll be here in no time!" she said into thin air.

Uncle Walter departed for the Mohican. Bickering the whole time, Aunt Dorothy and my mother made a desultory attempt at cooking supper on the big gas stove from which my grandmother had so long and so majestically ruled: this time, macaroni and cheese. We were seated before our identical platters, my cousins studying my deployment of the silverware, when Uncle Walter returned and, entering the dining room, announced to us all, "He says no." After a suspicious glance at the macaroni, he turned significantly to the adults, who rose as one and left the dining room, leaving me with my cousins. We heard "bloody bugger" through the door.

Kathleen, who had snapping blue eyes and jet black hair in tu-

bular curls that hung alongside her face, announced, "We're awfully sad over at our house." Antoinette, a plainer brunette with a
thin downturned mouth, looked on and remarked, "It's too bad
your father isn't here to help. Why is it he never comes?"

I couldn't tell her that the household melodrama was unbear-
able to him or that he was busy, in my mother's absence, making
the two-backed beast with his secretary. Instead, I replied, "He
has a job. He's on his way now. How fast do you expect him to
drive?" Both smiled: Anyone who couldn't broil in an old mill
town all summer long was to be pitied. I remembered with satisfaction the day this pair appeared at Horseneck Beach. They
looked like two sticks in their bathing suits, no butts but the same
superior smiles. Naturally, they started a shell collection, everything lined up according to some system.

I was preoccupied, having just reached the point where Doc
Holliday was moving silently behind the corral planks with his
sawed-off shotgun. Distantly, my mind was moving to the even-
tualities facing those men in that dusty patch of earth when the
door opened and Uncle Walter summoned me with a crooked
finger. I rose slowly to go out. My fears were aroused by the hauteur in the faces of my cousins, then confirmed when I saw my
mother and my two aunts. I first pinned my hopes on the slightly
skeptical expression of my aunt Dorothy, but when I saw my
mother's pride and the phony look of general forgiveness on the
face of my aunt Constance, I knew I was cooked. It was miracle
time again. Father Corrigan gazed with detachment, wig tipped
up like a jaybird: the services this family expected of me probably
struck him as verging on sacrilegious.

I clapped both hands over Uncle Walter's car keys as they
lightly struck my chest. "The Blue Roadmaster in front. Bring
your uncle Paul. You're the guy that can get this done. Get Paul
now and *bring him here.*"

Constance piped up. "He *is* your favorite uncle."

It was a straight shot to Mohican House, and at that hour there was enough room to park a thousand cars. The entire way, I was plagued by mortifying visions of unsuccessful parallel parking, but I was never tested. Spotted by pedestrians my own age—three swarthy males with ducktails—as I climbed out of the car, I adopted a self-effacing posture I hoped would make clear that I was not its spoiled young owner. Once it was locked, I plunged its incriminating keys into my pocket.

Paul answered the door to his apartment promptly, greeting me with the phrase "Just as I expected," and showed me in with a sweep of his arm. He wore a surprising ascot of subdued paisley foulard that complemented a sort of smoking jacket. His was what was once called a bed-sitting room, which perfectly described it. A toile wall covering with faded merriment of nymphs and sparkling brooks failed to create the intended atmosphere. "How'd you get here, Walt's car?"

"Yes," I said, as though it was obvious. Paul had a faint brogue this evening, a bad sign. I glanced around: his bed was beside the window that looked down into an alley and was made with military precision, including the hospital corners he had once demonstrated. There was a battered but comfortable armchair nodded over by a single-bulbed reading lamp, and on the other side a night table that held the only book Paul owned, his exalted Roget's thesaurus, which he called "the key to success" and which Uncle Walter blamed for his inability to speak directly on any subject. A gray filing cabinet a few feet from the foot of the bed supported an artillery shell that served as a vase for a spray of dried flowers.

Paul poured each of us a drink, and when I courteously declined mine, he said, "Why, then, our evening is at an end."

"I don't think I should drink and drive," I said defensively.

"Do it all the time," he said, "an essential skill. Never caught unprepared. Learn it while you're young. Bluestockings have given it a bad name." He used the same voice on me that he employed in testing insurance pitches, brusque shorthand best for indicating the world of valuable ideas he had for your future, take it or leave it.

I had a sip and, after little pressure, finished my strong drink; whereupon I was coerced to accompany John McCormack and my uncle Paul in "Believe Me If All Those Endearing Young Charms," a performance that, under the responsibility of my family assignment, I found so disturbing that I accepted Paul's offer of another drink. Next Paul recited a poem about Michael Collins, how he left his armored car to walk laughingly to his death, after which a silence made it clear that Paul was ready to hear my pitch. I was emboldened and terrified by the alcohol, and not entirely sure who Michael Collins was or why walking to his own assassination cheered him up. I suppose this contributed to my disorientation. The record playing in the background was scratchy, and the orchestra accompanying the various tenors sounded like a bunch of steamboats all blowing their whistles; at the same time, I could see the appeal of being drunk.

There was no use telling Paul his mother was dying. Walter had already said that. Not only did I feel utterly burdened, but being here gave me such an enduring case of the creeps that, years later, I voted against Kennedy, switching parties for the only time in my life. I now admit that I feared the loss of my standing as a miracle worker and longed to find a way of preserving my reputation, partly because it was so annoying to my father, who considered my mother's first home a hotbed of mindless nostalgia and an impediment to her conformity and compliance. I couldn't appeal to Paul's values because I didn't know what they were and because I suspected that beneath his lugubrious independence lay some kind of awful bitterness that, if uncovered, might turn my world upside down.

I had no strategy, and my heart ached. It was important to my grandmother that I deliver Paul to her side, and the only thing I could think to do was to tell him what she meant to me. I began with a head full of pictures, my grandmother folding her evening paper to rise from her rocker and embrace me when I returned from a day in North Park, of the harmony of her household, the smell of pies arising from her second kitchen in the basement, the Sunday drives after Mass when she was taken around the perimeter of her tiny kingdom and to the abandoned mills where she had once worked. I even thought of our life in the Midwest, when I'd longed for her intervention in a family slow to invent rules for their new lives. I was with her on the first visit to her husband's grave when, looking at the headstone of their little boy right next to my grandfather's, she said, "I never thought they'd be together so soon." A half century between burials: "so soon." She bent to pat the grass in the next space. "No keening," she had warned her children at my grandfather's funeral. And indeed, it was a quiet American affair.

I imagined I could touch on a few of these points and move Uncle Paul to accompany me back to Brownell Street, but I barely got started. I was seized by some force I'd barely suspected and astonished myself by choking on tears that spilled down my face while Paul watched impassively.

Once I pulled myself together, Paul stood and turned off the record player. He looked at me with chilling objectivity and then stated his position clearly. Moving to his filing cabinet, he began to rearrange the dried flowers in the artillery shell, awaiting my departure.

Driving the Roadmaster I became immediately hysterical. I saw myself rocketing through the railings of the Brightman Street Bridge and plunging into the nocturnal gloom of the Taunton River below. But the Buick rolled along like a ship and my panic abated.

As I parked in the dark of Brownell Street and turned off the lights, I could see the faces in the window: time to take my medicine. I hoped their seeing me alone would make it unnecessary to explain that I had failed, but Paul could be just behind me in his foreign car. Walter, my mother, and my aunts would not give up so easily. Perhaps my quite legitimate expression of defeat would help, assuming no one noticed my unsteadiness.

Like a jury they were waiting for me in the kitchen. Knowing my grandmother still lived, I was strengthened. Entering the back door, sole entrance for anyone but a priest, gave access to a hallway and the choice of going straight upstairs, to my bedroom, or into the kitchen, where I was expected. The great blue presence of my uncle Gerry opened the door for me. Walter, Dorothy, Constance, and my mother stared without a breath or movement. I could state that I had failed; I could indicate that I had failed; I could make a paper airplane with a handwritten statement that I had failed and sail it at those faces; but until I did I was *still* a worker of miracles and reluctant to step down. The silence lasted long enough that my uncle Walter elevated his chin sternly, more pressure than I could withstand. I shook my head: *no.*

I didn't look up until Walter summoned me to the bookless library. His fingers rested lightly on my shoulder as though I might not be able to find my way. Once we were behind closed doors, he reached an open hand for his car keys, which I deposited therein. "Have you been drinking?" I nodded, meek but with rising surliness, concealed in the booze that was now thrumming in my eardrums. "I suppose it was a condition of your negotiations." I nodded again, this time modestly. "Well," said Walter, "I would like to know exactly what Paul said." I felt reluctant to convey this information, perhaps out of lingering loyalty to my favorite uncle, who had so often thrown the baseball on the tenement rooftops for me to field, but in the end I felt it wasn't mine to keep.

"He said to tell you all that . . . that sick people depress him."

I returned to my room reconciled to my lost sainthood. For now, there was the OK Corral and its several possible outcomes. But that night, my grandmother died at last and nothing in the story of Wyatt Earp suggested an appropriate response, as he of course was dead too.

For the several days of the viewing, the wake, the funeral Mass, it was as if we were troops following orders. My mother kept slipping off, trying to check on my father's progress. First it was a flat, then they wouldn't take a check for gas, then a distributor cap, then the magneto, and later, when she told Uncle Gerry about the bad magneto, he said, with all his big-cop innocence, "Jeez, Mary, they haven't had magnetos in twenty years!"

My father arrived on the day of the wake, a hot day more like August than late September. Greetings were fulsome, given the gravity of the occasion, Dorothy frayed with grief and worry and Constance somehow politicizing it and making the demise of my grandmother refer mostly to her own need for importance despite having married a Protestant. My father always seemed extraordinarily brisk, compared to my mother's relatives, and more capable of defusing social awkwardness with sunny confidence. He hugged my mother so long that her sisters grew uncomfortable and abandoned the porch. As the baby of the family, she might be more "advanced," but it was not their job to bear witness to the decline of standards. It was my turn with my father, and my mother followed her sisters indoors.

"Come here, Johnny," he said, leading me to the trunk of his big sedan, which he opened with a broad revelatory gesture. There was his leather suitcase with its securing straps and, next to it, a ten-horsepower Evinrude outboard motor. Looking over his shoulder left and right as though fencing loot, he said, "These worthy folk are all indoors men, unlike you and me. They see the sky about twice a year. Now that the inevitable has come to pass, we're going to rent a rowboat, attach this beauty to the transom, and run down to Fog Land for some floundering."

I told him I could hardly wait, and he mussed my hair in approval. Later, I felt a pang at omitting to suggest that Grandma's departure was an impediment to floundering. I helped my father take his bag to Paul's old room and stayed with him for a short time because he seemed to forget that I was still there. He hung his clothes carefully and placed a bottle of Shenley's blended whiskey on the dresser. He lined up three pairs of shoes, in the order of their formality, walked to the window overlooking Almy Street, and heaved a desolate sigh. I left the room.

I suppose he was nearly forty by then and wore his liberation from what he considered the ghetto Irish with a kind of strutting pride. The circumstance of my grandmother's death was such that he would be forgiven for being a Republican and for condescending to the family with his obviously mechanical warmth. He was still remembered bitterly for summoning the family to the Padanaram docks to admire a Beetle Cat with a special sail emblazoned with I LIKE IKE. He now received news of Paul's disgrace with a serious, nodding smile. Aunt Constance, rushing about to prepare the funeral dinner for the family, brusquely and with poorly concealed malice gave him the job of opening a huge wooden barrel full of oysters. Standing next to me in the backyard, he confided in me. "Here I am in fifty-dollar Church of London shoes, a ninety-dollar Dobbs hat, a three-hundred-dollar J. Press suit, *shucking oysters*. When will I ever escape all this?"

I was afraid to tell him that I was enjoying myself. He pointedly reminded me that he always made note of whose side I was on. "This group"—they were always a *group*—"ain't too keen on getting out of their familiar tank town." He liked bad English for irony but was normally painfully correct about his diction. He viewed himself as an outdoorsman, almost a frontiersman, based solely on having taught canoeing at summer camp in Maine. "You'll find this outfit," he said, gesturing to my grandmother's house, "in street shoes." For my mother's family, the outdoors came in just one version: a baseball diamond. But his view of my mother's family could be infectious, and I went to our first meal with him now viewing them as a *group*, nervously calibrating the array of forces around the table.

My father never seemed particularly interested in me, except when my alliance offered him some advantage, or at least comfort, in disquieting settings like this household. My grandfather thought he looked like an Indian and once greeted him with, "Well, if it isn't Jim Thorpe! How are your times in the four-forty, chief? Leaving them in the dust?" Or, more succinctly, "How."

My grandfather drove the back wheels on the majestic American-LaFrance hook-and-ladder. "A good place for him," said my father. "Well to the rear."

I knew his stay here would be a trial, though it seemed the only voice that carried up through the floor, causing him to flinch, was Father Corrigan's. Religion was an empty vessel to him. When my mother compelled him to attend Mass, he did so with the latest Ellery Queen wrapped in the cover of the Daily Missal.

"Now the keening begins," he said. "Your grandmother was a fine woman, but all the noise in the world isn't going to get her anywhere any faster. When you hear them in the parlor tuning up, you may think they've gone crazy. This stuff's about to go the way of the Model T. You'll be able to tell your kids about it. The sooner it's over, the sooner I can go back to America and try to make a buck."

"Will I see Grandma again?"

"That's the sixty-four-dollar question, isn't it? Ask Father Corrigan. Old Padre Corrigan never had a doubt in his life. He'll tell you it's only a matter of time. Me, I'm not so sure. He'll have

Grandma crooking a beckoning finger from the hereafter even if you can't see it and he can. Poor fellow spent his life making promises to weavers with TB and loom mechanics with broken bodies. I guess he started believing it himself. You ought to hear him describe heaven. It sounds like Filene's department store."

Then he went off on the Irish. "Among the many misconceptions about the Irish," he said, "is that they have a sense of humor. They do *not* have a sense of humor. They have a sense of ridicule. The Ritz Brothers have a sense of humor"—I had no idea who the Ritz Brothers were but he held them in exalted esteem— "Menasha Skolnik has a sense of humor. You think the Irish have a sense of humor? Read James Joyce. You'll have to when you go to college. I did. You'll ask yourself, 'Will this book never end?'"

I always tried to agree with my father, even when I didn't understand him. "I see what you mean," I said, with an aching sort of smile.

"Here's a famous one," he said, as the wailing started downstairs. "'If it weren't for whiskey, the Irish would rule the world.' Do I like this. They're *only* charming when they're drunk. When they're sober, they're not only not *ruling* the world, they're ridiculing its hopes and dreams." This was entirely true of my father himself. He was a merry boozer but a bleak observer of reality when sober. The present moment was a perfect example. He saw no legitimate grief in the response to my grandmother's death, only posturing and inappropriate tribal memory. "Rule the world, my behind," he added. "'If it weren't for blubber, Fatty Arbuckle would set the world record in the high jump.'"

My relatives were certainly not ruling the world, and they went about their lives with high spirits. While their certainties like everyone else's were soon to be extinguished by the passage of time, their ebullience was permanent, and I say this having seen two of them expire from cancer. My father, on the other hand, was grimly obsessed with his health, and for some reason I associate this with his flight from his origins. I recall him explaining to my mother that he had missed making his Easter Duty on the advice of his eye-ear-nose-and-throat specialist to avoid crowds.

I went downstairs and sat among my relatives, some of whom hadn't seen each other for a long time, especially the ones from Lawrence, who seemed to have in common straitened finances and sat in their overcoats watching the circulation of plates of finger food. My aunt Dorothy, from Providence, wept copiously and in a manner that reminded everyone, I was sure, of the melodramatic nature so annoying to my grandmother that she pretended that Taffy longed to star in a soap opera. The Sullivans were there from across the street. Uncle Gerry, wearing his mounted policeman's uniform with its crossed straps and whistle deployed just under his left shoulder, stared straight ahead and moved his lips in authentic prayer. My physician uncle Walter maintained a look of dignified pragmatism, and I'm sure he knew we looked to him for deportment hints. We believed he understood life and death through actual experience and, unconvinced by Father Corrigan's merry certainties, wished he would say something about the afterlife.

Saddest of all was Aunt Dorothy, because her household meddling had expired with my grandmother and she was now wandering about without a self to give meaning to her acts. I thought of her with white holes for eyes, as in the standard depiction of zombies. She looked blank and confused and made clueless efforts to find chairs, answer the phone, and offer horrifying comfort to people she barely knew. Finally, Walter commanded, "You need a rest. I'm sure everyone will excuse you." At this she let out a somewhat lunar cry that made poor Mr. Sullivan, a surgical arch outlining the former position of his cigar, grab his wife and run for the door.

Aunt Constance served the funeral dinner with a kind of pageantry, abetted by her daughters, the two little shits Kathleen and Antoinette. Watching their stately entrance for each course, learned in that narcissistic training ground of First Communion, I could have, as Josef Goebbels once remarked, "reached for my Luger." The meal was a tribute to my grandmother and featured all her favorite dishes—swordfish (my father confided these small steaks were doubtless from a skillygallee, an obsolete term for the less desirable white marlin), corn on the cob, parsnips, and apple pie—and represented a maudlin idea of grieving. "They're gonna milk it," he said, when he heard the menu.

We were seated, Walter at the head of the table, my mother, father, and I in a row, Dorothy sniveling into the canned consommé preceding the main course, Kathleen and Antoinette, half crouched in their pinafores and ready for duty, Gerry upright as a man of the law. As Walter said grace, I watched my mother closely; her melancholy smile was less occasional than chemical, produced by the pills she took, ostensibly to raise an abnormally low blood pressure, as well as straight shooters from the vodka tucked in her suitcase. Like many of their generation, my parents believed in the absolute odorlessness of vodka and applied to its consumption none of the restraint of the blends whose broadly familiar aroma marked the user like a traffic light. My father sported his customary deniable supercilious smile. When cornered, he'd lay it to gastric distress or the unaccountable prelude to heartbreak, as when my mother walked out on him and he couldn't wipe the grin off his face and had to explain it.

The front door was carelessly slammed shut and Uncle Paul walked in, wearing his drab woolen officer's uniform with obvious moth holes, and commented that we looked a bit gloomy. Father Corrigan rose to his feet, held his napkin between thumb and forefinger, and dropped it to the table. With infinitesimal authority, Walter indicated with his eyes that Father Corrigan was to take his seat again promptly. Constance appeared behind Paul and, leaning around him, said in a shrill voice, "Just making certain there's a place set."

"Grab me a beer from the fridge," said Paul. Constance froze but my mother leaped up and chirped nonchalantly that she knew right where it was. My father patted her butt, eyes half-lidded with private irony as she swept past, and Paul smiled at his favorite relative, my mother; Uncle Gerry, rendered huge in his uniform by the smallness of the room, strode to the sideboard to turn on the big Sunbeam fan. He'd begun to sweat. Seated again, he asked Walter about various old folks of our acquaintance. Most got good health reports, except Mary Louise Dwyer and Arthur Kelly, who had, he said in a significant voice, "been in to see me." As to lip cancer Mr. Sullivan, "You couldn't hurt him with a tire iron."

"A corker," Gerry agreed.

Once my mother had deposited the beer in front of a greatly relieved Uncle Paul, Aunt Constance began to send in my cousins with a steady parade of dishes. Noticing my father, Paul nodded and said, "Harold." Constance shooed the cousins along from close behind, with no effect on their speed at all but reinforcing her position as culinary benefactress. She kept her husband behind in the kitchen as a kind of factotum and sous-chef; besides, he wasn't comfortable in what he not altogether humorously called Harp Central. He could have said it more clearly because no one cared what he said, all part of Constance's disgrace: she would have enjoyed greater standing if she'd been gang-raped by a hurley squad.

I'm not sure my father enjoyed much esteem either, and I think he knew it. He was well educated, hardworking, and ambitious, yet something set him apart, as though he had renounced a portion of his humanity to achieve his current station and had, moreover, abducted the baby of the family, my mother, to a dreary and stunting world where people made themselves up and were vaguely weightless. I realized with dread that, at this funeral meal, he was likely to take a stand.

"I wonder where she is now," Paul said, slurping his consommé.

"Where who is?" Walter asked coolly.

"Ma. Where Ma is."

Dorothy covered her mouth.

"Ma is in heaven," said Walter.

"You, as a man of science, say she is in heaven?"

"Absolutely."

"Well, good. I hear great things about the place."

Kathleen made a covert rotary motion with her forefinger at her temple; then, fearing she'd been observed, she pretended to adjust one of the tubular curls. She wouldn't look at me.

My father half rose from his chair, rather violently, shifting all attention to himself, as he reached across the table for a dish of lemons. "It's been a long time since I had a chance to enjoy a swordfish steak!" This fell discordantly upon me and anyone else who'd heard his theory of the skillygallee.

My mother said, "Wonderfully done, Constance, a beautiful meal." Constance gave a self-effacing curtsy. Dorothy stared at her food with white eyeholes and a half-opened mouth, and Gerry rubbed her back consolingly until she picked up her fork and prodded a parsnip. Since I eat too fast when I'm nervous, my mother put her hand on my forearm to slow me down. I looked up at her helplessly, wide-eyed.

Walter smiled all round and said, "This would be a good time to remember all the happy times we've had at this table, especially when Pa would have been in my place. We saw very little of Ma then. She just came and went from the kitchen, long enough to look after us. She sure looked after us, didn't she?

Generations of us. Me, Connie, Gerry, Mary, and you kids, right, Antoinette?"

Antoinette stood up from her seat. "My grandmother is a saint," she sang out, in a high mechanical voice. "She is being welcomed by the angels this very minute."

Paul blew up his cheeks and nodded.

"Kathleen?"

Kathleen rose and gazed around the room with her electric blue eyes. "Our grandmother—"

I knew I was next, and I felt the ironic expectations of my father, who loved to see me on the hot seat. I never really believed it was the test of character he claimed.

"—brought to our family the highest standards of piety and family concern, especially as to her devotion to Holy Mary Mother of God." Even knowing they'd been prepped, I asked myself where the two little hussies had come up with this chin music. I hadn't long to think about it, though; it was my turn.

"Johnny?"

I sat dumbfounded, a weird tingling in my scalp. My father looked at me with a faint smile and my mother gazed into her lap. Both seemed to understand I wasn't up to this. I had the whirlies.

"Why don't you stand up?" Uncle Walter said gently.

I rose slowly, the tightness in my throat making speech impossible. A glance at my father revealed ill-concealed hilarity. Uncle Paul was waggling his empty beer at Constance, who stood in the doorway bearing down on me with her eyes. The cousins looked like winners. Only a brief picture of my grandmother rescuing me from this, which she certainly would have, allowed me to break quietly into inarticulate tears.

Uncle Walter smiled sadly and said, "Thank you, Johnny. That's how we all really feel. You've done us all a big favor— thank you." As I sat down, my father's glance said he could hardly believe I'd pulled off this stunt. I could almost hear him saying, "Fast one there, M.B.," or, "Smooth."

Uncle Walter turned his gaze to my father but quickly looked away; my father was fussing with the napkin in his lap and plainly intended to say nothing at all about the passing of my grandmother. My mother stared at the side of his head, and I knew that in more private circumstances she would have been ready to raise hell. He surely knew ahead of time how brittle any words of tribute might have seemed. My mother's family were great at seeing through things, and he wasn't about to walk into a trap. Paul stood a carrot in the mound of his mashed potatoes and hummed "The Halls of Montezuma," satire that seemed some-how directed at my father. Kathleen and Antoinette were still smirking at me for crying, and I consoled myself with napalm fantasies as their mother stood between them, urging them to clean their plates while tossing me an artificial look of bafflement that suggested I'd lost a step or two to her darlings.

As Aunt Constance turned somewhat loftily to return to the kitchen and another unwelcome course, my mother, always in-genious when it came to defusing tension with her chaotic sense of humor, asked, "Where you going, Constance?"

She stopped but did not look back. "To the kitchen, Mary. Why?"

"Wherever you're going"—she pointed to the uncanceled first-class stamp affixed to Aunt Constance's behind—"it's going to take more postage than that!"

So we got some relief, and Constance could do no more than smile patiently through the laughter before continuing to haul food. The cousins were bouncing their heels on the rungs of their chairs, and I hoped their waning patience would undo all their prissy decorum. In the past I had seen their pandering, obse-quious grins turn into frustrated rage in a blink—ballistic in pinafores—and I could wish for that.

"Gerry, tell us about some crimes."

"Oh, Mary, nothing so exciting. Mostly just blocking jaywalkers with the horse. Ran down a purse snatcher on Sunday."

"That must have been satisfying."

"Yes, yes, it was. They slam into the old ladies to get the purses. We get a lot of broken hips, nice old ladies who might not walk again. When we catch the snatcher we take him up the alley and give him the same, couple shots with a paver."

We all admired this.

"What's the horse's name?" I asked.

Gerry lit up. "Emmett. From a farm in Nova Scotia." It was clear Gerry preferred Emmett's company to ours. Embarrassed to reveal so much emotion, he ran his finger around the tight collar of his uniform. "Seventeen-hand chestnut," he said in a choky voice.

"This is *real* food," Paul announced. "It's certainly not K-rations and, by cracky, she's no international cuisine."

"What d'you mean, *international cuisine*?" said my father. The rest of the family regarded him alertly. He seemed aggressive.

"Let me give you an example, Harold." Paul bounded back with startling volubility. "I was taken to a French restaurant in the city of New York with, if memory serves, a five-star rating from acknowledged experts in the field, and I don't mean Duncan Hines. Because there were four of us, all friends, I was able to sample each celebrated entrée, and I can report to you without prejudice that they all smelled like toilet seats. It gave me the fantods. I prefer a boiled dinner."

My father seemed ostentatiously bored. I had noticed the faint ripple of cheek muscles as he violently suppressed his yawns. His boredom became so pronounced it looked like grief and was probably taken for that. I knew better. I'd heard an argument start in his bedroom with my mother before dinner in which he stated that my grandmother was being "impetuously canonized," a claim my mother made no attempt to refute. She just called him a son of a bitch. "Ah," said he, "the colorful household vernacular."

Uncle Paul began to wail at the end of the table. It was astonishing. He looked around at his family and sobbed, not bowing or covering his head and face. A theory about traditional keening may have lain behind this, perhaps giving it a somewhat academic tone that didn't make it any less alarming.

"What's the matter, Paul?" my mother asked softly, which only raised the volume. I'd never seen anything like this before. I was thrilled at this splendid racket. Uncle Walter stood and placed his hands on Paul's heaving shoulders, giving them rhythmic squeezes, as the campaign medals tinkled. That seemed to calm Uncle Paul somewhat. Aunt Dorothy had begun a contrapuntal snivel, and Walter gently raised his palm for it to stop. Constance ran to the table with a glass of water, taking the position that Paul had something stuck in his throat. My mother held her cheeks, which streamed hot tears. Dorothy lowered the window, then the shade, and turned the Sunbeam fan up several notches until napkins began to flutter. Paul struggled to his feet, and Walter steered him slowly to the door as though fearing Paul would buckle.

My father jumped up and threw out an arm in Paul's direction with startling emphasis, a mariner spotting land. "For Christ's sake, tell him to pull himself together!" He was nearly shouting. There was something experimental in his exasperated tone.

Walter stopped, his back to us and his head bowed. He turned slowly, his head still bent, but when he was faced our way, I saw his eyes blazed.

"You would do well," he said to my father levelly, "to mind your own business." A terrible quiet followed.

Once Walter had steered a gasping, heaving Paul from the

room, my father sat in the ensuing quiet and wiped his lips with his napkin in thought. "Exactly," he said, as he rose and walked out of the room.

Constance soared in with the hot apple pie. I wondered why she always described things as being fresh from the oven, as she did again now. My mother had a terrific sweet tooth and fell on her slice with relish. Cocking her ear to a slight sound, she said, "He's heading up the stairs," and, at a series of thuds, announced, "He's packing his bag." She began to race through her pie. At the last mouthful, she grabbed my hand and stood me up. "We'd better see him off, or we'll never hear the end of it."

It was a moonless night, and the three of us gazed into the trunk of the sedan. My father slung his leather bag in and gave the Evinrude a comradely wiggle, looked at us, and smiled at the shabby building behind. "Goodbye," he said.

— — — — — — — — — — —

I thought my mother really had no chance to absorb the death of her own mother as long as my father was around. His general disapproval of her family and the ongoing need to argue about it must have drawn a veil over her feelings. I noticed too that though she had fallen nearly silent after my father's departure, she was also more efficient now in getting things done around the house, cooking and cleaning. She went to Mass every day, St. Joseph's, a short walk, and she usually brought me some little treat on the way home. She even had a carpenter come in to see to the sagging second-floor porch. Whatever tension was brewing between her and my aunt Constance must have come to a head, because Constance stormed out on her familiar slogan—"This is the thanks I get!"—and was not seen again before we left for home. Silence was not my mother's strong suit, but we spent a nearly wordless day where the Westport River opened onto the sea, wading in the salt mud for quahogs. "This is what I loved best when I was a girl" was nearly all she said. The clouds on the horizon made a band of light on the deep green Atlantic, and the breakers that lifted and fell with such gravity might have drowned our conversation, if there had been any. We must not have felt the need.

Aliens

Homer Newland, a partner and franchise specialist at a Boston law firm, had had a distinguished career and a very long one before retiring at seventy-five, when he was certainly still useful but had become more aware of the frequent need, when meeting new clients, of demonstrating that he still had all his marbles. So he indulged a lifelong dream and returned to live in the West, where he'd grown up but which in his long absence had made the place of his nativity hard to grasp.

For decades he had nursed his dream of going home, but when he moved back his dismay was all-consuming; Montana seemed like a place he had once read about in a dentist's office, and his daughter who lived there felt the pressure of his impending return. It reminded him of his early days in Boston, when he was always the only person anyone had met named Homer, and the name seemed to suggest risible rural origins. His internist, originally from Wisconsin, was named Elmer, and that seemed to help. Homer was a widower, after enjoying marriage for forty years to CeeCee, a pleasant alcoholic from Point Judith, Rhode Island. Their vacations were spent not in Montana, as he would have liked, but on the island madhouse of Nantucket, which he detested, as he did all seaside places. Too well-bred to cause the fuss that might have led to intervention, Homer's wife had boozed her way right off the planet and was buried among kin in the Point Judith churchyard, and Homer was back home in Montana, not quite comfortable and blaming a scholarship to Harvard

Law for turning his life upside down. His now-waning grief at CeeCee's death had been marked from the beginning by ambivalence; it was possible that either she or both of them were better off now that she was gone.

Twenty years ago, Homer sent their only child, Cecile, to a dude ranch, hoping to find a kindred spirit in his Montana romance, and it worked. Cecile met a local football star and settled down to raise two children, very much a local, soon treating her own father with that ambiguous humor reserved for out-of-staters. His grandchildren were precocious, in his opinion, and a bit crude, also his opinion. Cecile and her husband, Dean, were fairly crude themselves, always fighting and frequently separated. Homer had to make an effort to keep from finding everything somewhat crude in his old home place. Nevertheless, this further motivated him to retire there instead of visiting as he had been doing. He bought a nice place outside town with a view of the Absarokas, a long driveway, and a deep hundred-gallon-a-minute well. In his pleasantly interfering way, Homer could be quite forceful, causing more than a few unpleasant moments in his daughter's household, an ill-run enterprise at the best of times. He was determined to find his solace in nature but not having much luck at it.

The new quarters became in just a few years quite lonely. But Boston was long behind him and he didn't know what to do with himself. Nor could he account for the decades spent in Boston leaving so little trace. He couldn't go back there, he didn't have a wife, and he read himself into a hole. He brought himself excruciatingly up to speed on national and world affairs. In two years he would be eighty, and of all things he'd have liked a fresh start. He was remarkably fit for his years; maybe that was the problem. Considering his prospects without the alibi of decrepitude kept him on edge. He snapped at the propane man, not out of the blue—the lout had backed his big truck over a lilac—but a loss of composure uncharacteristic of Homer. He had generally been so-licitous, especially of tradespeople on whom he'd come to rely, and of the key gossips around the post office. Next, he quit greet-ing the UPS man and just let him leave things on the porch. He felt that some birds were bullying others at the feeder and started to fret about stepping in, before recognizing that this might just be some geriatric absurdity. He had enough money to keep man-aged care at bay, and he was determined never to need it.

On his not infrequent trips back to the city, he felt the extraor-dinary energy that seemed to emanate from the streets—staying only in hotels with thriving, even booming, lobbies—and on returning home he'd feel dissatisfied with land where all life seemed to have belonged to absent Indians and the blank faces of the neighbors. Believing that the great beauty of the place would have a possibly sweeping impact on an out-of-towner, he began to think of inviting a lady friend for a visit, a benign calculation that enlivened him considerably. At his age, a smorgasbord of widows lay before him. Surprisingly hale, several had undergone a kind of spiritual tune-up with the departure of their husbands and had become wonderful, even creative, company. There were a few with whom he'd had flings as much as forty years before.

Madeleine Hall was particularly vivid in his memory. He might have been in love with that one. Well, he was and God knows he acted it out. Homer felt that, blessed by longevity, he could be in a position to take advantage of this sentiment, and he elaborated upon the idea without losing sight of the fact that it was really about avoiding loneliness. He dismissed any notion of answering isolation with some fellow sufferer, since the thought of a woman who was herself lonely put him off: needy females had repelled him even in his youth, when neediness was more in style. He married CeeCee for her toughness, but then the drink got her. His greatest disappointment at his wife's dipsomania had been the decline of her contentiousness as she grew supine and content in addiction. And so he began to stray a bit, his handful of city flings thrilling him with their conflicts and rage. Married in Montana, Cecile had lost all contact with her mother and was strangely unsympathetic to her plight, viewing the addiction strictly as an extravagance not everyone could afford.

It was quiet at home, and then very quiet.

Homer and Madeleine's wonderful fling back in the fifties included risk-filled lovemaking right under the windows of her husband, Harry, a fund manager and broad-bellied former Princeton football star, and once they'd done it in the very home of Homer's passed-out CeeCee. Homer had wished Madeleine's interest in him originated in distaste for Harry. Unfortunately, it was sex and sex only; she adored Harry but he was now too fat, preoccupied, and plastered to fulfill what she considered a tiny part of her life. Madeleine's leggy tennis player's body was full of wanton electricity, and this memory was not entirely absent as Homer greeted a nice-looking old lady as she got off the plane. Her smile was the first thing that caught his eye—it was drawn off center—causing her to remark lightly, "I've had a stroke. Is it still okay?"

He took her in his arms and let the passengers find a way around them. He didn't quite understand his present desperation. His excitement to show her his house in the country, to introduce her to his daughter and grandchildren, had coalesced into uncomfortable urgency. The vacuum filled with a roar.

Madeleine had not been there long before she discovered Homer's neglect of the flower beds around the house, not that they amounted to much, nearly odorless rugosa roses for the most part. But she was not happy about the weeds in the hard ground that resisted her arthritic fingers, or about the signs of careless pruning. She could see that this was not anything Homer cared about. "I care about it," he protested, "but I'm not a gardener."

"We've got to get some water on them before I can do a single thing."

Homer tried to think of the implied time span of an improved rose bed and was apprehensive. "You see this," he said, indicating a faint ditch running around the perimeter of the beds. "This is how they were always irrigated. But it's a bit of trouble."

"How much trouble can it be?"

"You have to go up the river and turn some water into the ditch."

"And after that you've got water down here?"

"Yes."

"Then what's the problem? These roses are being tortured, and I can't get the weeds out of the ground."

Madeleine walked ahead of Homer as the trail progressed along the river and up through a chokecherry thicket. He was fascinated at her forthright progress, given that she did not know the way. He slyly let her lead them down a false trail that ended at the bottom of an unscalable scree slope, fine black rock shining in mountain light. She smiled to acknowledge that he probably knew the route better. At length they reached the head gate, an old concrete structure with 1927 scratched into the cement. In the bend of the river, it diverted water to ranches in the area, and in its steel throat snowmelt gurgled off to the east to meet with crops and fertilizer. Homer's place was not a ranch, but it still retained its small right to a share of water, just enough for a garden and a few trees. He seldom used it, but when he did he usually got a call from one of the neighbors who also used the ditch regularly and invariably addressed him as Old-Timer.

Downstream from the head gate, another ditch branched off, back toward Homer's place; he pulled the metal slide that held back the water and a small stream headed for his house. "This will be nice for the trees and flower beds."

"If it softens the ground, I can do something with it," said Madeleine. "You've just let things go, Homer. It looks like a transient has been squatting there."

"Madeleine, I'm doing something about it right now."

"How long will it take for the water to get there?"

"Not long." Actually, he didn't know.

Homer went back to the head gate, followed by Madeleine, hurrying along the path. He thought of that awful word *spry* and wondered why he imagined he might be exempt. *Spry* was supposed to be positive. It was awful.

A truck stopped on the road above them, a blue-heeler dog in back and rolled fabric irrigation dams piled against the cab. By the sound of the truck door being slammed, Homer knew this would not be a friendly visit. But he continued his adjustments, meant to preserve the water level of the ditch even after he had extracted his small share for the garden. Madeleine was looking up at the truck as its driver wheeled around the tailgate and started toward them. This was Homer's neighbor, Wayne Rafter, who raised cattle and alfalfa on the bench downstream. Wayne had a round red face, surmounted by a rust-brown cowboy hat with a ring of stain above its brim. He wore irrigating boots rolled down to the knee and carried a shovel over his shoulder.

He said, "What are you doing with the water?"

"We're sending a little down to the garden."

"You need to leave my head gate alone. You've got the whole valley screwed up."

Madeleine said, "That little trickle?"

"Stay out of this," said Wayne, without looking at her at first. When he did, he said, "What's wrong with your face?"

Homer answered that she'd had a stroke and was immediately

sorry he'd said anything at all. Wayne dismissed the explanation, saying that a lot of folks had had strokes. Homer felt a pressure he might not have if Madeleine had not been looking on.

"I do have a small water right attached to my property."

"Very small."

"But it *is* a right."

"Not if you don't use it. It reverts."

"I'm using it now."

"You're in the goddam way."

"I wonder if we should get a ditch rider." A ditch rider was appointed by the court to supervise the allocation of water.

"Do you have any idea what that costs?"

"It might be necessary if you prevent me from taking my water. Shall I arrange it?"

"No, don't 'arrange it,' Old-Timer. Just play with the water if that's what turns you on."

At this, Wayne marched off with his shovel over his shoulder and soon his truck was gone, a dog barking and running around in the bed.

Madeleine said, "Wow."

"Yep."

"Is that how they are?"

"Can be." Homer's insouciance concealed his humiliation.

Madeleine stared around herself into immediate space. Homer knew the remark about her face must have stung. Long ago, she'd been so careful about her looks, a little fashion-driven for Homer's taste but always ready to be seen, always lovely. They started back toward the house quite depleted by the encounter.

"Harry was truculent," said Madeleine. They found candles and Madeleine made their meal, a nice salad and cold cucumber soup good for a warm summer evening. "But I wouldn't say abusive. Abusive is when they focus on you. He just raged around, and whatever he might have done to me he did equally to the furniture."

In the sixties when, for whatever reason, CeeCee had started tying a scarf around her head, she acquired a reputation for heightened spirituality among acquaintances who didn't realize she was drunk. For them, she never passed out but was "transported." Part of this was abetted by CeeCee as an apparatus for her illness, and her conversation was increasingly ethereal as she discovered the allure of non sequiturs. Their neighbor, Dick Chalfonte, a thoracic surgeon, was enchanted, and Homer suspected that days spent out of town—some surreptitiously with Madeleine—allowed Chalfonte's fascination to be transmuted into something more tangible. Homer didn't like this thought at all but, because of Madeleine and his own fair-mindedness, found indignation unavailing; anyway there was some consolation if Dick Chalfonte was able to make contact with a soul drifting slowly to another world. It might have been that Homer wished he would take her away altogether, but of course this was unthinkable.

Madeleine rolled her napkin ring from side to side with her forefinger. "We used to think it was an affectation when you wore cowboy boots with your suit."

"And my Turnbull and Asser shirts. Of course it was an affectation. What else does a young man have? I was trying to make a name for myself, and in that town there didn't seem to be many possibilities left. Who's 'we,' anyway?"

"Harry and me, I guess. Harry thought you were a phony."

At night, they talked about poetry. Madeleine had a particular aversion to the poet H. D., whom she called "I. E." for what she called a perverse inability to say anything plainly. Homer feebly recited Wordsworth, to which Madeleine remarked she greatly looked forward to getting, spending, and laying waste her powers. And when Homer remarked that General Wolfe would have preferred to have written "Elegy in a Country Churchyard" than to have conquered Quebec, she urged him to stop thinking of poetry in terms of its public currency.

"I just read the funnies," said Homer.

They had twin beds with a reading lamp and nightstand between them, an easy distance for holding hands. The lamp could be adjusted so that Madeleine could read while Homer drifted off. She looked up from her book.

"Homer, are you afraid to die?"

"No."

"The Day of Judgment?"

"Nope."

"Homer, are you afraid of anything?"

"I'm afraid of rigor mortis."

She chuckled—"But exactly"—and went back to her book. It soon dropped to her lap. He watched her until she fell asleep, then slipped his hand free of hers and turned off the lamp.

Homer's daughter, Cecile—named for her mother, though unlike her in every way and never called CeeCee—phoned at about ten o'clock at night. Madeleine was asleep and Homer was setting out mousetraps, one for the cereal cupboard, one under the stove, and one in front of the refrigerator he hoped he would remember when he was barefoot in the morning. He didn't like this, but the humane traps were too humane to catch mice. He rotated the geranium on the windowsill to equalize its sun exposure and watched the grosbeaks and juncos scouring the ground under the empty feeder. Hawks sometimes killed juncos at the feeder; while nature might be red in tooth and claw, Homer worried about being complicitous in the death of the juncos. In fact, he'd twice moved the feeder to give the songbirds better cover from overhead but underestimated the hawks' capacity for swooping.

"Father, I'm having a yard sale tomorrow morning at ten. Can you help me look after the kids?"

"Cecile, I'm not so good at that." His tone was pleading.

"You'll be fine. They like you." This was a command. In fact, the children were quite distant with him. He thought he detected acid in her next remark. "You can bring your friend to help you." Cecile knew Madeleine's name perfectly well.

Homer was afraid of children. He could barely remember being one, and he really didn't understand them or why they acted as they did. He certainly didn't dislike children, but he found them emotionally opaque except when tribal or violent. Actually, he longed for Cecile's children to like him. But he was not always ready to test the idea, and they had rather peered at Madeleine on meeting her.

"You've got to do this. What's-her-name can help me with the sale. She'd just scare the kids. They don't know her."

"Why are you having a yard sale at all? Your furnishings are sparse now."

"Not sparse enough, buddy, not by a long shot. So get it together, Grandpa, and head on down here."

Cecile was always lightening her load, paring away at things, fixing a car that should have been traded, and he knew why: she was preparing for flight. She was readying herself for the moment when her life would change and she could escape. She had lost all her former levity, no longer introducing her father as a "forensic barber," and had recently had her breasts dramatically augmented, a move he viewed as panic inspired by those magazines at the checkout.

He helped Cecile prepare the yard sale while Judy and Jack, seven and two, still slept inside and Madeleine waited for them to

awaken. Cecile, a rag tied around her head, grunted enthusiasti-
cally as they hefted the NordicTrack to the sidewalk. A low egg-
yolk-yellow September sunrise was stretching shadows across
the street to lawns with uncollected morning newspapers. On the
pavement an old steel porch glider rested, his lower back pain reminding Homer how it had arrived. Also: a bread box, an early
microwave, percolator, a run of *National Geographic*s, a yoga mat,
a cactus, a birdcage, several of Cecile's college paintings in the
once universal style of Georges Roualt, a child's English saddle
with jodhpurs and boots (Cecile's), scenic place mats, a standing
ashtray with a lever that flushed the butts and ashes down a trap-
door, a silhouette of an Indian chief made with bullets, several
rugs, a Monopoly game, a Parcheesi set, a Coup Feret set, a
double-deck card holder for canasta, a checkerboard—these last
worried Homer, as it was hard to imagine Cecile without her
games—incidental Venetian blinds, canoe paddles, a Dutch oven,
and a mosquito net. Here we hit the strata of the ex-husband,
where lay the heart of the yard sale as they announced Cecile's
single status: commemorative whiskey bottles from Old Fitzger-
ald, I. W. Harper, Jim Beam, Ezra Brooks, and others, depicting
Man O' War, a largemouth bass, a fire truck, Custer's Last Stand,
the OK Corral, Elvis, W. C. Fields, cat-and-dog, rooster, turtle, an
Indian with a tomahawk on a white horse, a Florida gator, a black
rotary phone, the Run for the Roses, a Siamese cat, a kachina doll,
the Wyoming bronco, a raccoon, the Chevy Bel Air, Ducks Un-
limited, Van Gogh's *Old Peasant,* and there was also a set of train-
related decanters: engine, mail car, caboose, water tower. Homer
found it dizzying but Cecile assured him it would be the big draw
and she was right. One customer drove from Yakima, Washington, for the rotary phone, while a few more, drawn by the bottles,
bought other items, mostly small cheap things to satisfy the urge
for a transaction aroused by the bottles.

Cecile wanted to stay outside to guard the merchandise, so

Homer waited in the living room with Madeleine for the children to awaken. They felt so apprehensive they hardly spoke, and Homer looked around at the room as if through Madeleine's eyes. Only the front window admitted much light, enough to bleach the rug but not enough to lend any cheer. The living room of a single mother, he reflected, is a sad room. This one, containing so many things CeeCee had sent from Rhode Island, hoping for a response from Cecile, was especially sad. Even the old Aeolian player piano seemed to refer to cheerful times long gone by. The furniture was sad, the curtains were sad, the strewn toys were sad, the chandelier was utterly sad, but the china cabinet with its unemployed crockery was tragic. Over the fireplace there was still a color-saturated photograph of Dean, Cecile's ex-husband, in a classic football pose: knee raised, twisting off the opposite foot, ball tucked under one arm, the other projected, fingers spread wide, barreling toward an imaginary tackler.

"That's my son-in-law."

"What became of him?" asked Madeleine.

"Still in town. He's a bit impaired. He had an accident. They're separated."

"What kind of accident?"

Homer thought. There was a long version and a short version. He elected the latter. "He fell off a building."

"Good grief. But he's out of the picture?"

"Sort of," said Homer, with meaning.

"I see. Once they're in the picture," said Madeleine, "they're never really out of the picture, are they?"

How could my daughter have all this weight on her shoulders? His view might have been colored by his relationship with his grandchildren. He tried hard to charm and amuse them despite their lack of fondness for him. Still, he gave Cecile credit for an outstanding job: Judy and Jack were lively, curious, and confident. Also, they were calm. Judy was even a bit lofty. And why should they know him better? He never seemed to know exactly where he was, and the children could sense it. Jack once asked him if he was an alien.

"Why are you here, Grandpa?" Judy stood in her doorway, wearing her pajamas. She was seven and had chosen not to see Madeleine at Homer's side, another alien. Homer had imagined a situation in which the children adored her on sight.

"I'm looking after you and Jack while your mom has her yard sale." She was small with an oval face and burning black eyes. Homer's attempt to explain things had a whiny edge that he could tell annoyed her. Jack wasn't paying any mind and looked dopey. "Can you say hello to Madeleine?" He wondered whether he should have introduced her as Mrs. Hall, but he was some-what jealous of Harry Hall, long dead though he may have been.

"Me and Jack are against the yard sale."

"Of course you are," said Madeleine merrily. "I dislike change too. But how can we stop it?"

Judy stared at her as though she were nuts.

Jack stood at Judy's side, still half-asleep. To Homer, he resem-bled all two-year-old boys, though not nearly so fat as some. He had dark hair as his father once had, and it stuck out in a burr. He stared at Judy, awaiting her leadership. Then, as it was not forth-coming, he wandered to Madeleine and reached for her hand.

"Well, how does breakfast sound?" asked Homer, immedi-ately recognizing the absurdity of the question, as breakfast had no sound. The new acuteness about diction, with Madeleine lis-tening, produced this odd thought.

"Cheerios for me. Capt'n Crunch for him. Honey on mine. Sugar on his. The honey bear is over the toaster. It's on a paper towel because it was sticking to everything. The bowls are still in the washer. We don't use napkins, we use paper towels. Regular spoons, not soup spoons, and not too much milk."

It didn't take much for this to seem like drudgery. He was displeased by the cereal rustling from the waxed paper liners of the boxes into the bowls. It looked like packing material. "You don't have to sit here and stare at us," said Judy pleasantly. Madeleine strayed back out to the yard sale, doubtless to warm things up with Cecile. Homer watched her go.

"I didn't mean to stare. My thoughts were wandering."

"Do you find us obnoxious?" Judy asked.

Now Homer was wide-awake and attentive. "Judy, how can you ask such a thing?"

This was too plaintive. Her gaze darted over his face. "You seemed off in the clouds, Grandpa, probably thinking about your new girlfriend."

"It doesn't mean I find you obnoxious."

Jack poured his cereal into Homer's lap and, when Homer jumped up, started wailing as if his grandfather meant to attack him. In a moment, while Homer knelt on the floor, a rag in his hand and an icy feeling in his crotch from the milk, Cecile came in with no particular look of concern, quieting Jack and organizing another bowl of cereal. She pushed Jack's chair very close to the edge of the table, which seemed to make his movements less random. Jack just stared into his bowl, unsure what to do with it. Homer got up indecisively. Cecile said, "Your new friend is working the crowd." Jack waved his spoon jubilantly and then looked around to gauge its effect.

"Let's spruce them up and take them to the sale," she said, "a little poignancy to drive up prices."

A wet washcloth and extraordinary efficiency in lifting limbs or whole bodies into the apertures of their clothes had the two children spiffy in very short order, though it left them dazed. With Homer in the lead, Cecile herded the children from behind. Homer immediately mingled with amiable body language among the skeptics looking at the merchandise. Suddenly, Cecile cried, "Oh, no!" and whirled on Madeleine.

"What happened to the bottles?"

"A man came for them, a man in a wheelchair. He said they were his." Madeleine suddenly looked her age, with something comic about the makeup she'd applied so carefully.

"Did he pay for them?"

"He said they were his."

"Lady, I gotta tell you: this is a *sale*. You know, where objects are exchanged for money?"

"Yes, of course, I do know that."

"Who do you suppose got them?" Homer asked rather lamely.

Madeleine said, "He was in a wheelchair. I can't believe they didn't belong to him. In fact, I thought he said they *were* his."

"That cripple happens to be my husband. If you're around here long enough, you'll learn not to put anything past him." Cecile looked at the scattered offerings of her yard sale as though seeing them for the first time. She said, "I'm breaking down. Take Jack and Judy to see the kittens. You can go with him, lady."

"Her name is Madeleine." Homer started to back toward the outside door, guiding Madeleine by the elbow, the rigidity of which let him know that she was getting angry. "Where are the kittens?"

"Judy, honey, please show Grandpa and his lady friend the kittens. *Now*, Judy, okay? Her name is *Madeleine*."

When Homer looked back from the house, he saw that Cecile's interrogation of the customers must have been somewhat accusatory: they were fleeing.

Once in the house, he clapped his hands together and rubbed them briskly, as though he had a pleasant surprise in store. Judy's evaluating squint indicated his failure to convince. "Who would like to show me the kittens?" No answer. "Where are the kittens?" Let's try not making it a question. "I've been wondering how many kittens there are."

"There are two," said Judy, with authority.

"But I suppose Mrs. Hall and I can't see them. That's the feeling I'm getting from you, Judy."

After a moment. "You can see them. Follow me."

Towering behind Judy and Jack across the living room, in the unaltered light, past the gut-wrenching china cabinet, through the kitchen, into the pantry, and out to the garage, Homer tried to emanate modest obedience for fear Judy would change her mind, but she strode along, an algebra teacher of the future, until they reached a storage closet, where she pointed to a latch she couldn't reach. Madeleine, who seemed to have lost all confidence, trailed behind, utterly lost. Jack tried to crowd in front of Judy but she moved him aside so that Homer could open the door. When he did, he felt around the inside wall for a light switch until Judy told him, "Reach up and pull the string." He did as he was told and the resulting low wattage barely illuminated a room filled with discarded household goods: rugs, bath mats, cleaning rags, and worn-out towels. These formed a kind of rough nest next to which Judy sat, holding Jack's hand to keep track of him. She looked up at Homer and said, "They're in there." Then she looked over at Madeleine and said, "You're allowed to look."

Homer had to get on all fours to make an adequate inspection, and when he peered around he quickly found a gray kitten with vivid black stripes and black ears. He cupped his hand over it and felt the little motor start as it lifted its head against his palm. "Here's one," said Homer, and Judy was at his side at once. He smiled up at Madeleine, hoping to draw her in, but her face projected only some indeterminate fear. His knees hurt and he was concerned that in getting back up he would stagger.

"Where's the orange one?" Judy demanded.

"What orange one?"

Homer lifted the gray kitten to make way for Judy's inspection and felt the needle claws pricking his palm. Judy crawled around, lifting wads of fabric and old towels, which cast shadows up the wall, all the way to the back of the closet, where she stopped suddenly. "Here he is!" she cried. "He's dead!"

Judy was seated with her back to him for a long time, long enough for him to see her shuddering with silent weeping. He crawled over and pulled her into his arms, at which point the sobs became audible, and Jack, without any idea of why he was upset, joined in to make it deafening. Homer drew Jack to his side, and soon the quiet was broken only by Judy's snuffling. Homer felt mucus run onto the hand that gripped her tight, and he looked up at Madeleine with an expression of helplessness. When Judy began to calm down, he spoke very quietly about how the kitten was in heaven and how we all hope to go there someday; thinking to close his argument, he said, "Kittens are like all creatures, including us, Judy. They don't live forever, and neither do we."

The effect of this was to amplify Judy's anguish. "I know that," she said, indignant in her grief, "but I thought we all went at the same time!" Strangely, Madeleine nodded in agreement.

Homer could think of nothing to say. He would have had to care about the kitten to have been inspired to the right remark; Judy seemed to see through his dissembling. Besides, nothing was up to Judy's profound statement, which hung in the air. "I wish we did," he said, "it would be so much better. I don't know why we don't all go at the same time but we don't, and we have to accept that." That's that, he thought, take it or leave it. Besides, something troubled him about Madeleine's nod of agreement.

To make things worse, Madeleine's eyes began to fill, and Homer wondered if it was over that brute Harry Hall and his size-thirteen oxblood saddle shoes, ungainly even in death.

Homer could almost hear his booming voice: *Come on in, Homer. You like gin? I've cornered the market!*

Judy no longer cried, but she was very somber and far away. "Someone is responsible," she said.

"God!" barked Homer with exasperation. "God is responsible!" This yard sale was about to kill him. "Madeleine, is there anything I can do to make you feel better?" he inquired coolly. She was touching each of the children unobtrusively. She didn't know how to comfort them. He didn't know how to comfort her.

"Let's go to the living room. Maybe we can think better there." The children followed Homer, who, aware of his waning desperation to make anyone happy, followed Madeleine. In the living room, he looked around briskly, as though trying to choose among several marvelous possibilities. "Here, come sit here," he said, and indicated the bench in front of the old player piano. Judy's grief kept her from seeing through his various efforts to entertain her. They obeyed with dull bafflement as he loaded a roll of music and started pumping the pedals. "Pretend you're playing!" he called out, over the strains of "Ida Sweet as Apple Cider." Looking at each other, the children put their hands on the keys, which snapped up and down all around their fingers as Judy took over the pumping and Jack howled like a dog; soon they were caught up in it.

Inexplicably, Madeleine began doing a graceful if somehow cynical foxtrot with an invisible partner. Homer stared at her, arms hanging at his sides. The noise was unbelievable. Into the space between Madeleine's arms, Homer placed Harry Hall and his big belly.

Homer darted out the front door to the yard sale, where Cecile was persuading a pregnant teenager that the light-dark setting on the toaster still worked. Four or five others grazed among the offerings, concealing any interest they might have had, though a middle-aged man in baggy khakis and an Atlanta Braves hat was bent in absorption over a duck decoy lamp that had never been completed. "Dark Town Strutters' Ball" poured from the house, stopped abruptly, then resumed with "I Want a Girl Just Like the Girl Who Married Dear Old Dad." Homer could hear Madeleine joining in with a sharp, angry contralto. When the teenager replaced the toaster on the card table and wandered off, Homer said, "One of the kittens died."

Staring at the unsold toaster, Cecile said, "You're shitting me. When it rains, it pours. *My God,* what's with the piano?" Holding a cigarette in the center of her teeth she blew smoke out of either side of her mouth.

"Go in and comfort Judy. I'll try to sell something till you get back."

"No reasonable offer refused." At this two or three browsers cocked their heads, which Cecile noted. "Just kidding, of course." She went inside and Homer surveyed the prospects, holding his lapels like an expectant haberdasher. No one met his eye and, instead of rubbing his hands together, he plunged them into his pockets and considered the weather: low clouds, no wind. The player piano stopped abruptly and the shoppers all looked up with the silence.

Homer went over to the man still examining the duck decoy lamp. "Why don't you buy it? It's beautifully made. It works. I can't imagine any home that wouldn't be improved by it."

"I'm just trying to picture the sort of people who wanted this in the first place," said the man. "This doesn't look like a duck, it looks like a groundhog. I hate it. I really hate it."

"The people who wanted it in the first place are my daughter and her husband," said Homer.

"My condolences," said the man, before he turned to go.

Homer stared hard and said, "Go fuck yourself." He could hardly believe he'd said it. It was like a breath of spring, such vituperation.

"Get in line, Pops."

Cecile returned and muttered, "Bugs Bunny on low. Usually holds them. Your friend is resting on the couch with a washcloth on her head. She looks like she's on her last legs." A very thin older man in a navy-blue jogging suit with a reflective stripe down the pant legs was interested in the NordicTrack. He had an upright potbelly, bags under his eyes, and a cigarette in his mouth that made him turn his head to one side to examine the distance meter on the machine. Homer watched Cecile approach within a foot of the prospect, but the man went about his examination without acknowledging her. He knelt to examine the bottom of the machine, then sat back on his haunches, removed the cigarette, and bethought himself. When he finally stood, he said something very brief to Cecile. She seized her head in both hands while he puffed and looked the other way. When she came back to Homer with some bills in her hand, she said, "I got creamed but it's gone." The new owner was trying out his new machine, the cigarette back in his mouth. A gust of wind showered Homer and his daughter with cottonwood leaves. Wild geese creaked above. Soon there'd be ice on the river.

"You seem to have gotten over the bottle collection," said Homer. He saw the American flag go up a pole across the street, a hedge concealing whoever raised it.

"Guess again."

"Why don't you go and ask Dean to give them back?"

"That's what he's trying to accomplish. The whole issue has been over him having anything I need."

"Does he?"

"Yeah, the bottles." She stared hard at him. "I know exactly what you're thinking, exactly. You're thinking, How can anyone lose themselves in such trivia?"

"Nope."

"Well, I'm not going to dignify this by fighting over it. But don't you ever look down your nose at me. Just because things haven't exactly worked out doesn't make us white trash."

"It's beyond me why you'd have such a hateful thought. Your mother would have felt the same way, if you had ever deigned to share your thoughts with her."

Homer had already decided that he would retrieve the bottles. By that time the sale would be over and the awful things would be part of the desolation of the living room again. When he asked his daughter why none of the other customers had mentioned the theft, she said, "The only one he had to fool was your friend, and I guess that wasn't too hard."

Homer just let it go. It was hopeless.

He went inside to check on Madeleine. Without removing her hand from over her eyes, she said, "I feel terrible for losing those horrible bottles," and when he tried to speak, she waved him away. He went back outside and watched the tire kickers and the idly curious begin to drift away, leaving four who looked like real buyers. Out of the blue, he wanted to make a sale. Homer thought they were couples but, after considerable study, could not match them up. He became fixed on this task as a difficult crossword puzzle, but finally he sighed and gave up. He was wary of misreading anyone as he had the duck-lamp guy. He couldn't believe the two redheads were together, because he'd never seen that before; which left the two short ones, and that pair seemed less unlikely. Their gazes crisscrossed like light beams, giving nothing away. Homer wondered whether they were like our ancestors, wary and footloose. The red-haired male took sudden notice of the American flag ripping away in the wind across the street, and Homer realized he was avoiding eye contact. No sale.

He returned to the house, where he found the children sitting on either side of Madeleine. "We're discussing their Halloween costumes," she said, her warmth restored. "Judy is going as a punk rocker and Jack is going as a traffic cone."

Homer said, "Let's get out of here."

Cecile was still outside, cleaning up after the sale, tossing everything toward the garage. Madeleine and Homer paused on the sidewalk for a moment. It seemed not unreasonable that Cecile might say a word or two to them, but she didn't. Homer wondered whether his daughter had developed this awful carapace on account of being raised by a helpless mother. Once inside his car, he said, "Can I take you to dinner?"

"We're going to get those bottles," said Madeleine.

"Oh, you don't want to go there. That's a real can of worms."

"Bring it on."

Imagining for a euphoric moment that Cecile's ex-husband would see the light quickly, Homer reluctantly agreed to go to Dean's house. Wait till she gets a load of this! was his uncharitable thought. It was getting dark as he started the car.

"I'll buy the bottles," Madeleine cried.

"That won't solve it."

She said, "I thought I'd seen everything."

He stepped up onto Dean's porch and rang the bell, nearly embedded in careless layers of house paint. He had a reassuring hand on Madeleine's back. There was some sort of somber music coming from within. The door began to open. He wanted to help but knew that Dean liked doing this sort of thing himself. The door opened wide, revealing the interior of what was little more than a cottage, single story by necessity, with the kitchen and living room adjacent to the front door. Then Dean rolled around into view. He had a smile on his big soft face, and the weight of his head seemed to be sinking into the expanding circles of his neck. One hand poised birdlike over the controls of his wheelchair. None of the waywardness was gone from his sky blue eyes. On the television screen, an aircraft carrier was sinking with slow majesty. Homer was relieved to find that the dirge he'd heard at the door was not just something Dean was listening to.

Homer introduced Madeleine and Dean greeted her warmly, and they followed him into the house.

"That's a new wheelchair," commented Homer as he made his way past Dean. There was very little furniture but the gas fire log made a twinkling, habitable light, concealing the bareness of the room. "Brand-new," said Dean. "Haven't even knocked the paint off it." There were some trophies on an old library table and milk crates filled with paperbacks, a cheesecake calendar on the far door, which led to the bathroom. The young model, naked on a white fur rug, was holding an automobile muffler.

"Front-wheel drive. Watch this." Dean pivoted around the back side of the door and, with a graceful thrust of the chair's motor, swung the door to and latched it. "Onboard battery charger," he said, leading Homer into the living room. "Actually got to pick the color. That last chair wasn't nearly enough for quads, more for limited-leg-use folks."

Madeleine said, "I'll bet you can go anywhere you want." She seemed to like Dean. Maybe it was just for leaving Cecile. Homer was glad to see it. He knew Madeleine had had about all she could stand.

"Hell, I'm on the town again."

He wheeled over in front of the television, on which the funeral of Princess Diana played: it was an anniversary on an odd year. "Madeleine, check this out: here she is again!" Homer didn't know where this was headed but he was encouraged by the friendliness with which Dean addressed Madeleine.

There were slow panning shots of Diana's cortege interspersed with scenes from happier times, including those with paramour Dodi Fayed at the beach; then the mayhem with the paparazzi and the fatal limousine chase with the drugged chauffeur ending in underground calamity.

Moving to the side, Homer determined that the shaking he

saw in Dean's body was caused not by grief but by laughter. Madeleine noticed and said sharply, "She died young!"

Dean said, "It's a start."

"*What?*"

Dean turned it off with his channel changer, and as the picture sank to a blue dot he said to Madeleine, "None of that would have happened if she'd been fat."

Two years earlier, Dean had attended an after-game Cats-Griz party at the Nez Perce Inn, a dependably rowdy annual uproar, and fallen from a second-floor balcony into the parking lot with a freshly opened beer in his hand. He woke up the next morning, hungover and paralyzed. He had been out of work, but now he was running for mayor.

The commemorative bottles were lined up on the floor next to the north wall, receiving the last light of the day. Dean said, "There they are."

"Let me take them back to Cecile," Madeleine said reasonably.

"Over my dead body." His lips were drawn flat across his teeth. He was quite menacing.

"Ohhkay."

Homer could see that Madeleine was not happy. She would bolt at the first opportunity. All the mean people, all the open space, seemed to be closing in upon him at once.

"I don't like disappointing you, Madeleine. Or Homer neither. But those bottles are mine."

"No doubt they are, but I'm the one who let you take them, and now it seems I'm in trouble. You ought not to have done that to a lady. Besides which, you have two beautiful children and you continue to poison your relationship with them over your bottle collection. I'm an out-of-towner and I don't get it. Cecile has quite a job with those children. She could probably use some help as opposed to battling over a collection of whiskey bottles."

Homer was impressed at the practical way Madeleine swallowed what must have been her distaste for Cecile.

"I'm lucky she isn't feeding them sardines with the mother-seagull glove to make them think they can fly. Do tears embarrass you, Madeleine?"

"Not at all."

"Homer's seen all this before. I blubber, and he just goes with it." He swept his hand down his face, but it continued to glisten. "The bottles don't belong to Cecile. I bought those bottles full and I emptied them in my own home. They're a monument to better days. So, here's what you tell Cecile: no dice. Also, where's the phone decanter?"

"Yakima," Homer said, rather pleased he could supply this fact.

"I emptied that phone last New Year's Eve. Cecile was up-stairs watching the ball come down on Times Square. When she showed up, do you think she wished me happy New Year? No. She said, 'Shit-faced in a wheelchair is a look whose time will never come.'"

Madeleine gazed at Dean for a long moment, with wonder or compassion Homer couldn't say, though he struggled to understand. He seemed to expect that she would say something wise, should she finally speak, but all she said was, "I give up. Perhaps the bottles are happier with you."

━ ━ ━ ━ ━ ━ ━ ━ ━ ━

Madeleine couldn't make it all the way that night, but Salt Lake City was a hub and gave her several options for the morning, and there were shuttles to the hotels near the airport. She assured Homer that she had loved visiting the West and learning first-hand that it was, as all had promised, breathtaking. And just think: once in Salt Lake, you could go direct or change in Memphis, Atlanta, Minneapolis, Chicago, Detroit, Cincinnati—all those cities!—and still get home. Homer seemed downcast at these prospects, but she assured him it had been a treat catching up.

The Refugee

Errol Healy was going sailing to evade custody in one of the several institutions recommended for his care. He believed the modest voyage from his berth in Cortez across the Gulf of Mexico to Key West was something he could handle. All therapeutic routes in which he was described as having a labile affect and deficient insight had proved ineffective, and friends and professionals alike felt the trip might help him reconstruct events in a way positive to his well-being. In particular, his boss at the orange groves urged him to pull himself together or else, and he realized with a panic that losing his job would, under current circumstances, not be endurable. In contrast to the skepticism he directed at mental health professionals, he ascribed almost supernatural powers of healing to an old woman in Key West, Florence Ewing, whom he'd not seen for so many years that it was questionable whether she still lived in Key West or lived at all. In many of his plans these days, he was reduced to superstition, and the mestizos he managed in the groves, who had won his friendship and peculiar loyalty, were superstitious about all things, hanging their charms everywhere, from their old cars to the branches of orange trees. Errol, quite sensibly, thought it was absurd to describe someone who was drunk all the time as having "a labile affect and deficient insight." Better to note that a do-or-die crisis seemed at hand and something had to be tried if body and spirit were to be kept together. His body was fine.

Years ago, he'd had a sailing accident. As a result, his closest friend, Raymond, was lost at sea, and the meaning of Raymond's death, nagging and irresolute, continued to consume him. The customary remedies were unavailing, and he intended to resort to this soothsayer of his past. His employer, the owner of numerous large orange groves, had agreed to this final shot: after that, he was on his own. This ultimatum was not offered lightly: Errol, a fluent speaker of Spanish, had a loyal crew who would disperse in the event of his firing. The employer, a patrician cracker who also owned a large juice plant in Arcadia, Florida, said something that really caught Errol and made him see his plight more clearly. "I just can't have someone like this. Not around here."

It was evening before Errol boarded *Czarina*, unfurling her jib to gain enough headway to sail the few yards to her mooring. Not far away, a big ketch with the steering vane and ratlines of a long-range cruiser tugged politely at her rode. Otherwise the tideway, lit by stars, was empty. He went below to the galley, turned on a lamp, and made a drink, then carried it to the cockpit, where he sipped and watched the clouds make their way in a moon-brightened sky. He brought the bottle with him and refreshed his iceless drink from time to time, feeling the deep motion of the boat as the incoming tide lifted her against the weight of her keel.

Errol awoke as the sun crossed the side of the cockpit. As usual, he was sick and disgusted but with the rare luxury of not being guilty over something he'd done the night before. He declined to throw the empty bottle overboard and sentenced himself to live with it a few hours more. He had wisely provisioned the galley already—wisely because he hardly had the strength for a shopping trip now—but was in no mood for food. He remained stretched out, waiting for his mind to clear.

Errol made his way around the yawl, raising the mizzen first so that she swung on the mooring facing upwind. Raising the main seemed to take all his strength, the hard stretched halyard in his aching hands, but the sail went up and the halyard somehow found its way to a cleat and *Czarina* trembled under the steady luffing of the mainsail. Errol went forward and cast off the mooring, and *Czarina* began to drift backward toward the dock. Errol released the mizzen sheet and drew in the mainsail; *Czarina* bore off into the tideway. He trimmed the mizzen and the yawl sank down onto her lines and beat across the harbor, tacking here and there to avoid anchored boats. Errol was glad she had no engine: an oily bilge would have been disastrous in his current state.

He sailed south in shallow water past islands covered with winter homes and islands which had been declared wildlife refuges. There was occasional traffic on the Intracoastal Waterway and to the east, towering from the mangroves, a baseball stadium. Cumbersome brown pelicans sailed on air currents, suddenly becoming arrows as they dove into schools of fish. *Czarina* was moving well, rail down and tracking her course insistently. A northwest wind was building, and Errol planned to evaluate the seas once he reached the pass. He would venture out into the Gulf and make a decision. The leeward side of the foredeck had begun to darken with spray as the wind increased, and he could hear the telltales on the leech fluttering. Exultation at the little ship's movement cheered Errol at last, and he went below to examine his larder. He cut up an apple into a bowl of dry cereal, then poured Eagle Brand condensed milk over it. *Czarina* had sailed herself contentedly in his absence, and he sat down to eat with an inkling of happiness.

The tide was falling through the pass, building up steep seas. A big new-moon tide, it sucked channel markers under and left streaming wakes behind them. Errol was anxious to begin his voyage and, nearly certain he would be turned back, he beat out toward the Gulf of Mexico and the dark sky to the west.

Because of the running tide, the faces of the waves were steep and the little yawl seemed to be ascending skyward before reaching their crests. The long slopes at the backs of the waves were almost pleasant as she ran down them, the centerboard humming in its trunk and a fine vibration coming through the tiller. But by the time he passed Johnson Shoals and began to contemplate a long trip in these conditions as opposed to the immediate sporting challenge, he grew apprehensive. There was green water on the deck racing toward the scuppers, the bottoms of the sail were dark and soaked, and he was getting shaky again. This development was something he meant to observe from afar.

He came about and headed downwind toward Cayo Costa, avoiding whatever temptation he might have had to press on in this small boat, and in the face of obvious peril that would have been the real loss of nerve. Better to shake himself miserable in a safe anchorage than abandon himself to the fatal and picturesque.

Pelican Bay was a protected anchorage in the middle of a state park, and its oceanic zephyrs were personalized with the smells of hot dogs and hamburgers from the many boats anchored there. Errol was ill equipped to cope with this banality, and he looked beyond the mouth of the bay to the increasingly raging seas of the Gulf with melancholy and regret. By tomorrow, the winds should have diminished and clocked around to the northeast, which would make the hundred-mile open-sea crossing to Key West one long reach. Meanwhile, the high-spirited shrieks of children made him furious. That the powerboats looked like huge tennis shoes only added to his general dissatisfaction with the world. Nevertheless, his belief that all his problems would go away once he reached Key West brought him a kind of grim cheer; recently and in an hour of unsurpassed bleakness, when the landscape of his failures seemed almost to afford death a dismal glamour, he'd had a kind of satori in which he'd either remembered or imagined an old woman of infinite wisdom who could see him on to a better place. In years past she'd done this for him and for several dissolute friends, among whom he remained the sole member whose life seemed to be slipping through his

own fingers. The occasion of his vision was less than august: trying to please a new lady friend, he'd lost a toe while mowing her
lawn at midnight, and the pain as he sat in a crowded emergency
room, a bath towel around his foot, a tall to-go cup in his lap,
seemed to summon forth a vision of a livable future spelled out
by the old lady in Key West. He had to get there and he would,
once the wind was in the northeast.

About fifty yards away, a man stood in the stern of a dilapidated launch, hands on his hips, playing Beethoven's Fifth Sym-
phony from a boom box at high volume. He seemed to be
challenging anyone who might wish to interrupt his attempt to
educate waterborne vacationers. Errol was having difficulty ignoring this. Presently, a cigarette boat filled with young people
pulled anchor and relocated near the loner in the old launch.
They played rap music on their much more powerful sound system while mimicking the crablike moves of hip-hop. Errol ran-
sacked his boat for booze and miraculously found a six-pack
of warm beer made with water from the Rocky Mountains
wrapped in a bundle of canvas in his sail-repair supplies. He tin-
gled with the excitement of discovery as he remembered hiding
it from a woman who'd come aboard one morning, an attractive
woman who'd gone nuts, shouting invitations to a coast guard
station in her underwear. Errol permitted himself to sample the
beer. Feeling better, he mused over the old fellow's persistence in
playing Beethoven; and with the second can, he began to enjoy
the undulations of the half-clothed youths in the cigarette boat.
The arrival of a private helicopter overhead, ruffling the entire
surface of the harbor and tossing the smaller craft merrily, made
him bless whatever gods had dropped off the six-pack. He re-
treated to the cabin and assumed the cooler view that would become necessary if the hilarity continued to spread over Pelican
Bay. His simple ambition—to avoid insanity—seemed in danger
of deteriorating into misleading annoyance. Still, he was smart

enough to know that the curtain would fall again. It was only a matter of time.

After a short and troubled nap, Errol rigged a hand line and small jig that he dangled from the side for only a short time before bringing a snapper aboard. He held it in front of him, its fins braced, bright eyes seemingly fixed upon his. He rapped it over the head with his cleaning knife, and as it stiffened, shivered, and died in his hand, tears filled his eyes. He cleaned it, placed the two fillets in a skillet on the single-burner alcohol stove, and, after examining the fleshless frame of the fish and thinking it looked like a good plan for a snapper, he threw it overboard. A seagull flew straight from the Beethoven boat, where it had been working the owner for snacks, and carried off the remains. The cigarette boat was now motoring slowly among the other anchored boats, treating them to the latest urban sounds. The helicopter was gone. "Why do we 'clean' fish?" Errol said aloud. "They are not dirty." He chuckled as though he'd made this remark for genteel company, then grimly contemplated pulling anchor and sailing for Key West. The wind had not come around sufficiently but surely it would; staying in this public anchorage any longer would only put off the help he needed to avoid calamity and, more important, polishing off the beer would make it unavailable for the voyage, when its service to morale in stormy conditions would be invaluable.

Therefore, he raised the sails, pulling the halyards until they squeaked in the jam cleats. They luffed loudly as the boat drew back on the anchor rode, the boom bouncing against the mainsheet traveler, the tiller swinging from side to side as though the boat were being steered by a ghost. The anchor came up covered with turtle grass, and Errol laid it on deck, cleaning the weeds and throwing them overboard before lashing the anchor into its chocks and returning to the cockpit. He sat down and pushed the tiller to one side. The boat drifted backward and swung, until the sail filled and she reversed direction. *Czarina* then moved swiftly, rail down, toward the entrance to the bay.

As he sailed out the pass, he felt the slight easterly shift of the still-powerful winds. The faces of the waves were still tall but less abrupt and the rudder never lost its bite as it had on his first crossing. The sky was gray, but it was higher and faintly light-shot to the west. He trimmed the sails until, at due south, there was no pressure on the helm and the yawl sailed herself. His only job would be to adjust the sheets to keep this heading as the wind clocked around to the east.

The coast soon disappeared and he found himself making good progress in the open water; the Gulf of Mexico, and the greater regularity of the seas, uninfluenced by tide and shore, made the little boat lope along with a purpose. Errol had a few sips of his beer, but he could already tell he was not going to drink too much. He occupied himself with housekeeping, making up the pipe berth below, folding his oilskins and stowing them in their locker, draining the icebox into a bucket and pouring the water overboard. He pulled the floorboards and sponged out the salt water that had come on deck and gotten through the deck ventilator, which now poured fresh air through the cabin, arousing the smells of cedar and old varnish. On the bulkhead a framed photograph had discolored over time, a picture of himself much younger, a man, and a woman, the same age. Underneath, it said *Pals*.

Back in the cockpit, he unspooled a hand line with a large silver spoon and single hook over the stern. It danced and dove a hundred feet behind the boat and seemed to raise Errol's spirits further. He wished he had some sort of flag to raise and then remembered that he did have just the thing. He dug around in the cockpit locker among dock lines, fenders, and life jackets until he found the flag of the Conch Republic, the imaginary nation of Key West from its days of hippie utopianism, an era Errol seemed to have trouble escaping. He raised it to the masthead on the flag halyard and liked seeing its pink and yellow conch and sunburst against an increasingly blue sky.

The compass indicated he was now heading for Yucatán and so further adjustment to the sails would be necessary. This was the result of the steady easterly shift of winds and clearing weather. The seas were ever less violent, and within an hour the skies had cleared entirely and the Gulf had regained its characteristic dusty green placidity under towering white clouds. It occurred to Errol that his drinking days were behind him. Oh, joy! Not another shit-faced, snockered, plastered, oiled, loaded, bombed, wasted minute ever again! No more guilt, remorse, rehab, or jail! Free at last!

Calming down, he remembered that his hope lay in his visit to Florence Ewing, the good witch. She had seen right through him in days past and found something redeeming. She would again. He could have taken the bus and gotten there straightaway, but he had arrived by sea the last time she'd put him right, and though it was decades ago he was sure she could do it again. He knew better than to alter any of the details. His mestizos, trustworthy and industrious, would keep the cracker's groves in order until he returned.

A frigate bird followed him at a great altitude, a perfect flier that barely needed to move its wings, an elegant black zigzag watching his wake for bait fish. He daydreamed about what it would be like to be a bird like that, a seabird with that great altitude and horizon. No big thoughts, of course, just "Where's the fish?" Like being a fine athlete, everything vision and muscle memory, Ted Williams watching the ball compress on the bat, no attitude, a simple there-it-is. Roar of the crowd same as wind or traffic, just worthless noise. If I were a bird, that six-pack wouldn't glow like radium, a screeching come-hither.

The yawl was making wonderful progress. With the slowly

clocking wind and more moderate seas, she sped along on a controlled reach that might scarcely need adjustment before Key
West. The coast soon disappeared beneath the eastern horizon,
and for a pleasant half hour a pair of young dolphins surfed in
the quarter wave before peeling off for more interesting games.
Huge schools of bait, shadows in the pale Gulf green, erupted
like hail falling on the water as predators coursed through and
terns dove at them from above. The leeward deck was dark with
spray all the way to the transom.

In late afternoon, he sailed through a congregation of
Louisiana shrimp boats, nets draped from trawling booms as they
awaited nightfall. And at dusk a big ketch rail-down passed a
couple miles to the north of him, heading for Yucatán. Errol
lashed the tiller and went below to warm some soup over the
blue alcohol flame. He ate it slowly, sitting on the companionway
step and looking at the clouds swaying back and forth above the
cockpit, their undersides pink at the approach of sundown. As he
gazed south, he wished he could do this forever. Maybe once he'd
been saved, it would be possible. At least he could go to the islands for a spell, which islands it was hard to say. What difference
did it make? he thought irritably, as though being cross-examined
about the islands. For a moment, he fretted about islands all running together and being required to distinguish between them.
Now his ears were ringing.

Then it was dark, a comfortable dark with stars coming up
in tiers, and a quarter moon hung outlined in haze. The tiller
throbbed gently in Errol's hand and the lubber line on the compass rested quietly on his course of 180 degrees. It seemed that
since his boat went in the water all things were sweeping him
gently toward this destination. The hours slipped by until the
loom of Key West lit the southwestern sky in a pale glow, calling
for a "cocktail," a cause for celebration even Errol found suspicious. He might have felt misgivings.

Sails had to be trimmed again as he beat his way past the sea buoy and up the ship channel toward the bright skyline of the city. He didn't feel he had time to go all the way around Tank Island to get to Garrison Bight. Instead, he sailed on until he broke out into the Atlantic, and then broad-reached up Smathers Beach before turning in toward the desalinization plant and a dismaying number of bright lights and even automobile traffic. Dropping the mainsail, he lashed it to the boom, and crept up the channel under the jib and mizzen between small anchored boats backlit on black water. Spotting an empty slip, he dropped the jib and mizzen and glided very slowly to the dock. As he stepped ashore to secure the yawl, he suddenly felt frightened, but the feeling passed. He was briefly without momentum, a situation efficiently solved by one of the beers. Furthermore, last call was still hours away.

He kept inhaling deeply, surprised after his long absence at the familiarity of Key West night air, the particular humidity, the scent of more flowers than occur in nature, salt water, and faint indications of humanity: tobacco, perfume, automotive exhaust. It was a perennial aroma occasionally subsumed by a single smell, new house paint or Sunday-morning vomit. All in all, it made his heart ache.

Key West seemed a most appealing landfall. Old-timers used to tell him that before the aqueduct and plentiful fresh water, the place was a kind of gooney-bird island, not much greenery and plenty of exposed cap rock and coral. Now it was as lush as Hawaii, an easier sell.

The bartender had a deeply fissured, weathered face, a gold chain around his neck, de rigueur before Key West went literary; also, solidarity with the Cubans. He returned with Errol's drink.

"I quit drinking over eleven thousand days ago," said the bartender, whose name was something to do with *dog:* Coon Dog, Hound Dog, Blue Dog—Errol forgot. "And it was no mistake."

Dog-something seemed to be studying Errol, probably re-membered Errol no better than Errol remembered *him*. Errol clearly recalled that the bartender drove in one day from Boston about a quarter-century ago with a blue-eyed dancer he was very proud of and who wasted no time in absconding with one of the entrepreneurial hippies, a corrupt prep-school boy from Colum-bia, South Carolina, who was restoring a conch house.

"What about that Caroline? You still see her?"

"That was quite long-lasting, wasn't it? No, I haven't seen her in ages." Caroline was from New Orleans, a beautiful girl with thick auburn hair who reminded everyone of Gene Tierney. She had a genuine New Orleans Brooklyn-Southern accent. She was languorous and virginal, with a promise of depravity so instinc-tive in New Orleans girls that it must have been devised by their ancestral mothers. Some logged feverish turns in town before going home, marrying Tulane doctors, and raising little magnolia aristocrats to replenish the Garden District. But Caroline was dif-ferent from all the others; she and Errol had been engaged to be married. He hadn't cared about anything else at all. He stood be-side his stool and said, "Well, I suppose."

"Nice seeing you."

"Same."

"You remember West Coast Anita?"

"I remember Anita."

"There were two Anitas, Anita and West Coast Anita."

Errol was anxious to go. Looking toward the door, he asked, "Which one had the flag in her tooth?"

"West Coast Anita."

"What about her?"

"Anita stayed too long at the fair. She had an out-of-body ex-perience in the Turks and Caicos, and they had to take her down on the beach and shoot her."

Errol said, "I must be missing something." He counted out his tab on the bar. "Well," he said, "I'm off to see Florence Ewing."

He didn't know why he was not cordial to Dog-something, one of those citizens you can't quite remember, though he tells you that you and he go way back. Perhaps it was the sense that one was about to be drawn into something or discover that one had failed to recall a debt. A group strode in, three women and a man with low gray bangs who cried out, "But wait: right after the car crash, we come in with the Japanese flutes!" The women were awestruck as he swept his arm toward the table he had selected for them. One, forefinger to a dimple, hung back, contemplating the flutes in her imagination.

Night Dog! That was it!

From here he could see shrimp boats between the buildings on Lower Caroline Street. He and Raymond had backed the old ketch in here one winter to pull out the Vere diesel that had turned into a half ton of English rust in the bilge. They'd built a gallows frame of old joists they got when the Red Doors Saloon was remodeled, and all the wallets fell out of the walls from a century of muggings. They lifted the great iron lump on a chain fall and swung the dead engine to the fish docks. Thenceforth, they sailed her without the engine. She went that way into Havana, but Raymond was not aboard.

Florence Ewing lived on Petronia Street, a street frequently in the *Key West Citizen* for scenes of mayhem; but this was the more sedate upper Petronia, now part of a district renamed by realtors the Meadows, a tremendous leap of the imagination. Florence was born in the house over eighty years ago and, though Errol hadn't seen her in some time, his every hope was pinned on her being still alive.

She had gone to sea with her father, a turtle captain, when she was eleven and could still describe the Moskito Coast of

Nicaragua in detail. By sixteen, she was a chorus girl in New York; she married at seventeen back home and stayed married for over sixty years to her physician husband. A precondition was that they never leave the Petronia house. Dr. Ewing, an Alabaman and a sportsman, struggled with this, turning the old carriage house into a kind of dominoes hall for his cronies, building a stilt shack past Mule and Archer keys where he fished and played cards on weekends in his old Abaco launch. He delivered thousands of Key West babies, who stayed until the tourist boom pushed them up A1A to the mainland; some were even his own, begotten on lissome Cuban teens. When Raymond Fitzpatrick and Errol Healy went into partnership, they lived around the corner from Florence; and during some of the fraught hours of their business life, Errol found himself being quietly counseled by the very sensible and spiritual Florence Ewing. You could say they became close, cooking meals for each other or watching Johnny Carson. And it was not a matter of an old widow needing company. *Errol* needed the company; Florence was wholly self-sufficient. Errol was cautious about imposing on her, though he supposed he must at times have tested her patience. He never went there high, more consideration than anyone else got, and he tried to keep the more outrageous ladies from battening onto her and declaring her a role model. He didn't know how she created such peace. Others noticed and sought her out; they believed she had the power to sanctify and heal those who had lost hope. He marveled that she didn't run them all off, or even judge them, or, just once, tell them she was *too tired*. They were her subjects. For some she was an oracle; for a few a last chance. She had learned forgiveness and discovered its mighty power.

He made the trek from the bar in the fragrant early evening, taking enough time to gaze upon the Laundromat still lifes, those all-night getaways where girls of yore rode the tumblers and fornicated on the washing machines. Notions and grocery stores still open were nevertheless somnolent. Here and there among the renovated houses miraculously a few remained tumbledown as before, with gutted refrigerator kingfish smokers in the backyard. Many of the houses were tall and attracted the eye, making you look upward, at a sky that let you know that you were surrounded by the sea. Elsewhere, rainwater cisterns had been converted into atmospheric soaking tubs, leaves and rotting fruit were made to disappear, and services created to secure the things bound to fail when the city was astonished by some intrusion of nature, such as a storm. Life sometimes tested absentee owners. When, after a half year, remembering the fresh air and clean linens, the truce with vegetation, the ringless tubs and toilets, the owners returned to find fetor and mildew, the inconvenienced rats and fleeing roaches and bellicose fighting chickens who had moved into the lap pool, there was seldom anything so untoward as a demand for return of caretakers' fees. Slaves of their own vacations, the owners began by negotiating.

He cut through a lane behind the library on Fleming to gaze at a house where Caroline's friend Frances Mousseau had lived, working on a romantic play, a gnomish tale of Cajun high jinks set in the Atchafalaya Swamp. Errol thought Frances, a racist Creole from Plaquemines, too dull-witted for passionate folly; nevertheless, upon learning she'd been disinherited, she jumped off an ocean liner. Had a passenger watching the moonrise from a cheap cabin not seen Frances go by his porthole, her absence might never have been noticed. While characteristic notions of the day included a dreamy version of suicide, Frances was quickly forgotten.

Errol walked to Fleming, where he had lived with Caroline and Raymond, at least one Anita, and a few others, sharing the rent and parceling out all the small rooms. He remembered believing this lack of privacy was assurance that his love for Caroline would remain undisturbed. But Caroline could make men find original ways to hurt themselves, even his late, great best friend Raymond. Holding the iron railing, he looked up at the old house, which had become a bed-and-breakfast, Fronds, with a sign in front: NO CHILDREN. NO PETS. In that house, Errol felt all he had left behind.

There was still light in Petronia, brighter along Georgia, and indeed in the garden at Florence's house someone was toiling late, a middle-aged man in khaki pants and work shoes whom Errol did not recognize. The grounds were in ominously poor shape. Though infinitely polite, Florence had always gotten a lot of work out of her people, some of whom were of remarkably little account, reverting to their torpid ways as soon as they left her.

When Errol told the gardener that he had come to see Miss Ewing, the man stood back from him uneasily.

"She's in there." He made little secret of his inhospitability. But the gardener could not have known how much Errol had riding on this. "And who are you?"

"An old friend from Fleming Street."

He gave this some thought. "You want to go in, go in."

"Yes, of course." So he went up the steps, and on the gardener's peremptory "Don't knock; she can't get to the door," he let himself in. He felt shaky.

Except for the soaring lines of the old shipwright's staircase and the few glints of a high chandelier, he couldn't see much of anything. Just this was enough to make him feel quieter as his soul expanded safely into Florence Ewing's sanctum, the house that turtles built, furnished from wrecks, including a grand piano made of African mahogany, said to have killed a man as it came aboard. Here, nearly a century ago, Florence was delivered by a black midwife from Great Inagua who, she claimed, taught her to conjure, a tale the young people made her tell again and again. Compared to the conventional mummery with which they had arrived, conjury held great attraction. Florence owned dozens of lacquered boxes, little private containers of silver and enamel that could furnish coveted storage for secret things, and sometimes she made gifts of them. Secrets were everything in Errol's circle, and they all worked at suggesting they were full of them. It was not for everyone and especially not for Errol and Raymond, who made a handsome living transporting souls from Cuba, their earnings disbursed not by driving big cars or hiring interior decorators, but rather by throwing banquets.

Dividing the foyer from the living room was an old theater flat with a great big moon sparkling on an empty sea that created an obstruction to direct entry. Errol called out, "Florence," and got no reply. There was a blue spider with a body shaped like a pentagram lowering itself slowly on a single strand of silk; from afar came the sound of a ship signaling the harbor pilot. He stepped around the theater flat and wondered why he had waited so long. He felt weightless as he gazed, soaring and uncertain, at the ghostly figure of his redeemer.

The living room had become her bedroom and the chandelier that Errol had glimpsed from the other side was seen to hang over her bed, an old gas-burning model that had been converted to electric and was now a garland of mostly expired little bulbs. He remembered best her big ormolu bed, formerly on the second floor, a table beside it supporting a water pitcher, a vase of anemones, and several small bottles. Florence was propped against many pillows and covered by the palest blue counterpane. The room was fresh and the bedclothes looked buoyant and clean; someone must be looking after her. Errol wished he could have slipped in beside her, to begin pouring out his heart in crazy familiarity, to detach himself completely from his own story and watch it sail out into the air like a ribbon.

As he entered she gazed at him with eyes that were opalescent. He greeted her and told her who he was. She said nothing, and he drew up the only chair, one so straight-backed and uncomfortable that he wondered if she ever had visitors. Florence had grown so very old, with a diaphanous quality of something about to turn to powder. Yet she was as elegant as an ancient Spanish altarpiece. Errol almost wished some of the others were here, especially Raymond Fitzpatrick, of whom she was so fond. Or even Caroline, whom Florence disliked; here they could have all finally come clean. The last time Florence spoke to Caroline, she told her that she saw right through her, and Caroline gave her no chance to elaborate. Florence smiled until Caroline got up and left.

It didn't seem to matter that neither of them spoke. Errol was fascinated that he could slip back into Florence's house and feel that the fabric of consolation had never been torn. He decided then and there that he would just talk, just pour it out. He was far too desperate to do it conversationally, and she looked as though she might not have the strength. She could always ask him to stop, but it had been a long ride and he needed to talk.

"Florence," he said, "I've been gone a long time." He could see her eyes sharpen somewhat, and he wanted to get the mechanical tone out of his voice. "I moved up to Canada for a while." That reminded him: there used to be a number of French Canadians around town, Separatists in Speedos, who told the girls they'd planted the mailbox bombs in Montreal. It was a very effective line and kept the bulk of the Separatists out of inclement weather. "Now I'm in citrus. I'm responsible for four huge groves in Hendry County, frost-free high ground, the best. Caroline and I split up quite a while ago." He'd mistakenly thought this would induce a reply. "She's up in New Orleans, three beautiful kids. They all swim. Remember how crazy Caroline was about swimming? Jumping off the White Street pier? And remember Jackie L. Dalton? Used to play his songs for you on the guitar? He's a huge hit, just huge, got his own jet plane." He caught himself mimicking with his hand the jet plane flying through the sky. "Fills big stadiums," he added weakly.

For an instant his head was empty. Then he wanted to talk again.

"Those days seem so long ago. But that's nothing to you, is it? Not when you've seen Cay Sal from the deck of a schooner. Really, I think all of us were just pitiful, just homeless and pitiful. Didn't know anything. Worse came to worst, declare yourself a carpenter. There was that awful song, 'If I was a carpenter and you were a lady,' started all that mess. Then some people couldn't get out of it, and after they left here they couldn't ask *you*, so a lot of them took off more or less empty-handed. It wasn't your fault and I don't know what you got out of listening to all that, and here you are doing it again and I'm starting to feel better already. I'll be honest with you; I *had* to come here. In a way, it's my last chance. I said to myself, Miss Florence Ewing will not permit me to go on like this.

"I didn't really move to Canada, I just said that. I didn't move anywhere. I moved my body several times but nothing else moved. I was like that four-hundred-pound lady bouncer at the Anchor they called Tiny. We were there a thousand times and nobody ever saw Tiny move. I'm kind of like old Tiny, but in my case the body is the only thing that *did* move. Let me clear that up: I *went* to Canada, I went to Red Deer, Alberta, but it just didn't work out, and anyway Canada won't let me back in. It's not like I meant to mislead you about that.

"By the way, it's sure nice nobody smokes in here. I can smell all that longleaf pine just like the day your granddad nailed it up. When you used to get us to do a little work around here, we'd run into those gumbo-limbo joists and break our tools and you'd just laugh. I think me and Raymond pretty much covered that old turtle route in that black Nova Scotia ketch we had together, a real little ship. We probably saw as much of the tropics as anybody."

He looked off to one end of the room where the tall windows had darkened and a breeze lifted the long curtains. The four live bulbs in the chandelier were little help and Errol was at the point of thinking Florence had passed away.

"That last trip, coming across the stream in a northern gale, a big wave took Raymond right off the helm and away. I came up for my watch and there was no one at the wheel. Not a soul." He delivered a hearty laugh but there was a scream buried in it. "I realize there are plenty of people who said it didn't exactly happen that way, and I *hope* you believe me. But I got the boat home, got her tied up at the desalinization plant, and walked to Caroline's house. She wasn't there. She wasn't going to *be* there. Well, what do you know about that, Florence? I'll bet you imagined you were through with all that. I kind of wish you'd answer me or say something. I'll bet you figured we had used you about up. Surprise, surprise. You know what? Just goes to show you, Raymond is the legend we all knew he would be. I can tell you that I have failed to make—uh, to make an appropriate accommodation. I am a drunkard and I really felt I better get back down here for a little visit, see what you had to say about all this, help a person more or less sort of *stand* it."

Florence Ewing did not say a word. Errol could feel her opal eyes enter his soul. He knew that if he did not tell the truth she would not offer him absolution, and even then there was no certainty, no promise, no assurance that her powers would work or that he would ever be whole again. It had been half his life since he'd known what hope felt like. In Florence Ewing's face it seemed everything was accepted as morning accepted light. He was joyous that he'd had enough mother wit left to make the trip, to place himself in the way of this illumination.

"Florence, you don't have to talk."

He rose from his chair and sat at the corner of her bed and thought. Carter and Castro were going to show the world we could be friends and they declared a race from Key West to Cuba. Errol and Raymond entered the race with no hope of winning, and they agreed they wouldn't try to bring any souls back with them. The manifest showed just the two of them in both directions: Errol Healy and Raymond Fitzpatrick.

Errol couldn't tell if he was talking or just thinking. Florence's eyes took him in with even greater opalescence, and he wondered whether she was reading his mind. He thought he could hear himself speaking, maybe just part of this dream, a disquieting dream that suggested the possibility that he wasn't even here at all, that he would be awakened by an attendant of some sort, someone he would be unable to recognize. He never wanted to be in any form of custody.

All the boats knew a gale was predicted. Everyone leaving the ship channel at sundown thought they would reach the middle of the stream sometime after midnight. There was a crowd by the coast guard dock, all the sunset watchers and dogs and jugglers there to see them off, grand prix yachts and cruisers and local dope captains in anything they could lay hands on, from J24s to backyard trimarans. It had the feeling of a big parade, with Errol and Raymond's the only ship customarily dedicated to profiteering at the misfortune of refugees.

They were going to Cuba! The sun set behind them kind of cold, and for a few hours right into the darkness they were on a beam reach in fifteen to eighteen knots from the north, and the ketch had her rail right at the water, pulling a quarter wave higher than the transom. They had an overlapping jib that was almost too much for her, but this was perfect sailing for a heavy English ketch, and her rock-elm ribs creaked under her. They had a bottle of Courvoisier to sip, and Errol chattered about all the good things in their lives, all their tax-free money, and about Caroline and sailing forever and someday settling down with her, with their own crabbing pier for the kids, with a flounder light and maybe a picture album of the days when Raymond and Errol were young in a dangerous trade, when everyone they did business with had a gun.

At some point, Errol realized that Raymond hadn't said a word. He was a very direct man, an honest man. He never spoke for effect and Errol had long ago learned that something was coming when he was quiet like this. Well, something *was* coming. Raymond said that he had never intended to join this race. He came so he could talk to Errol man-to-man. And what he had to say was that when they got back to Key West, he and Caroline were moving to New Orleans. That by the time they got back she would already be gone.

"Raymond was at the helm and I was sitting in the foot well with my back to the companionway. I could see all the way to the last glow on the horizon, and Key West was under the western horizon except for the loom of its lights. I felt I should say something. I actually felt I should say something *out of our friendship.* But nothing would come. I kept trying to picture Caroline, and she would come to me all outlined; it's hard to explain. But I couldn't say *anything.* I guess I thought we should go back, but if I said we should go back, that would really make it . . . really make it official. So I never said, Let's go back, and we pushed on toward Cuba.

"At about two in the morning, the gale was rising and we put a double reef in the main, a real adventure because she had an old-fashioned boom that overhung the transom by ten feet, and getting the bunt tied in all the way to the leech was dangerous."

Again, the thought returned that he was not actually speaking and this was only a dream, but Florence's gaze seemed to indicate absorption and whether he was thinking or speaking seemed not to matter. In fact, this is how he remembered it was with Florence Ewing. It was what they'd all looked for: the trance she'd cast from her past mysteries.

"The wind really came up fast, and since it was blowing against the direction of the stream the seas were bad. At first we could see the spreader lights of the other yachts, and then we couldn't even see that and all around us it was just the black wave faces in our running lights. Without saying anything, I changed places with Raymond and took the wheel. He went below and stayed there for a long time as the seas built and the ketch began to groan under the strain and yaw worse and worse, especially as we came down the faces. Several times I could feel her try to broach, but I was able to head up and keep her on her feet. I later heard the seas had been over twenty feet. Boats were dismasted and *Black Magic*, a Great Lakes yacht, killed her helmsman in a standing jibe. One of the dope captains on a Stone Horse disappeared entirely, the only boat out there without a self-bailing cockpit. No one ever found the tin cans full of money he'd buried all over Key West, but his girlfriend went around in a haze, carrying her shovel and knocking on doors, trying to get in people's yards.

"Raymond came partway up the companionway and I could barely hear him over the storm. He said, 'The jib's got to come off before we lose control.' I knew it was true, but all this time I had been thinking, and I wasn't sure if I cared whether we controlled the boat or not. As it was, I had trouble. Even twenty-five tons of oak and lead seemed to lose traction in those seas.

"Typical Raymond, he went forward hand over hand toward the foredeck. I kept her on course until he eased the halyard and the jib started down. I turned her upwind and the jib collapsed,

Raymond on top of it lashing it with wild, violent exertions of his arms. I bore off, and as I did so we were lifted on a huge wave. We stayed atop it for a long moment, Raymond facedown on the foredeck, and then we started into the trough, which was just a long, bottomless hole. What had made me change direction? I felt the boat pick up speed as we went down and it had begun to yaw as the sea hissed out behind the keel. It seemed like it yawed harder and harder. The spokes on the wheel just tore at my hands, and either I lacked the strength or I—or I—it got away from me. The wheel got away from me . . . and we broached. The next wave buried us from starboard and the bow went under, beyond the forward hatch, then over the brow of the house. She stayed like that for a long time, and when she came up, the ocean was pouring off the crown of the foredeck. There was no one there.

"The Cuban came aboard in Havana and read the crew manifest. He said, Where's the *otro hombre*? I said I came by myself. He left and came back with another guy in a green uniform with a machine gun. He spoke English. I said there had been a language problem with the first guy. I told him the *otro hombre* washed overboard on the western edge of the stream where it changed color. He believed me. I don't think it's that unusual to Cubans to wash overboard."

The gardener came quietly into the room. Errol couldn't tear his gaze away from Florence, because he felt any second now she might speak. He was hoping she would. She pulled herself up and looked at him intently, all phosphorus gone as her eyes blackened and some beads rolled off the counterpane and tinkled to the floor. Errol could tell she was going to say something.

"Are you with the termite people?" she asked. Errol didn't reply and Florence repeated her question, this time with some agitation.

The gardener pushed past him and leaned over Florence so she would be sure to hear him. "They can't come without they tent the place," he said to her. "And they can't tent the place if you in it, 'cause they pump it full of poison." She let out a moan. The gardener spoke in a more conciliatory voice. "The exterminator been every week," he told her, as if he was singing her a song. She seemed crushed at the news.

"Is he the one with his car all fixed up like a rat?" asked Florence urgently. "Has big ears on it like a rat?"

<hr />

The old house on Fleming was the obvious choice, as long as they had a room with a tub available. He stopped first at Tres Hermanos for some supplies. The front door was wide open to the air, and a desk had been set up in the front hall. Here sat the clerk reading the newspaper, his treated blond hair swept forward from a single spot. Without looking up, he asked how he could help and Errol told him he wanted a room with a tub.

"No can do."

"No rooms?"

"Not with a tub."

"There's a tub in the last room on the second floor."

"That's a *suite*. You said you wanted a *room*."

"I'll take the suite."

"It's not the same *price* as a room."

"I understand."

The clerk looked up finally. He regarded the paper bag from the Cuban *tienda*. "Is that all you have to your name?"

"Yes."

"Usually, when we rent the suite, it's to someone with a *suitcase*."

"I'll bet that's right." The clerk had no idea what a problem lay before him.

Despite all the heavy, almost operatic furniture and tasseled drapery, the room was recognizable. He remembered its old bare wooden bones, the sparse secondhand furnishings of that time, the Toulouse-Lautrec poster and its rusty thumbtacks. The names were streaming at him. The gardener had told him he was wasting all that noise on Miss Ewing; he declared that Miss Florence Ewing had upped and cleared out during a previous administration and wouldn't know him from Adam.

The water made a deep sound in the old tub. Errol pulled a chair next to it and placed the bag where he could reach it. He filled the tub, calculating how deep it could be without the mass of his body overflowing it. The water looked so still, so clear, with light steam arising. He undressed and got in, sliding down until the water was as high as his throat. Errol remembered taking bread scraps to the birds in the small town where he grew up; and when he reached toward the chair next to the tub, he saw the birds again, how they rose in a cloud. He was alert enough to enjoy this slide into oblivion, to picture a million oranges rotting on trees as his mestizos dispersed into Florida barrios, and at first he confused the shouts he heard with those of his boss, the cracker, the juice king of Arcadia and citrus oligarch who made his life so wearisome. A cloud of blackbirds rose from the rotting oranges around a small man shouting in the grove. . . .

It was the desk clerk and two police officers, but the desk clerk alone, soaking wet, was doing all the shouting. "He ruined my beautiful hotel!"

One of the officers, a small portly Cuban, asked, "You call this a hotel?"

"Get him out of here! Pump his stomach, do something!"

To the skeptics in the emergency room, Errol said, "Must be some kind of bug."

Grisly days at Keys Memorial passed slowly. The nurses knew what he had done and several considered it a mortal sin, a view that produced grudging service and solitude beside otherwise busy corridors. At checkout, the accounting office having assumed indigence expressed surprise at his Blue Cross. He started to explain but all that came out was *citrus*. He was too numb to speak and wondered whether he had done himself permanent harm. Perhaps I am now feeble-minded, he thought. But really his heart was lighter for having survived the outcome of a long obsession.

He spent the rest of the morning buying provisions. The yawl was just as he had left it, but for a light coating of ash from the island's heroic burning dump. A fishing boat was being swabbed down by two Cubans in khakis and white T-shirts who from time to time tossed a fish from the scuppers to a pelican waiting modestly on the transom. The tide had dropped, leaving a wide band of barnacles around the pilings, and Errol moved his spring lines until the boat stood away from them. Provisions were stowed in the galley; the water he had acquired on the mainland was still in good supply. He washed the deck down with seawater, sweeping the ash over the stern, and checked his watch. The bars had just opened. He stepped off the boat and headed uptown, stopping at a phone booth to call his employer, the owner of the groves and juice plant. He told him he'd gotten a much-needed rest and would be back among the oranges in no time flat. He'd left the Latino crew detailed instructions sure to see them through every waking moment. "I'll just bet," the grove owner said, adding, "You're the damnedest feller I ever met."

"Anyway, you said you'd go along with me on this," said Errol.

"To a point," said the cracker. "There's a limit to everything."

— — — — — — — — — —

All he remembered was walking through the door of the Bull and Whistle Saloon and not much of that. He had sufficiently conquered disgust to realize he was in the Gulf Stream, the sun just rising, and he felt a bleak pride that he could manage the yawl in his present condition. He sank and rose among the ultramarine troughs and saw golden strands of sargasso weed at eye level. Flying fish skittered off breaking wave edges, and the three that landed on deck he gutted and laid in the sink. By the end of the ten days promised him by the cracker, the mestizos would be gone and jobless. The oranges would fall and fruit wasps would rise in a cloud. He couldn't let that happen. He couldn't let himself put words to his dismal pride in belonging to the manager class, but he clung to it nonetheless.

Wherever it was going, the little yawl was sailing well. Errol stood on the deck hanging onto the backstay and looked down into the Gulf Stream and the almost purplish depths. The rudder made a long trailing seam at the surface; he could see all the way to the end of the blade as it vibrated under the force of the boat's progress. The sun had dried the decks, and only the leeward side remained dark with sea spray.

Errol started to search out details of the previous night but nothing came. He had a good many of these blanks now, trailing into the past. Sometimes they unexpectedly came to life, filled with detail. He called them "sleeping beauties" in an attempt to assign some value amid what he realized was simple creeping oblivion. He even knew that his current behavior—indifference to where he might be headed—was customary following a blackout, and not unrelated to his frivolous attempt to do away with himself; the feeling would soon give way to extreme concern for his situation and all-round fearfulness. As strength returned he would be amused by these comical swings, even a bit jubilant, and the cycle would begin again, its force undiminished by familiarity. His excuse was that life was repetitious anyway, without quite realizing that the source of despair's enduring power was that it was always brand-spanking-new.

The yawl climbed each swell toward its breaking crest with steady progress, its thin wake like a crack in glass, until a moment when the view from the helm was blue sky and the whitest sea clouds; then hissing down the back slope into the trough to begin the climb again. In one ascent, he saw in the thinnest part of the rising wave a big iridescent fish that vanished as the sea swelled around it.

He merely wondered where he was going.

By afternoon, he more than wondered. The pleasant breeze from the southeast had gone round to the southwest and picked up considerably. Moreover, his spirits had sunk and he began to picture his restive mestizos, the towering cracker unfurling from his Mercedes to shout dismay at the ground covered with rotting oranges. But there was still time before all that happened, before the mestizos dispersed to the work camps at Okeechobee and their cramped prospects. He hadn't really been their friend but he spoke their language and they shared his whiskey, and that was enough, relatively speaking.

The blue of the sea was still reflected by the clouds, but instead of gliding down the backs of waves, the yawl seemed now to push its way down them, the wind driving the bow deeper and deeper until only inches remained before seawater came aboard. It was time to reef.

Errol turned the yawl into the wind and she stopped, wallowing in the rolling ocean, the boom jumping from side to side until he sheeted the mizzen in and she held quietly, nose to wind. With eagerness and relief, Errol went from thinking to doing this work: releasing the main halyard to lower the mainsail, securing the first reef at the luff cringle, and then drawing down the leech until the sail was a third smaller. By tying in each of the fifteen reef points, he secured the loose stretch of decommissioned sail hanging below the boom in a tight, efficient bunt. The main halyard was raised until it hardened; he eased the mizzen, trimmed the jib and main, and the yawl resumed her course for an unknown destination, once again gliding down the waves with her nose up and her decks dry.

Back at the tiller, he regarded the sweat pouring off his body as a result of his exertions and knew it carried poison away. He first thought it behooved him never to land, but awareness of his limited stores made him reject this foolishness. As misery approached, the romance of annihilation seemed to recede, and he wondered why his bouts of self-destruction always occurred on a rising tide of self-love. He knew that the worse he felt the harder he would try to get somewhere and survive. First he had to find out where he was. He had missed his chance at a noon shot of the sun with the sextant and would have to wait for the stars.

The erasure of the previous night left him with no information about his departure; all he knew for certain was that he was in the Gulf Stream, heading for either Cuba or the Bahamas. At this rate, he would reach one or the other during the night, and he really ought to find out which one it was.

He lashed the tiller and went below to cook the flying fish on the alcohol stove, frying them until they were crunchy and taking them back to the cockpit on a tin plate, where he watched the white top of each wave racing along a blue edge before turning into white spume and blowing away. Terns hunted fish overhead and sometimes rained down onto baitfish pushed to the surface by predators beneath, mostly unseen but sometimes showing a dark fin slicing through the turbulence.

Lying back, Errol watched the mast move against the sky, a repeated crossed loop, the infinity sign. He had begun to feel sick. It started as pain just behind his forehead and spread down his spine; as the pain moved into his limbs over the next several hours he began to tremble. By sundown his entire body was shaking and he began dragging things from the cabin—sail bags, an army blanket, the canvas cockpit cover—covering himself with these to the height of the coaming so that only his face showed and the arm that connected him to the tiller. These too were shaking, and unless he kept them locked his teeth rattled audibly. His course was taking him to some part of the vast world of rum and his mind traced a path between this universe and a wallet still fat with banknotes. This wallet, pressed uncomfortably against his buttock, could have been left in the cabin, but the prospect of misplacing it on arrival in the land of rum was such that he wished to verify its whereabouts continuously by the discomfort it produced. Sunken-eyed and desolate, he watched the stars rise from the sea, and he knew he was meant to find out where he was. But the sextant in the far end of the cabin with the sight tables might as well have been on the moon; he knew he couldn't hold it steady enough to take a fix. Instead, he made a crude estimate in his mind of where he might be. The wind was in the first part of the southwest shift; hence the building seas after the quiet of the prevailing southeasterly. He knew he sailed on a starboard tack perhaps ten or fifteen degrees east of the wind, which meant only that he was headed for islands of various sizes, histories, and languages and not the open Atlantic. Beyond that he couldn't say how far he'd gone since he'd departed from a hole in time somewhere behind him.

He vomited the flying fish onto the sole of the cockpit and moaned as malodorous drool poured from the corner of his mouth. His hand on the tiller was a claw by now and the shaking had grown sufficiently violent that he heard himself thump against the cockpit seat, where he stretched out under the heap of things he'd brought from the cabin. He recognized that he wouldn't be able to steer much longer and wished that, while he'd had the strength, he'd heaved to and stopped the boat until a better hour. It was too late now. He lashed the tiller in place and let the wind pick his course out of a hat. The one advantage of this much misery was that he could quit caring, a welcome detachment from his suffering, suffering that would end in the Isles of Rum. At this point, he heard a bitter laugh fly from his mouth, a raspy bray that produced another just like it, then another as they fed off each other, and finally a picture of himself braying at a colossal rum bottle, which inspired bleak masturbation on the cockpit floor. After that, he could only hold his head up by resting his teeth on the seat.

A calming spell of defeat overtook him as he lay on his back looking up at the sail as it passed the stars. Though he recognized them all, he was somewhat absorbed as they flowed in one side of the sail and out the other with a purpose—though not his, of course; he had no purpose. He was not purpose, he was pulp. He cast about for consolation, grimly congratulating himself for being childless. But he remembered that his mestizos trusted him. Of course, they were grateful to anyone who learned their language in this coldhearted nation. But more. He worked beside them, made sure they were paid, while the cracker often inclined to contrive withholdings. The mestizos knew Errol was not so devious, and a working alcoholic appealed to their sense of shared desperation and defensible self-destruction. Indeed, they shook their heads in sympathy when he came to the groves sick, picked things up when he dropped them, carried his ladder. In the depths of his misery, this was all Errol could find, but under the circumstances it seemed quite a lot. Perhaps he was beginning to turn the corner, but first there was more vomiting to be done and the last of the flying fish went over the side. Miguel, Delfin, Juan, Machado, Estevez, Antonio, were their names. Good men.

He slept, but lacked the humanity to dream.

The yawl sailed on into day without his attendance. For hours the decks shone bright with dew and then dried as the sun arose. The telltale streamed from the masthead in the freshening breeze and the water was no longer purple as she had crossed the stream; now she pulled her thin seam of wake across the blue water of a new sea, one that grew steadily paler until the yawl's own speeding shadow on the bottom preceded her, then rose to meet her when she ran aground.

Unavailing curses poured from the companionway as Errol emerged to view his misfortune. The jib, the main, and the mizzen displayed their same wind-filled curves and emphasized the sheer peculiarity of the boat's lack of motion. Looking in every direction, he could see only more bars and the dark shapes of coral heads, any one of which would have sunk the boat. Noon was rapidly approaching, and he dug out his sextant to take a sight of the sun, though he mirthlessly noted the irony of having two pieces of information, latitude and the proximity of the bottom.

The sight reduction from his battered book of tables gave him to conclude that he was somewhere in the western Bahamas. He should pride himself on his effortless crossing of the stream, he thought sardonically. Once he'd accepted that he was immobile, he felt an unexpected wave of security at the calm translucent waters around him, the coral gardens that were pretty shadows beneath them, and he marveled at having sailed so far into this gallery before going aground on forgiving sand. The full moon was a few days away. If he was not too surely embedded on this bar, he had an excellent chance of floating free on a spring tide. He had enough food and seemed to exult in this absence of choices; he explored the idea that he was content to be stuck.

The days began to pass, each more peaceful than the last. He had begun to think of his boat as an island, and in fact he could walk all around it or swim among the coral heads where clouds of pretty reef fish rose and fell with him in the gentle wash. He caught lobsters and boiled them in salt water while Radio Havana played from the cabin. He stretched out in the cockpit and read Frantz Fanon, experiencing pleasant indignation. After the first night, he had dragged a mattress from atop the quarter berth into the cockpit, and he slept there, watching expectantly as the moon grew full to bring the big tides that would float him off. Then, for better or worse, his life would resume. The boat had begun to float tentatively, lifting slightly at the bow only to ground again when the tide fell, but release would come soon.

The last day Errol knew that at high tide, a few hours from now, the yawl would float, free to sail away. He took the opportunity to give the bottom a good scrubbing, breaking down the new barnacles with the back of his brush and then sweeping them off. Down tide, hundreds of tiny fish gathered in a silver cloud to eat the particles of barnacle. With the full moon, the weather changed and dark clouds gathered against the western sky. He would have to look for shelter as soon as he was under way, or at least find enough seaway to heave to. A storm was coming.

He waited in the cockpit into the afternoon, and around three, with a light grinding sound, the yawl lifted off and turned into the wind. The anchor line, which had hung slack when he'd walked the anchor out into the shallows, rose and grew taut. If this were a safe anchorage, he would wait out the storm, but the anchor wouldn't have to slip much under the force of the wind to put him atop the coral. He reduced the mainsail before ever departing, taking the sail down at the second reef to a cleat on the mast. The line leading to a cringle on the leech he wrapped onto the reefing winch and drew that down until the main was little more than a storm trysail. He brought the anchor aboard, hand over hand, the rode dropping into the anchor locker until the anchor was at the stemhead, streaming turtle grass and small snapping creatures; there he secured it and returned to the mast to raise sail before the yawl could make much sternway.

Once sail was up, the yawl began to move obediently. Errol stood at the tiller, carefully conning his way through the dark coral heads in their white circles of sand. The shadow of the boat scurried alongside him on the rippled bottom. Gradually the shadow shrank, then vanished, as he found blue water. With a rising thrill, Errol set sail for the unknown. He knew that any piece of land at all was on the trail to hell, and that this ocean road put a good face on oblivion. A bad storm was coming; he meant to embrace it. The first passage would be fear, but the other side—if he could get there—was what interested him as being the country of death or freedom, unless it turned out they were the same thing.

It was the season of equinoctial storms, and the halo around the sun made Errol see in this something of a larger plan for him. Still, the little yawl was indifferent to such things, a thought whose absurdity he recognized without quite believing. Like most sailors, he did not regard his ship as inanimate and extended his senses out to all her parts the better to understand the whims of the sea. This impulse came of a great desire to survive that he was not sure he owned. Nevertheless, he believed his ship wished to live, and perhaps he would defer to her out of respect for the adage that a good ship is one which, when her master can no longer take care of her, takes care of her master.

Her purposeful obedience let Errol work his way through the coral heads to the dark blue of deeper water. Once she had way on, she never hesitated in stays—unless the man at the tiller was entirely lacking in skill—and moved from tack to tack like one of the domino players at the Cuban-American Hall in Key West. She'd been built forty years ago by a tidal creek in St. Michaels, Maryland, with a bottom of yellow pine from a church made by slaves, the marks of whose axes could still be found inside a hull so thick and hard that screws had to be drilled first; the topsides were single-length planks of Atlantic white cedar, the deck of native pine and canvas, Sitka spruce spars that had come on a train from Oregon a long time ago. When he reviewed her various attributes, as he often did, Errol began to feel responsible for her, and he recognized its absurdity without believing it. Whatever juju he believed her to possess was not mitigated by the fact that her previous owner was shot in a card game and she had sunk into desuetude at Garrison Bight until Errol rescued her for past-due dock fees and a modest bribe to the city council. He'd never find another boat with the marks of slaves' axes in her timbers. She went up on jack stands at Stock Island, neglected sculpture among the shrimp boats, slowly returned to life by Errol and friends until launching day, when in an alcoholic crisis he sailed her away to the Dry Tortugas, anchoring in Mooney Harbor under the shadow of Fort Jefferson, to await a new day. His gratitude toward his little ship was evident in his belief that she had treated him like a cherished dependent and hung on her anchor, keeping a fresh breeze across his bunk until such time as he could return to the tiller like a man. When that day came, he sailed right past Key West and all his previous sins, and fetched up at Cortez, his current berth, where he met the cracker at a party on the latter's sixty-foot Hatteras; and there he began his apprenticeship in the orange groves, where his command of Spanish was put to service exploiting the cracker's laborers. Errol suffered no more than most over the plight of his fellow man, yet this was a bit of a problem. Some of the men were refugees from violence, and their children, though occasionally visited by well-meaning social workers from the State of Florida, clearly expected massacres at any time and so avoided anyone who was not obviously a mestizo peasant. One way or another, the oranges continued to head for the juice plant at Arcadia, and Errol came to be trusted by these lost souls, who forgave his being a *perro infermo* or perhaps even liked him because of it.

The job now was to get to deeper water and plenty of it before getting knocked around by the storm. He had no destination other than the knowledge that in this ocean you could not go far before striking some community or another, a bit of shelter, perhaps some refreshments. The problem was that his slowly clearing mind wasn't sure it wished to arrive. The gradual illumination—cramps, headaches, and diarrhea notwithstanding—was a substantial reward in itself, and the reattachment to reality bore a religious quality, or at least rootless excitement. He imagined the storm as a cascade of invigorating challenges.

A set of line squalls formed across the horizon, driving columns of seabirds before it, a thunder-filled cross-winded trough of weather. He traversed five miles of broken sea to sail right into them, lightning jumping around over the spar, an uprush of fragrant supercharged sea in omnidirectional winds. Each cell had its own weather and light, from near darkness and pandemonium to a fluorescent stillness walled by rain. Thus far, a pleasant exercise, for he sailed right through the squalls for a better view of the gray sky beyond, scudding clouds and building seas where a barometric trench made the rules.

Foresight suggested that he feed himself in the time available. He lashed the tiller and went below to light the alcohol stove, dumping a can of chicken noodle soup into a pot. The yawl's steady progress had acquired a kind of leaping motion, and he stirred the soup impatiently, as though that would shorten the time it took to heat it. He raised and lashed the weather cloths beside the bunks and stowed the few loose objects in their Pullman nets: a bottle of aspirin, a notepad, a dead cell phone, the Frantz

Fanon book, a Key West telephone directory, spare winch handle, and flashlight. When he returned to the stove, a wisp of steam rose from the soup, but there was no time to enjoy it as the yawl was knocked onto her beam ends by the crush of wind, imprisoned in a bad angle by the lashing on her tiller. When Errol looked up through the companionway, a graybeard arose in the dim light, its top blowing off into spume, and subsided. It was a grim black-and-white movie, *Down to the Sea in Ships,* Clara Bow the It Girl, and dying whales. This sort of respite from reality had previously been his accommodation; but for better or for worse, reality would be back plowing irony before it.

Errol half crawled into the cockpit from the companionway and snapped on his lifeline. Once the tiller was free again, the boat rose to the gusts and relieved some of the lateral pressure that had her on her side. The pool of water in the self-bailing cockpit roared through the scuppers and emptied quickly. The frontal storms that had met his requirements for a manageable challenge were beyond him now; in their place, the wind came in an unimpeded fetch from open ocean in a scream. The incessant movement of the boat gave him the sense that they were being chased by the increasingly enormous waves, whose breaking crests gleamed unpleasantly. A cabinet burst open in the galley, discharging all his canned goods, and when Errol looked below he could see the food racing about on the floor.

The yawl rose as each great sea swept past with an uncanny hiss. His steering the boat now consisted entirely in keeping the stern presented to the waves and preventing the yawl from broaching as she sped down their backs. Thankfully, he detected a rhythm in this and, being able to feel the rise of sea without looking, made the proper adjustments through the memory of his muscles. Though reefed to a fraction of its original size, the mainsail seemed hard as iron and its leech buzzed like an electric saw.

The black faces of approaching waves were so steep that Errol quit looking back; they were at the height of the spreaders and it seemed another degree or two of pitch and they must fall on him. If they did, they did: he wouldn't watch that.

A rain began, and then a pelting rain, which after a time flattened the sea. Now the yawl whistled along, seeming to enjoy its velocity undeterred by the recent mountains of water, the speed of wind for the moment little more than an inconvenience. Errol took this opportunity to go below and confront the disorder of the cabin. It was mostly canned goods and he stowed them frantically, knowing the calming rain wouldn't last.

When the violent motion of the ship resumed, he was reluctant to go above. He pretended the cabin was insufficiently tidy and lingered over trifles, the charts that needed rolling, the celestial tables that had somehow landed on the wrong shelf; he even renewed the paper towel on its roller. All this housekeeping betrayed a grim comedy as he was flung about performing it.

A boarding sea fell with a thud on the cabin top. He watched the water roar through the cockpit, overwhelm the scuppers, and pour over the transom and the untended helm. He felt the weight of it press against the little yawl's buoyancy in repeated attempts to overwhelm it. Recognizing a plausible run-up to drowning, Errol was swept by lethargy, not the same as peace but fatalist stupefaction. He was not afraid to die but very frightened of drowning, of filling his lungs with seawater and sinking to the bottom of the ocean; nothing could be more alien unless it was on another planet. That of course was just how his friend Raymond had departed, having once remarked that it would be an appropriate end for anyone who had trafficked in refugees. This thought produced in Errol an unexpected return of the heebie-jeebies. He forced himself into the cockpit, and there he saw that the great waves had begun to cascade and he was sure the end was at hand. This gave him some peace at least. Now he went about his business managing the ship, exercising what few options remained.

He replaced the reefed main with a storm trysail, now the only sail on the boat. He'd thought that the double-reefed main would be good enough but it wasn't. If it had loaded up with seawater, it would have been big enough to take out the mast. Amid gusts that sounded like gunshots, he sheeted the trysail to leeward, lashed the tiller in the opposite direction, and produced a plausible version of heaving to: the yawl drifted and forged slightly into the wind, fell off, forged, and fell off again. The sea was now covered by flying spindrift, a gruesome fuzz that extended to the glittering wave tops. Errol could bear to see no more and went below and crawled into a bunk but was soon flung onto the floor where the oozing bilge emerged between the planks. He crawled in again, lashed up his weather cloth so he was secured in the bunk, laced his fingers behind his head, and entertained himself with ideas of death while disdaining those of drowning, fish eating his flesh, descent to a lightless sea bottom, et cetera. In the Pullman net beside him was a Cuban statuette of the Madonna, the gift of a refugee physician; he turned it until it faced him. "Our Lady," he said. He liked her face. She looked a bit Cuban, actually; he was pleased she was not so universalized as to seem inhuman. He stared into the tiny face as the senseless chaos of the sea tried to destroy his home. The face grew larger and came toward him. He was falling in love.

It was time to go topsides once again. He didn't realize how peaceful the cabin had been until he was in the cockpit. The hove-to yawl seemed to follow a cycle. At the bottom of the troughs there was a kind of peace. This created a leeward eddy that moderated some of the more fearsome violence. At the same time, the troughs were so deep they actually protected him from

the wind. Once the yawl rose to the crests again, the full force of
the wind and its attendant shrieks could be felt.

It was with welcome detachment that he observed the behavior of his boat and concluded that there was no more he could do
for her; she had managed thus far, and to be ready to cope with
any great change in conditions he would have to sleep. He hoped
that the cooler sea temperatures outside the stream would re-
strain the storm, but there was as yet no sign of that. He went
below once again and secured himself in his bunk, feeling, as he
fastened the weather cloths that kept him from rolling out, an
odd coziness that he guessed came from his now-rapt gaze upon
his Madonna. It was not that he possessed a single religious con-
viction, but knowing millions worshiped her was consoling. He
wished now to be among the millions, and this was a start. If he
lived till daybreak, he would address his gratitude to Allah as
well as Our Lady, and to their millions of worshipers, his fellow
humans.

First, he asked Her forgiveness for not helping Raymond
back into the boat. True, he had not pushed Raymond overboard.
The ocean had done that: the jib boom had come adrift and was
beating a hole in the deck; Raymond had gone forward without
his lifeline; the bow buried in a green sea and when it came up, in
a white cloud of spindrift, Raymond was no longer there. He
floundered alongside the passing hull, reaching toward Errol.
The split second of ambivalence—as though Raymond were
being swept to New Orleans with Caroline—was all it took, and
Raymond was gone. Caroline had had her fling with pirates and
was careful the next time to latch on to someone with a future
and an office.

He asked to be forgiven. Caroline was raising beautiful children in the Garden District, driving them to their swimming les-
sons from her home on Audubon Street, and Raymond, who had

not known home ownership, was at the bottom of the sea. Errol understood that he was being shriven by the same sea and held the statuette in his fist, praying for forgiveness. Expecting his boat to crack open at any time and release him to his fate, he believed his request was legitimate. Certainly he'd never felt anything quite like it before. Such sobbing pleas were something he'd never heard from himself, as though he were being disemboweled by his own voice. His grief was possession and infancy, far more urgent than the storm and something of a deafening joyride. At one odd moment, he burst into laughter.

He wished to live. He stared into the face of the little statue, absorbed by her high Latin coloring and carmine lips; she was devouring him with her eyes. He felt himself sink further into his bunk supinely awaiting her kiss. "You gorgeous bitch," he murmured.

If he could tell by the weight in his limbs, he had awakened from a long sleep. He moved his eyes and took in his surroundings warily. It required some time for him to understand what had changed so completely: the boat was still. As the cabin was sealed against breaking seas, he could not see outside, and the air within had become sultry and fetid. He untied the weather cloths and swung his feet out onto the sole, glancing at the gimbaled lamps that had swung so violently in the night. They were motionless, though their oil was splashed around underneath him, indicating to his relief that he had not imagined the storm. He reached a hand gratefully to the cedar planks of the hull, still cool, still fragrant, perhaps still trees. Pines and oaks and cedars had carried him safely.

He was always given one more chance: it was frightening. The sight of the Madonna, moreover, gave him a queasy feeling.

It reminded him of awakening in the bed of a woman who clearly didn't remember meeting him. But the Madonna didn't say a word. He got to his feet, startled that he was wearing no clothes; he looked around and discovered them tossed on the opposite bunk. He pulled on his shorts and went topsides.

"The Dawn of Creation," he thought, with a giddy impresario's flourish: the sea, ultramarine and pierced by sunlight, was still in every direction, no birds, no fish, no clouds, just the blue of heaven as it awaited completion. It crossed Errol's mind that by existing he intruded upon all this vacant magnificence. He preferred this more solemn view of so heroic and empty a vista. He considered his pill-gobbling episode in Key West with shame as trivializing the question posed by this empty sea, where eternity had stored the materials for a fresh start.

Errol went below and directed his optimism toward feeding himself. He had a beautiful round Macintosh apple, which he sliced carefully on the galley sideboard, and a piece of Canadian cheddar. He disguised the staleness of a hunk of Cuban bread by toasting it over the alcohol flame of his stove and basting it with tinned butter. The coffee soon bubbled in the percolator and filled the cabin with its wonderful smell. As he pictured Raymond sweeping past the hull, he could nearly imagine forgiving himself. But when he speculated on how many miles astern Raymond might have been before he drowned, he failed to add relief or prospects for forgiveness to his detachment.

His mood didn't last as he discovered how wide-ranging his hunger was. He gazed about at his breakfast and inventoried the other things he might eat. The tea cake, in the cabinet under the sink, excited him, as did the small tinned ham whose container he vowed to respect as long as necessary. The cornucopia of food that he had stowed here and there—even the pineapples under the floorboards!—unconsidered during the storm began to reform in his mind.

Admiring Caroline as she hung her bathing suit on the line behind the house on Petronia, Raymond had said, in a reflective tone, "I love 'em with that hunted look, don't you?"

After a moment, Errol had said, "No."

It came to him now: here resided one of the roots of hesitation as Raymond swept past the ketch. A boat that weighed almost fifty thousand pounds would not stop on a dime; there was that. Or turn in fewer than several of its own lengths. Even luffing up, the ketch would forereach farther than a man could swim in those seas. That knowledge could have been embedded too—couldn't it?—the sort that produces indecision, and indecision produces hesitation, and hesitation produces unfortunate accidents as opposed to murder.

At noon, he took a perfect sight of the sun. The boat was unmoving and the horizon a hard clean line. With the sextant to his eye, he measured the elevation and then went below to try for a signal on the radio direction finder. Haitian Baptist Radio was in its customary spot, and by combining its direction from the boat with the noon sight of the sun, he knew for the first time where he was. The information was sickening.

When Raymond was lost over the side, Errol reported the accident to the coast guard and gave them his position. Was it not right here? He went back to the cockpit and looked around the yawl at the stillness of the sea and its plum blue depths under a quiet sky as though he would recognize the scene of many years ago. This, he knew, was absurd. Surely he had simply superimposed the two pieces of information in an unreliable mind. He pounced on the idea that the accident had happened in the stream, and clearly this was not the stream. He had the celestial fact that the stream lay to the east of his current position, information that should have protected him from the sense that he had been directed to revisit the site of the misfortune. But the Gulf Stream moves like a great blue snake and there were times when this spot on the planet was indeed in its trail. Still, he didn't believe it.

Recently, Errol had become more superstitious, and as he was at base a practical man he ascribed the change to two things: alcohol and hanging around with peasants who buried things at work sites as health talismans or to ward off accidents. On occasions of birth and death, his workers tied *ex votos* in the orange trees. He had twice visited a palm reader in an old strip mall on the Tamiami Trail, a service he took sufficiently seriously to pay for it. Dressed in a bronze-colored gown decorated with sequins and designs from the horoscope, she had a snubby Scandinavian face and the flat *A*s of Minnesota. When he pointed out that her interpretations of his lifeline were diametrically different on separate occasions, that his heart line on one visit indicated that he was devious and unreliable while on another that he was courageous in the face of impediment, she called him a "motherfucker" without a moment's hesitation, then, relenting, told him his barred sun line made him vulnerable to jealousy and that he must always exercise caution. He paid her grudgingly but thought about her remarks as he stood before the tattoo parlor next door while tourists battled for position on Route 41.

He was prepared to consider that he was back at the scene of the accident, and only recently this would have been enough to cast him into a black hole. But his guilt was changing. His superstition had begun to be attached not to the consequences of Raymond's being swept away but to the belief that trafficking in refugees had given rise to Raymond's death and his own long slide toward the abyss. When he remembered the myriad plastic Madonnas in the jalopies at his groves, like little scenes of lynchings, hanging from rearview mirrors or from the branches of orange trees, and the impure thoughts aroused by the little chicas who brought food to their men in the groves as well as a tremor of excitement among them, feral gusts of flesh and spirit, he began to realize that you pay for *all* your sins, and if that was superstition then so be it. It was the implied lesson of the mestizos. What he should have done for his friend no longer mattered; *he was guilty of everything.* The wish to be forgiven poured from him as a moan directed to the sea; he could think of no one else. Still, there was a glimmer of solace in acknowledging his superstition that every bird, every cloud, every flash of light had a message for him, now and in eternity.

A light breeze, a zephyr, arose from the southeast, and Errol could smell some sort of vegetative fragrance, some hint of land. He untied the reef nettles and reefing lines and raised the main. Its folds were full of freshwater from the storm, and it showered down on him as the sail went up. There was just enough air to pull the boom into position and the jib barely filled, but a serpentine eddy formed behind the transom and the boat was moving once again.

He sailed half the day at this slow pace and the water grew paler blue as the bottom beneath the hull came near. There were more birds now, and when the horizon thickened with the mangrove green of land it was as he expected. He kept on in this direction, now recognizing that he couldn't live on the open sea. He would have to make his way home to his grove workers, who would fare less well without him under the cracker and to whom he owed his last allegiance. In this, time was running out: he would reprovision, look for a hole in the weather, and sail home, determined to find there the strength to withstand evil.

A scattering of cays lay before him, Cuban, Bahamian, it didn't matter; both were far from empire. As he drew nearer, he was surprised to see stands of coconut palms emerge from the mangrove shoreline. These cays were more substantial than he had guessed they'd be—a better chance to take on some water, a nicety he'd overlooked during his Key West tear, a better chance of finding some helpful souls. He stopped the boat before he was much closer, as a bar arose before him bright with its reflective sand bottom. Beyond it he could see a protected turtle-grass sound but, at first, no way through to what would be a superb anchorage. Where the palms were concentrated at the shore, boats were drawn up, and after he'd tacked back and forth for an hour, unsuccessfully looking for an opening, he saw two figures at one of the boats pushing it into the water. One of the men sat in front, elbows on his knees, face in his hand, while the other sculled vigorously from the stern with a long oar.

Errol watched with rising apprehension, not so much at what these two might have in mind for him but at the fact they were humans at all. In a short time, they were alongside, two tall black men, shirtless, barefoot, in a crude plank skiff with a coconut-shell bailer, a grains for catching lobster. Errol bade them good afternoon, as the man in front reached a hand to the rail of the yawl to keep the skiff from bumping. This man replied inaudibly and Errol determined only that he'd said something in Spanish and that rather shyly. Errol decided he would not let on that he too spoke Spanish until he had a better idea of what these fellows had in mind for him. The man holding the rail, with the refined features of an Indian, kept his eyes downcast while his companion boldly boarded the yawl. The miserable detachment with which Errol had long encountered people he didn't know had somehow disappeared—perhaps during the storm—and he greeted his uninvited guest somewhat heartily as he asked in English what he could do for him. Putting his hand on the yawl's tiller and wiggling from side to side, the man explained in pidgin Spanish, which Errol pretended not to understand, that if he wished to land he would have to be piloted over the bar. For an instant, Errol thought of revealing his Spanish but thought better of it. Instead, he made some obtuse gestures indicating the boat, the land, the water; at which the man at the tiller—a dignified and classically African-looking man, older, Errol now saw, than he'd first thought, even maybe the father of the other man—at which the older man said in exasperated Spanish to the man still in the skiff that he didn't know what this white man wanted but that if he wanted to go to the inside anchorage, he would need their guidance. At this, with disconnected and resolute stupidity, Errol gestured around at the boat in general and then pointed to the island, where water and some of the consolations of dry land awaited him. He could stay on the boat and incur few obligations by mingling with these people.

The two men understood, and at this the fellow in the boat secured the painter of the skiff to a stern cleat of the yawl and came aboard with a shy nod to the owner. The older man glanced about the deck of the boat to determine how the rigging ran and then drew the jib sheet in and cleated it. The yawl eased into motion once more, not much as the wind was faint, swung around, and, as the man at the tiller made several more adjustments with a smile and a shrug directed at Errol, sailed straight at the bar, tugging the skiff behind. As Errol stiffened, the helmsman shook his head and measured a distance to the floor with his hand, suggesting plenty of water, then waving into space as if to shoo all cares away. Errol could see nothing but the gathering shallows, changing color alarmingly as they sailed forward. He resigned himself that they would be aground in minutes, hoping his shipmates knew of a rising tide.

At the moment of impact, a miraculous thread of dark green appeared in the bar, barely wider than the yawl, and the man at the helm followed it quickly and efficiently like a dog tracking game as he crossed the bar into the small basin. He continued sailing nearly to the shore and then rounded up, stopping the boat. Errol went forward and let go the anchor. *Czarina* dropped back slowly until the rode tightened and she hung in the light breeze. "A well-behaved vessel," said the helmsman in Spanish. Errol gave him a puzzled smile. The three went toward shore, passing a post driven into the bottom to which was tethered a huge grouper, arriving at a long dock so decrepit it resembled part of a Möbius strip. The black men led, waving Errol along, and he followed on a path between old shell mounds, and soon came to a clearing with several houses made of salvaged timbers and monkey thatch, then around those houses to a well. "Wada," said the older man with a smile. Errol looked down the well, not more than fifteen feet deep, with a bucket on a wooden windlass contraption and various ladles, two of which were cut down Coca-Cola bottles and the other coconut shells like the bailer in the skiff. When they went back to the clearing, Errol following obediently, several people, probably family members, had appeared from the houses, two women of indeterminate age, a very old man, and a teenage boy with dreadlocks. All smiled. At this, Errol turned to his hosts and told them in Spanish that he was quite comfortable speaking Spanish. The two men laughed and pounded his back.

"You were espying on us!" said the younger.

On reflection, the older man seemed less pleased with this deception. "What besides water do you wish from us?" he asked rather formally.

"I'm not sure I even need water. I was looking for a place to rest. I've been in that storm, you see."

"Yes, that was a storm."

"I'm a bit tired."

"Of course you are tired. One hardly drifts about in such a situation. Great exertion is called for."

"I have to admit, I nearly lost my nerve."

"Evidently you didn't, for here you are. You have a safe anchorage, and this place is good for rest if nothing else."

Caught up in this colloquy, Errol was reduced to a small bow.

"You're our only guest," said the younger man. "We ate the others."

General laughter.

"Wrong ocean," said Errol. General appreciative laughter except from the old man, who seemed a bit disoriented. Errol had a whorish need to include all in admiring his wit and rested his glance on the old man long enough to determine that he was blind.

It was agreed that he would go on sleeping on the yawl and borrow the skiff for transport. One of the women, tall and Indian-looking, with a bright yellow-and-black cloth tying her hair atop her head, informed him in English that when dinner was ready someone would come to the shore and make a noise. Noting his pause at her choice of language, she said, "I from Red Bays."

The older of the two men who'd brought him said, back in Spanish, "You'll come, of course."

Errol bowed all round and said, "Enchanted."

All replied, "Equally."

Errol returned to his boat, rowing past the great fish swimming slowly around its stake, tying the skiff alongside and climbing back into the yawl and the security it offered, especially after its latest and probably worst storm. He found himself disturbed and so particularly dreading the dinner that he made himself sit in the cockpit and puzzle over his aversion to such companionable people, an aversion so strong that he only abandoned the thought of sailing off when he admitted he'd never find the way back over the bar. Isolation seemed to have the attraction of a drug, and he reluctantly intuited that he must not give in to it. He'd have been less apprehensive about that dinner if it had been at the White House, but he believed, if he could pass this small social test, he could begin to escape the superstitions and fears that were ruining his life.

He had a short rest on the quarter berth with its view of blue sky over the companionway. The stillness of the yawl was a miracle, and he laid his palms against the wooden sides of the hull in a kind of benediction, or at least thanksgiving. For now at least it gave him the feeling of home.

He smelled buttonwood smoke. The sun was going down and he had to close the companionway screen to keep out the mosquitoes that always seemed particular to their own area: these were small and quick, produced a precise bite that was almost a sting, and couldn't be waved away. Presently, he heard someone beating on a piece of iron. Poking his head out the hatch, he saw the younger of the two men announcing dinner with two rusty pieces and gave him a wave, upon which the man retired up the path between the shell mounds. A fog of buttonwood smoke lay over the water at the mangrove shoreline.

He pulled the skiff onto the beach and secured its painter to a palm log, which, judging by the grooves worn in its trunk, was intended for that purpose. He pulled his belt tighter and straightened his shoulders before heading up the path for dinner. Excepting the woman from Andros, the group, including the blind old man, were sitting by the fire watching strips of turtle roast over the glowing coals; which the older of the two men raked toward him. The remains of the turtle were to one side, heaped within its shell, and seemed to have concentrated a particularly intense cloud of mosquitoes. When Errol saw the rum being passed around, he reassured himself that the supply would be limited. No liquor stores out here! he thought, with creepy hilarity.

The unhesitating first swallow made everything worthwhile and was followed by an oceanic wave of love for his companions. When the Andros woman came to the fire with plantains to be roasted, he reached the rum out to her. The younger of the two, Catarino, seized his hand, said, "No," and took the bottle himself. The woman from Andros cast her eyes down and went on preparing the plantains. At Errol's bafflement, Catarino explained. "She is our slave."

Looking at the bottle of rum and wondering why Catarino was so slow in raising it to his lips, Errol asked, "How can that be?" He wondered if he had misunderstood the Spanish word but he repeated it, *esclava,* and had it confirmed. He reached for the rum but it went on to the old blind man.

Catarino patiently explained further. "As you can see, she is black."

Errol emitted a consanguineous giggle lest his next statement give offense and dispel the convivial atmosphere and—he admitted to himself—result in the withholding of the rum. "But all of you are black, aren't you?"

The blind man threw his head back and in a surprising rumble of a baritone asked incredulously, "Black *and* Spanish?" Catarino looked at him sternly.

"We are as white as you, sir. I hope this is understood."

"Oh, it is, it is," said Errol, with rising panic.

The older of the two men, Adan, gazed at him with a crooked smile and said, "You must be hungry."

Not seeming to hear him, Errol asked, "Will she eat with us?"

"Clearly not," the blind man rumbled. "The American would do well to turn to our repast and that which makes all men brothers." He held up the bottle. Errol decided not to express his thought, *Except the slaves,* again less out of principle than a fear of causing the rum to be withheld. When the Andros woman came back to the fire, Errol asked her in English what her name was and she told him Angela. The others nodded their incomprehension but encouraged this foreign talk with smiles.

"I'm told you're their slave."

"They believe that," she said complacently.

"And it's because you're black?"

At this, she stopped and gave voice to what was evidently dispassionate consideration. "How amusing I find this. I am a Seminole Indian. My great-grandfathers came to Red Bays in cayucos. Why else would the University of Florida send us so many anthropologists? We are all Indians in Red Bays. Why else would they bring us T-shirts from the Hard Rock Cafe and expensive tennis shoes to earn our trust, if we were not Indians?"

The others nodded happily; they were enjoying her indignation and seemed to understand that it was based on a discussion of her slave status.

"These disgraceful Spaniards don't understand that they are blacks. They think their language protects them. How they'd love to be Indians!"

"Were you captured?"

Angela couldn't control her mirth. She held the turban around her head with both hands and jiggled from head to toe with laughter. The others united in what seemed to be real pleasure, and she looked at them and rolled her eyes at the absurdity of the white man. This rather calmed things because, as his fellow whites, the Spanish-speaking blacks did not want to throw in their lot with their slave too emphatically. They wished to project that they were compassionate slaveholders who followed the dictates of humanity.

The rum landed back in Errol's hands, and all the others, including Angela, generously relished his enthusiasm as he raised it to his lips and kept it there for a long time, not fully understanding how ravenous he was. But when he lowered the bottle something in his gaze caused them to fall silent. The moment passed as interest turned to the turtle and plantains. Noticing that Angela sat by herself on the step of one of the driftwood shacks, Errol asked her if she thought of herself as a slave.

She replied, "Don't be a fool."

"Oh, well," said Errol, in odd contentment. Confusion could be pleasant when you were drinking; it kept the mind whirring agreeably. He began to eat, taking pieces of turtle from spits over the sputtering buttonwood coals. The teenager with dreadlocks was wholly focused on the food and neither laughed with the others nor in any way seemed to know he was not alone. The only other woman, a heavyset Spanish-speaking black, watched Errol with sullen attention as though he were there to present a bill or a summons. The blind man staring with white eyes across the fire into the darkness cupped his hands in front of him, into which Adan and Catarino placed pieces of food. Catarino asked Errol if he was enjoying his meal.

"I certainly am!"

"And the rum suits you, does it not?"

"Very agreeable."

"Sometimes it is more important than food, no?"

"Sometimes," said Errol.

Adan smiled at his food and asked, "Sometimes?"

Errol waited before answering. "I believe that is what I said."

Catarino gave Errol a jovial thump on the back and returned the bottle to him. The wind had shifted slightly, and Errol moved closer to the buttonwood smoke to be free of the vicious little mosquitoes. When he glanced at Angela, sitting away from the fire, Catarino explained that mosquitoes didn't bother black people.

"How is it that she is your slave?" Errol asked. At this, the blind man spoke in a surprisingly firm voice.

"Her man drowned."

"Is that so?"

"Yes, that is so," said Adan. All except Angela seemed quite sad to reflect upon this event. "We didn't take her back to her country. That would be against the law. Those blacks have laws no one can understand. With her man dead, she wished to throw in with us, but we were barely surviving as it was. You see how it is. We offered to let her come and be our slave, as that is entirely natural and appealing to blacks. As you see, she accepted."

"Which only proves our point," Adan added.

Errol took another slug of rum and gazed around at his companions, who seemed to him, as best as he could tell, to all be black. Then he thought of something. "What color do you think I am?" The three looked at each other. It was Catarino who finally spoke, his smile full of accommodation.

He said, "We haven't decided."

"I can't take mosquitoes at all," said Errol nervously. "Never could. They drive me nuts!"

The blind man said, "Have some more of that aguardiente. To enjoy your meal, you must calm your nerves."

Adan looked pensive. "They served wine at the Last Supper. If we had not been prepared to offer refreshment to our guests, perhaps the turtle would not have offered himself to us. All things are connected. Even you, sir, are connected to us, if only in that we share a clearing which we made of sufficient size with our machetes as to offer you a place at our meal." He smiled pleasantly. "Surely we knew you were coming."

Errol's expression of gratitude was interrupted by a burp, which brought a change of mood and all went about eating with a purpose, all except Angela, who paced about, desperately waving away the mosquitoes.

The sun must have awakened Errol, balled up next to the extinguished fire, the sun that caused the mosquitoes to retreat into the mangroves. Errol didn't seem to remember where he was, and indeed his body was disagreeably unfamiliar. No parts of it seemed to fit together any longer and all were consumed by burning and itching. He felt his face with swollen fingers. His lips were drum tight, his eyelids so thick he could see them, and his cheeks lumpy with bites. He had lost his shoes, then remembered they'd been laced. Someone had taken his shoes. In any case, his swollen feet would no longer be contained by them. He lay back, let his mouth fall open, and gazed at the sky.

Once there was sufficient water in his boat, he could call it provisioned and begin the voyage home. He had hand lines and a shoebox full of diamond-shaped silver spoons: he would have fish and freshwater and that was enough. All this horror, this mis-shapen body, was temporary. Steps toward atonement had been taken; more could be promised. He remembered his mestizos and the groves. He tried reckoning how long he'd been away, but no exact answer was required. The cracker's deadline had come and gone: he had broken his covenant with the mestizos and by now they were dispersed, thrown once again to fate, to wander the labor camps at Immokalee or Belle Glade, offering the days of their lives for sugar, citrus, and white men. His, like theirs, were the inconveniences of hell.

Certainly it lay in his power to arise, thank his hosts, sail away, and, against the cadences of wind and sea, sort through his many failings and the invoices for atonement that accompanied them. There was no mess so great it could not be broken down into a manageable sequence, a bill of lading for debts to oblivion.

As he stood, his buttocks abraded each other in special misery. My God, he wondered, how did they get in there? He began scratching himself all over. He hurried from one place to another as no sooner did he palliate some mad insistence than it appeared in another place. He was writhing and dancing without leaving his small spot in the dirt.

Something caught his eye.

Angela, arms wrapped around her sides, was lost in shaking, silent mirth. He stopped and stared at her through indignant, swollen eyes. He walked over to her, the pressure of edema squeezing up his calves with every step. She smiled at him when he arrived. She had unwound her turban and twisted it around her hands, allowing her hair to spring out in all directions. In his present condition, that hair struck him with its terrible vitality. There was something thrilling about it. She ṣaid, "I tink it will rain. And dis is my great day. Dey have freed me."

"That's nice," said Errol sarcastically. His disfigured lips distorted this offensive speech but Angela seemed not to notice. "Are they still sleeping?"

"Oh, dey gone."

Errol could not lose his snide tone. "Where exactly is there to go?"

Angela answered him imperturbably. "Miami." Errol considered this for a remarkably short time.

"They took my boat?"

"Oh, yes."

Errol seemed unsurprised. He considered levelly that he was without choices. His despair was such that the possibility of solace could only lie in the evaporation of all his options. Never before had he sensed himself greeting his destiny with so little resistance. It was an odd luxury to contemplate this, pants unbuttoned to accommodate his itches, spread fingers hanging at his sides, and a face whose risibility could now be enjoyed only by Angela, who had the upper hand of observing him.

An implement of sorts leaned against the shack. A corner of salvaged iron had been secured to a hardwood limb from which the branches had been removed with many wraps of rusting wire. Angela handed this to Errol and ordered him to follow her up the path through the mastic and wild palms. As they walked, Angela told him of the brothers' dream of taking their father, the blind man, to Miami, where they had been told you could buy eyeballs on the black market. There had been much in the air about family values, but Errol had never imagined they'd be honored at his expense. Perhaps he didn't really mind as he followed Angela with his new implement. Musing on the current arrangement, he wondered whether she was his owner and what color they each were, since the evidence of his eyes had proved insufficient.

Bright-hued birds flashed through the opening made by the path; near the flowers of tall vines, clouds of hummingbirds rose and sank, competing for nectar with surprising ferocity. A bananaquit, an urgent little yellow bird, danced down the path ahead of him, landed, and then scurried off like a mouse.

The path opened atop what Angela said was an old burial mound, and there he saw a garden under the morning sun. Errol briefly wondered what sorts of people were buried here but doubted that Angela knew. She showed him how things were arranged, the peppers, the tomatoes, the staked gourds, the new melons concealed under dark leaves glistening with dew. A pleasant smell arose from the tilled ground. A tall palm hung over the scene, and from its crown of leaves the sound of parrot nestlings descended.

At the still-shaded end of the garden, wild vegetation had encroached on the perimeter. She showed him where he must start.

Gallatin Canyon

The day we planned the trip, I told Louise that I didn't like going to Idaho via the Gallatin Canyon. It's too narrow, and while trucks don't belong on this road, there they are, lots of them. Tourist pull-offs and wild animals on the highway complete the picture. We could have gone by way of Ennis, but Louise had learned that there were road repairs on Montana Highway 84—twelve miles of torn-up asphalt—in addition to its being rodeo weekend.

"Do we have to go to Idaho?" she asked.

I said I thought it was obvious. A lot rode on the success of our little jaunt, which was ostensibly to close the sale of a small car dealership I owned in the sleepy town of Rigby. But, since accepting the offer of a local buyer, I had received a far better one from elsewhere, which, my attorney said, I couldn't take unless my original buyer backed out—and he would only back out if he got sufficiently angry at me. Said my attorney, Make him mad. So I was headed to Rigby, Idaho, expressly to piss off a small-town businessman, who was trying to give me American money for a going concern on the strip east of town, and thereby make room for a rich Atlanta investor, new to our landscape, who needed this dealership as a kind of flagship for his other intentions. The question was how to provoke Rigby without arousing his suspicions, and I might have collected my thoughts a little better had I not had to battle trucks and tourists in the Gallatin Canyon.

Louise and I had spent a lot of time together in recent years, and we were both probably wondering where things would go from here. She had been married, briefly, long ago, and that fact, together with the relatively peaceful intervening years, gave a pleasant detachment to most of her relationships, including the one she had with me. In the past, that would have suited me perfectly; it did not seem to suit me now, and I was so powerfully attached to her it made me uncomfortable that she wasn't interested in discussing our mutual future, though at least she had never suggested that we wouldn't have one. With her thick blond hair pulled back in a barrette, her strong, shapely figure, and the direct fullness of her mouth, she was often noticed by other men. After ten years in Montana, she still had a strong Massachusetts accent. Louise was a lawyer, specializing in the adjudication of water rights between agricultural and municipal interests. In our rapidly changing world, she was much in demand. Though I wished we could spend more time together, Louise had taught me not to challenge her on this.

No longer the country crossroads of recent memory, Four Corners was filled with dentists' offices, fast-food and espresso shops, and large and somehow foreboding filling stations that looked, at night, like colonies in space; nevertheless, the intersection was true to its name, sending you north to a transcontinental interstate, east into town, west to the ranches of Madison County, and south, my reluctant choice, up the Gallatin Canyon to Yellowstone and the towns of southeast Idaho, one of which contained property with my name on the deed.

We joined the stream of traffic heading south, the Gallatin River alongside and usually much below the roadway, a dashing high-gradient river with anglers in reflective stillness at the edges of its pools and bright rafts full of delighted tourists in flotation jackets and crash helmets sweeping through its white water. Gradually, the mountains pressed in on all this humanity, and I found myself behind a long line of cars trailing a cattle truck at well below the speed limit. This combination of cumbersome commercial traffic and impatient private cars was a lethal mixture that kept our canyon in the papers, as it regularly spat out corpses. In my rearview mirror, I could see a line behind me that was just as long as the one ahead, stretching back, thinning, and vanishing around a green bend. There was no passing lane for several miles. A single amorous elk could have turned us all into twisted, smoking metal.

"You might have been right," Louise said. "It doesn't look good."

She almost certainly had better things to do. But, looking down the line of cars, I felt my blood pressure rising. Her hands rested quietly in her lap. I couldn't possibly have rivaled such serenity.

"How do you plan to anger this guy in Rigby?" she asked.

"I'm going to try haughtiness. If I suggest that he bought the dealership cheap, he might tell me to keep the damn thing. The Atlanta guy just wants to start somewhere. All these people have a sort of parlay mentality, and they need to get on the playing field before they can start running it up. I'm a trader. It all happens for me in the transition. The moment of liquidation is the essence of capitalism."

"What about the man in Rigby?"

"He's an end user. He wants to keep it."

I reflected on the pathos of ownership and the way it could bog you down.

"You should be in my world," Louise said. "According to the law, water has no reality except its use. In Montana, water isn't even wet. Every time some misguided soul suggests that fish need it, it ends up in the state supreme court."

Birds were fleeing the advance of automobiles. I was elsewhere, trying to imagine my buyer, red-faced, storming out of the closing. I'd offer to let bygones be bygones, I'd take him to dinner, I'd throw a steak into him, for Christ's sake. In the end, he'd be glad he wasn't stuck with the lot.

Traffic headed toward us, far down the road. We were all packed together to make sure no one tried to pass. The rules had to be enforced. Occasionally, someone drifted out for a better look, but not far enough that someone else could close his space and possibly seal his fate.

This trip had its risks. I had only recently admitted to myself that I would like to make more of my situation with Louise than currently existed. Though ours was hardly a chaste relationship, real intimacy was relatively scarce. People in relationships nowadays seemed to retain their secrets like bank deposits—they always set some aside, in case they might need them to spend on someone new. I found it unpleasant to think that Louise could be withholding anything.

But I thought I was more presentable than I had been. When Louise and I first met, I was just coming off two and a half years of peddling satellite dishes in towns where a couple of dogs doing the wild thing in the middle of the road amounted to the high point of a year, and the highest-grossing business was a methamphetamine tent camp out in the sagebrush. Now I had caught the upswing in our local economy: cars, storage, tool rental, and mortgage discounting. I had a pretty home, debt-free, out on Sourdough. I owned a few things. I could be okay. I asked Louise what she thought of the new prosperity around us. She said wearily, "I'm not sure it's such a good thing, living in a boomtown. It's basically a high-end carny atmosphere."

We were just passing Storm Castle and Garnet Mountain. When I glanced in the mirror, I saw a low red car with a scoop in its hood pull out to pass. I must have reacted somehow, because Louise asked me if I would like her to drive.

"No, that's fine. Things are getting a bit lively back there."

"Drive defensively."

"Not much choice, is there?"

I had been mentally rehearsing the closing in Rigby, and I wasn't getting anywhere. I had this sort of absurd picture of myself strutting into the meeting. I tried again to picture the buyer looking seriously annoyed, but I'd met him before and he seemed pretty levelheaded. I suspected I'd have to be really outlandish to get a rise out of him. He was a fourth-generation resident of Rigby, so I could always urge him to get to know his neighbors, I decided. Or, since he had come up through the service department, I could try emphasizing the need to study how the cars actually ran. I'd use hand signals to fend off objections. I felt more secure.

Some elk had wandered into the parking lot at Buck's T4 and were grazing indifferently as people pulled off the highway to admire them. I don't know if it was the great unmarred blue sky overhead or the balsamic zephyr that poured down the mountainside, but I found myself momentarily buoyed by all this idleness, people out of their cars. I am always encouraged when I see animals doing something other than running for their lives. In any case, the stream of traffic ahead of us had been much reduced by the pedestrian rubbernecking.

"My husband lived here one winter," Louise said. "He sold his pharmacy after we divorced, not that he had to, and set out to change his life. He became a mountain man, wore buckskin clothes. He tried living off the land one day a week, with the idea that he would build up. But then he just stuck with one day a week—he'd shoot a rabbit or something, more of a diet, really. He's a real-estate agent now, at Big Sky. I think he's doing well. At least he's quit killing rabbits."

"Remarried?"

"Yes."

As soon as we hit the open country around West Yellowstone, Louise called her office. When her secretary put her on hold, Louise covered the mouthpiece and said, "He married a super gal. Minnesota, I think. She should be good for Bob, and he's not easy. Bob's from the South. For men, it's a full-time job being Southern. It just wears them out. It wore me out too. I developed doubtful behaviors. I pulled out my eyelashes and ate twenty-eight hundred dollars' worth of macadamia nuts."

Her secretary came back on the line, and Louise began editing her schedule with impressive precision, mouthing the word *sorry* to me when the conversation dragged on. I began musing about my capacity to live successfully with someone as competent as Louise. There was no implied hierarchy of status between us, but I wondered if, in the long run, something would have to give.

West Yellowstone seemed entirely given over to the well-being of the snowmobile, and the billboards dedicated to it were anomalous on a sunny day like today. By winter, schoolchildren would be petitioning futilely to control the noise at night so they could do their schoolwork, and the town would turn a blind eye as a cloud of smoke arose to gas residents, travelers, and park rangers alike. It seemed incredible to me that recreation could acquire this level of social momentum, that it could be seen as an inalienable right.

We came down Targhee Pass to Idaho, into a wasteland of spindly pines that had replaced the former forest, and Louise gave voice to the thoughts she'd been having for the past few miles. "Why don't you just let this deal close? You really have no guarantees from the man from Atlanta. And there's a good-faith issue here too, I think."

"A lawyerly notation."

"So be it, but it's true. Are you trying to get every last cent out of this sale?"

"That's second. The first priority is to be done with it. It was meant to be a passive investment, and it has turned out not to be. I get twenty calls a day from the dealership, most with questions I can't answer. It's turning me into a giant bullshit machine."

"No investments are really passive."

"Mutual funds are close."

"That's why they don't pay."

"Some of them pay, or they would cease to exist."

"You make a poor libertarian, my darling. You sound like that little puke David Stockman."

"Stockman was right about everything. Reagan just didn't have the guts to take his advice."

"Reagan. Give me a break."

I didn't mind equal billing in a relationship, but I did dread the idea of parties speaking strictly from their entitlements across a chasm. Inevitably, sex would make chaos of much of this, but you couldn't, despite Benjamin Franklin's suggestion, "use venery" as a management tool.

Louise adjusted her seat back and folded her arms, gazing at the sunny side of the road. The light through the windshield accentuated the shape of her face, now in repose. I found her beautiful. I adored her when she was a noun and was alarmed when she was a verb, which was usually the case. I understood that this was not the best thing I could say about myself. When her hand drifted over to my leg, I hardly knew what to do with this reference to the other life we led. I knew it was an excellent thing to be reminded of how inconsequential my worldly concerns were, but one warm hand, rested casually, and my interest traveled to the basics of the species.

Ashton, St. Anthony, Sugar City: Mormon hamlets, small farms, and the furious reordering of watersheds into industrial canals. Irrigation haze hung over the valley of the Snake, and the skies were less bright than they had been just a few miles back, in Montana. Many locals had been killed when the Teton Dam burst, and despite that they wanted to build it again: the relationship to water here was like a war, and in war lives are lost. These were the folk to whom I'd sold many a plain car; ostentation was thoroughly unacceptable hereabouts. The four-door sedan with a six-cylinder engine was the desired item, an identical one with a hundred and fifty thousand miles on it generally taken in trade at zero value, thanks to the manipulation of rebates against the manufacturer's suggested retail. Appearances were foremost, and the salesman who could leave a customer's smugness undisturbed flourished in this atmosphere. I had two of them, potato-fattened bland opportunists with nine kids between them. They were the asset I was selling; the rest was little more than bricks and mortar.

We pressed on toward Rexburg, and amid the turnoffs for Wilford, Newdale, Hibbard, and Moody the only thing that had any flavor was Hog Hollow Road, which was a shortcut to France—not the one in Europe but the one just a hop, skip, and a jump south of Squirrel, Idaho. There were license-plate holders with my name on them in Squirrel, and I was oddly vain about that.

"Sure seems lonesome around here," Louise said.

"Oh, boy."

"The houses are like little forts."

"The winters are hard." But it was less that the small neat dwellings around us appeared defensive than that they seemed to be trying to avoid attracting the wrath of some inattentive god.

"It looks like government housing for Eskimos. They just sit inside, waiting for a whale or something."

This banter had the peculiar effect of making me want to cleave to Louise, and desperately, too—to build a warm new civilization, possibly in a foolish house with turrets. The road stretched before me like an arrow. There was only enough of it left before Rigby for me to say, perhaps involuntarily, "I wonder if we shouldn't just get married."

Louise quickly looked away. Her silence conferred a certain seriousness on my question.

But there was Rigby, and, in the parlance of all who have extracted funds from locals, Rigby had been good to me. Main Street was lined with ambitious and beautiful stone buildings, old for this part of the world. Their second and third floors were now affordable housing, and their street levels were occupied by businesses hanging on by their fingernails. You could still detect the hopes of the dead, their dreams, even, though it seemed to be only a matter of time before the wind carried them away, once and for all.

I drove past the car lot at 200 East Fremont without comment and—considering the amount of difficulty it had caused me in the years before I got it stabilized and began to enjoy its very modest yields—without much feeling. I remembered the day, sometime earlier, when I had tried to help park the cars in the front row and got everything so crooked that the salesmen, not concealing their contempt, had to do it all over again. The title company where we were heading was on the same street, and it was a livelier place, from the row of perky evergreens out front to the merry receptionist who greeted us, a handsome young woman, probably a farm girl only moments before, enjoying the clothes, makeup, and perquisites of the new world that her firm was helping to build.

We were shown into a spacious conference room with a long table and chairs, freshly sharpened pencils, and crisp notepads bearing the company letterhead. "Shall I stay?" Louise asked, the first thing she'd said since my earlier inadvertent remark, which I intuited had not been altogether rejected.

"Please," I said, gesturing toward a chair next to the one I meant to take. At that moment, the escrow agent entered and, standing very close to us, introduced himself as Brent Colby. Then he went to the far end of the table, where he spread his documents around in an orderly fan. Colby was around fifty, with iron gray hair and a deeply lined face. He wore pressed jeans, a brilliant white snap-button shirt, cowboy boots, and a belt buckle with a steer head on it. He had thick, hairy hands and a gleaming wedding band. Just as he raised his left wrist to check his watch, the door opened and Oren Johnson, the buyer, entered. He went straight to Louise and, taking her hand in both of his, introduced himself. It occurred to me that, in trying to be suave, Oren Johnson had revealed himself to be a clodhopper, but I was probably just experiencing the mild hostility that emanates from every sale of property. Oren wore a suit, though it suggested less a costume for business than one for church. He had a gold tooth and a cautious pompadour. He too bore an investment-grade wedding band, and I noted that there was plenty of room in his black-laced shoes for his toes. He turned and said it was good to see me again after so long. The time had come for me to go into my act. With grotesque hauteur, I said I didn't realize we had ever met. This was work.

Oren Johnson bustled with inchoate energy; he was the kind of small-town leader who sets an example by silently getting things done. He suggested this just by arranging his pencils and notepad and repositioning his chair with rough precision. Locking eyes with me, he stated that he was a man of his word. I didn't know what he was getting at, but took it to mean that the formalities of a closing were superfluous to the old-time handshake with which Oren Johnson customarily did business. I smiled and quizzically cocked my head as if to say that the newfangled arrangements with well-attested documents promptly conveyed to the courthouse suited me just fine, that deals made on handshakes were strictly for the pious or the picturesque. My message was clear enough that Louise shifted uncomfortably in her chair, and Brent Colby knocked his documents edgewise on the desk to align them. As far as Oren Johnson was concerned, I was beginning to feel that anyone who strayed from the basic patterns of farm life to sell cars bore watching. Like a Method actor, I already believed my part.

"You're an awfully lucky man, Oren Johnson," I said to him, leaning back in my chair. I could see Louise openmouthed two seats away from Brent Colby, and observing myself through her eyes gave me a sudden burst of panic.

"Oh?" Oren Johnson said. "How's that?"

"How's that?" I did a precise job of replicating his inflection. "I am permitting you to purchase my car lot. You've seen the books: how often does a man get a shot at a business where all the work's been done for him?"

Brent Colby was doing an incomplete job of concealing his distaste; he was enough of a tinhorn to clear his throat theatrically. But Oren Johnson treated this as a colossal interruption and cast a firm glance his way.

"It doesn't look all that automatic to me," he said.

"Aw, hell, you're just going to coin it. Pull the lever and relax!"

"What about the illegal oil dump? I wish I had a nickel for every crankcaseful that went into that hole. Then I wouldn't worry about what's going to happen when the D.E.Q. lowers the boom."

"Maybe you ought to ride your potato harvester another year or two, if you're so risk-averse. Cars are the future. They're not for everybody."

Oren Johnson's face reddened. He pushed his pencils and notepad almost out of reach in the middle of the conference table. He contemplated these supplies a moment before raising his eyes to mine. "I suppose you could put this car lot where the sun don't shine, if that suits you."

Johnson having taken a stand, I immediately felt unsure that I even had another buyer. Had I ever acknowledged how much I longed to get rid of this business and put an end to all those embarrassing phone calls? I wanted to hand the moment off to someone else while I collected my thoughts, but as I looked around the room I found no one who was interested in rescuing me—least of all Louise, who had raised one eyebrow at the vast peculiarity of my performance. Suddenly, I was desperate to keep the deal from falling apart. I gave my head a little twist to free my neck from the constrictions of my collar. I performed this gesture too vigorously, and I had the feeling that it might seem like the first movement of some sort of dance filled with sensual flourishes and bordering on the moronic. I had lost my grip.

"Oren," I said, and the familiarity seemed inappropriate. "I was attached to this little enterprise. I wanted to be sure you valued it."

The deal closed, and I had my check. I tipped back in my chair to think of a few commemorative words for the new owner, but the two men left the room without giving me the chance to speak. I shrugged at Louise and she, too, rose to go, pausing a moment beneath an enormous Kodachrome of a bugling elk. I was aware of her distance, and I sensed that my waffling hadn't gone over particularly well. I concluded that at no time in the future would I act out a role to accomplish anything. This decision quickly evaporated with the realization that that is practically all we do in life. Comedy failed, too. When I told Louise that I had been within an inch of opening a can of whup-ass on the buyer, I barely got a smile. There's nothing more desolating than having a phrase like that die on your lips.

It was dark when we got back to Targhee Pass. Leaving town,

we passed the Beehive assisted-living facility and the Riot Zone, a "family fun park." Most of the citizens we spotted there seemed unlikely rioters. I drove past a huge neon steak, its blue T-bone flashing above a restaurant that was closed and dark. There were deer on the road, and once, as we passed through a murky section of forest, we saw the pale faces of children waiting to cross.

"What are they doing out at this hour?"

"I don't know," Louise said.

I made good time on the pine flats north of the Snowmobile Capital of the World, and I wondered what it would be like to live in a town that was the world capital of a mechanical gadget. In Rigby, we had seen a homely museum dedicated to Philo T. Farnsworth, the inventor of television, which featured displays of Farnsworth's funky assemblages of tubes and wire and, apparently, coat hangers—stuff his wife was probably always attempting to throw out, a goal Louise supported. "Too bad Mama Farnsworth didn't take all that stuff to the dump," she said.

We had the highway to ourselves, and clouds of stars seemed to rise up from the wilderness, lighting the treetops in a cool fire. Slowly, the canyon closed in around us, and we entered its dark flowing space.

The idyll ended just past the ranger station at Black Butte, when a car pulled in behind us abruptly enough that I checked my speed to see if I was violating the limit, but I wasn't. When the car was very close, the driver shifted his lights to a high beam so intense that I could see our shadows on the dashboard, my knuckles on the steering wheel glaringly white. I was nearly blinded by my own mirrors, which I hastily adjusted.

I said, "What's with this guy?"

"Just let him pass."

"I don't know that he wants to."

I softened my pressure on the gas pedal. I thought that by

easing my already moderate speed I would politely suggest that he might go by me. I even hugged the shoulder, but he remained glued to our bumper. There was something about this that reminded me strongly of my feeling of failure back in Rigby, but I was unable to put my finger on it. Maybe it was the hot light of liquidation, in the glare of which all motives seem laid bare. I slowed down even more without managing to persuade my tormentor to pass. "Jesus," Louise said. "Pull over." In her accent, it came out as "pull ovah."

I moved off to the side of the road slowly and predictably, but although I had stopped, the incandescent globes persisted in our rearview mirror. "This is very strange," Louise said.

"Shall I go back and speak to him?"

After considering for a moment, she said, "No."

"Why?"

"Because this is not normal."

I put the car in gear again and pulled back onto the highway. The last reasonable thought I had was that I would proceed to Bozeman as though nothing were going on; once I was back in civilization my tormentor's behavior would be visible to all, and I could, if necessary, simply drive to the police station with him in tow.

Our blinding, syncopated journey continued another mile before we reached a sweeping eastward bend, closely guarded by the canyon walls. I knew that just beyond the bend there was a scenic pull-off, and that the approaching curve was acute enough for a small lead to put me out of sight. Whether or not this was plausible, I had no idea: I was exhilarated to be taking a firm hand in my own affairs. And a firm foot! As we entered the narrows, I pinned the accelerator, and we shot into the dark. Louise grabbed the front edges of her seat and stared at the road twisting in front of us. She emitted something like a moan, which I had heard before in a very different context. Halfway around the curve, my tormentor vanished behind us, and although my car seemed only marginally under control, the absence of blinding light was a relief as we fled into darkness.

When we emerged and the road straightened, I turned off my lights. I was going so fast I felt light-headed, but the road was visible under the stars, and I was able to brake hard and drop down into the scenic turn-off. Seconds later, our new friend shot past, lights blazing into nowhere. He was clearly determined to catch us; his progress up the canyon was rapid and increasingly erratic. We watched in fascination until the lights suddenly jerked sideways, shining in white cones across the river, turned downward, then disappeared.

I heard Louise say, in a tone of reasonable observation, "He went in."

I had an urgent feeling that took a long time to turn into words. "Did I do that?"

She shook her head, and I pulled out onto the highway, my own headlights on once more. I drove in an odd, measured way, as if bound for an undesired destination, pulled along by something outside myself, thinking: liquidation. We could see where he'd gone through the guardrail. We pulled over and got out. Any hope we might have had for the driver—and we shall be a long time determining if we had any—was gone the minute we looked down from the riverbank. The car was submerged, its lights still burning freakishly, illuminating a bulge of crystalline water, a boulder in the exuberance of a mountain watershed. Presently, the lights sank into blackness, and only the silver sheen of river in starlight remained.

Louise cried, "I wish I could feel something!" And when I reached to comfort her she shoved me away. I had no choice but to climb back up to the roadway.

After that, I could encounter Louise only by telephone. I told her he had a record as long as your arm. "It's not enough!" she said. I called later to say that he was of German and Italian extraction. That proved equally unsatisfactory, and when I called to inform her that he hailed from Wisconsin she just hung up on me, this time for good.

WOLVERHAMPTON
LIBRARIES